• Praise for Krista Davis's Pen & Ink mysteries

"Clearly this book was writter ¹

"The mystery is pleasantly twisty
ters—whose backstories lend ther
this carefully crafted cozy series."

"The theme was unique and new, the characters were relatable and entertaining, the mystery was unpredictable, and the writing was excellent." —*Night Owl Reviews*

"I love a book that immediately grabs my attention and this new debut series does that. This was a well-written and fast paced whodunit that was delightfully entertaining. The author did a good job in presenting a murder mystery that had me immersed in all that was happening." —*Dru's Book Musings*

Praise for Krista Davis's *New York Times* Bestselling Domestic Diva series

"This satisfying entry in the series will appeal to readers who enjoy cozies with a cooking frame, like Diane Mott Davidson's Goldy Schulz mysteries." —*Booklist*

"Reader alert: Tasty descriptions may spark intense cupcake cravings." —*The Washington Post*

"Davis . . . again combines food and felonies in this tasty whodunit." —*Richmond Times-Dispatch*

"Loaded with atmosphere and charm." —*Library Journal*

"A mouthwatering mix of murder, mirth, and mayhem." —Mary Jane Maffini, author of *The Busy Woman's Guide to Murder*

"Raucous humor, affectionate characters, and delectable recipes highlight this unpredictable mystery that entertains during any season." —*Kings River Life Magazine*

Krista Davis is the author of:

The Domestic Diva Mysteries

The Diva Cooks Up a Storm
The Diva Sweetens the Pie
The Diva Spices It Up
The Diva Serves Forbidden Fruit
The Diva Says Cheesecake!

The Pen & Ink Mysteries

Color Me Murder
The Coloring Crook
Murder Outside the Lines
A Colorful Scheme

A
Colorful
Scheme

KRISTA DAVIS

Kensington Publishing Corp.
www.kensingtonbooks.com

KENSINGTON BOOKS are published by

Kensington Publishing Corp.
119 West 40th Street
New York, NY 10018

Special book excerpts or customized printings can also be created to fit specific needs. For details, write or phone the office of the Kensington Sales Manager: Kensington Publishing Corp., 119 West 40th Street, New York, NY 10018. Attn. Sales Department. Phone: 1-800-221-2647.

The K and Teapot logo is a trademark of Kensington Publishing Corp.

ISBN: 978-1-4967-2466-3 (ebook)

ISBN: 978-1-4967-2465-6

First Kensington Trade Paperback Printing: September 2022

10 9 8 7 6 5 4 3 2 1

Printed in the United States of America

To Virginia Jeppson Moore, my dear friend.
What fun we had!

ACKNOWLEDGMENTS

Many thanks to my good friends Ginger Bolton, Alison Brook, Laurie Cass, Peg Cochran, Kaye George, and Daryl Wood Gerber. They are always just an email away to share joys and lows.

While this book is about writers, none of the characters are based on anyone. We are a varied lot and I had fun inventing these people.

My good friends Betsy Strickland, Amy Wheeler, and Susan Smith Erba are sweet to put up with my endless questions, and this time Susan kindly shared her recipe for lemon drop martinis. Yum!

As always, I must thank my editors, Wendy McCurdy and Elizabeth Trout, who catch my omissions and make my books better!

Special thanks to my agent, Jessica Faust, who is always on top of things and one step ahead of me!

Broken crayons still color.
—Unknown

CAST OF CHARACTERS

Bride—Jacqueline Liebhaber
Groom—John Maxwell
Liddy Maxwell Woodley—John's sister
Walter Woodley—Liddy's husband
Mr. DuBois—the Maxwells' butler
Florrie Fox
Peaches, Florrie's cat
Veronica Fox—Florrie's sister
Linda and Mike Fox—Florrie and Veronica's mom and dad
Sergeant Eric Jonquille—Florrie's boyfriend
Bob Turpin—Color Me Read employee
Arthur Bedlingham—author of literary novels
Evan McDowell—Arthur's assistant
Mia Woodham—artist
Wayne Ridley—Mia's friend
Sloan Rogers—literary agent
Margarite Herbert-Grant—book reviewer
Gabriella Archambeau—romance author
Griffin Corbyn—thriller author and Gabriella's husband
Buzz Powers—author of new thriller
Cara Melton—waitress and aspiring reporter
Grady and Celeste Sorello—wedding guests

Chapter 1

I thought someone had been following me, so when Mr. DuBois shouted and banged on the door of the carriage house, I was momentarily alarmed. I peeked out the window to be certain it was him. When I opened the door, he barged in and demanded, "Is Miss Jacqueline here?" He panted as if he couldn't catch his breath.

It was most uncharacteristic of Mr. DuBois. He had been trained as a proper butler. Pounding on doors and shouting ranked right up there with the most egregious sins in his mind. But that only made his question and behavior more worrisome.

My sister, Veronica, who was acting as the wedding coordinator, leaped out of her chair, spilling coffee on her bathrobe. She reminded me of our mother when she took a moment to catch her breath and then with forced composure asked sweetly, "Did you lose our bride?"

Mr. DuBois, who watched far too much true-crime TV and was prone to seeing murder everywhere, closed the door behind him. "She is not in the mansion. I have searched from the basement to the attic. She is simply gone."

I froze for a moment. Was she being followed, too? "When is the last time anyone saw her?" I asked.

Veronica nodded at me, her head bobbing with too much vigor, thus exposing her true level of anxiety. "Excellent, Florrie!"

"I last saw her yesterday evening around nine, I believe. I asked if they wanted anything before I retired for the night."

Elderly Mr. DuBois was petite, always impeccable. He had worked as the butler for the Maxwell family for decades. John Maxwell, adventurer, professor, and heir to the Maxwell fortune, was my boss, which was how I came to reside in the small carriage house behind the mansion. He owned the Color Me Read bookstore but had neither the time nor the inclination to manage it and relied on me to do it all, from payroll to selecting stock, hiring, and paying the bills. At night and on my days off, I indulged my artistic side by drawing adult coloring books.

"I trust you have seen the professor this morning?" I asked.

At that moment, there was a brisk knock at the door. Mr. DuBois opened it and John Maxwell strode in. Tall and dignified, he was the type of man who commanded attention. Despite his age, he remained decidedly handsome. His well-trimmed beard was black at the bottom but curiously changed to snow-white along his jawline and sideburns, then his hair morphed back to black at the top of his head. He glanced around the open room. "She's not here?"

"I'm afraid not," I said. "Are you sure Jacquie didn't have plans? Breakfast with a friend? Some kind of spa treatment?"

Veronica frowned at me. "I would have known about anything like that."

Somewhat bashfully, Professor Maxwell asked, "You're not hiding her here? That silly thing about not seeing the bride on the wedding day?"

"I'm afraid not," I said. "Have you notified the police?"

"No!" cried Veronica.

We all looked at her.

"Not yet. It's her wedding day. I'll admit that it's usually the groom who takes a runner, but maybe she has cold feet. Maybe she just needs a breather before everything gets underway."

Professor Maxwell gazed at Veronica silently. "Perhaps you're correct. DuBois, did you hear anything in the night?"

"I'm afraid I slept soundly."

"What about the alarm system?" I asked.

DuBois glanced at Professor Maxwell. "We didn't turn it on. With so many guests in the house, we were afraid someone might trigger it if they wandered out for a breath of fresh air or for a cigarette. I believe a few of them are smokers."

Professor Maxwell turned to look at my clock collection. "We'll give her two hours. If she hasn't called or turned up, then we'll go to the police."

I wondered if he was thinking about Jacquie's previous disappearance. Jacquie was Jacqueline Liebhaber, the well-known romance and women's fiction author. She had been Professor Maxwell's second wife.

They had one child, a girl named Caroline, who had been kidnapped at a young age and never found. The loss of Caroline had worked its way between them with Jacquie pursuing psychics and John partaking in wild adventures, all of which eventually led to divorce. Years later, when Jacquie found herself in a troubling situation, she sought John's help, which brought the two of them together again.

That time she had been missing for days. Her agent had been so worried that she hired a private detective to find Jacquie. That she had vanished before was concerning yet something of a relief as well. It worried me because I hated to imagine that she had had a change of heart about the professor and was now an aging runaway bride. He would be devastated. She could at least have told one of us so we wouldn't worry all day, wondering if we should cancel the minister and wedding accoutrements.

I nodded and hoped I sounded reassuring when I said, "I bet she turns up."

Professor Maxwell stiffened. "I'm going out to look for her."

"I shall stay by the phone in case she calls," said Mr. DuBois, holding up a wireless landline phone as though it were proof of his intentions.

The minute the professor was gone, Mr. DuBois said, "I'll bring coffee over."

Half an hour later, he rolled a serving cart into the carriage house. *Coffee* turned out to be croissants, eggs Benedict, and a fruit salad in jewel tones. The reds, oranges, and greens glistened under a sauce. "I have left a buffet at the mansion for the few late-rising guests."

Mr. DuBois had been formal but polite to me when I moved into the carriage house, but he made no secret of his disdain for my cat, Peaches. Since then, Peaches and I had wormed our way into his good graces.

Veronica vaulted toward the table and picked up a croissant. "Oh my! Does the professor eat like this every day?"

Mr. DuBois tsked at her. "Did you think I serve him boxed cereal in cold milk?" He busied himself, placing a covered plate in my oven.

For a moment Veronica appeared chastened, but her humor returned quickly. "How the other half live, eh?"

The three of us sat down to eat. Even though I was busy being indulged, I noticed that Mr. DuBois wasn't eating.

"I, um, may have notified the police," he said quietly. "Sort of. Not really. Not officially, you understand."

Veronica choked on her breakfast. In between coughs, she

croaked, "You didn't! You know how they feel about the press. If they get wind of this . . ."

Mr. DuBois poured more coffee for her.

Normally a missing bride wouldn't be of much interest to anyone outside the families and friends involved. But Jacquie's books sold worldwide.

"How would one unofficially notify the police?" I inquired.

"One might have phoned a friend on the police force."

Veronica's eyes grew large. "Florrie and I aren't properly dressed yet!" She jumped to her feet, but it was too late. Someone rapped on the door.

I tightened the sash on my own bathrobe of flowing silk the rich color of red plums, a gift from my parents. I peered out the window in the door. "I believe your police contact has arrived, Mr. DuBois. Relax, Veronica. It's Eric."

I opened the door and smiled at him. He planted a quick kiss on my lips, the polite sort employed in the presence of others. But the grin on his face told me how happy he was to see me.

I could feel a flush rising up my cheeks. I was a bookish type, perfectly content to stay home with my tabby cat, Peaches. All I needed was a good mystery or my sketch pad where I drew pictures for my coloring books. I loathed bars, dance clubs, and other noisy places packed with writhing people trying to meet Mr. or Ms. Right.

Growing up, I'd been called names like squirt, brains, and Goody Two-shoes. I was the big sister, yet the smaller one. Veronica and I were only a couple of years apart in age, but we couldn't have been more different. Veronica had long slender legs, the kind short woman envied, and blond hair that she wore in a sassy cut. She was athletic and loved nothing more than a great party. She knew the trends, had always been popular everywhere she went, and frequented local bars and events.

The day I met Eric, I only dreamed that he might be interested in someone like me. His eyes were a bright cornflower blue, and his sandy hair fell in loose curls. He looked like the sun had kissed him, though I would never tell him that. It was an unbelievable stroke of good fortune that he had responded to my 911 call just over a year ago, and even more miraculous that he was as drawn to me as I was to him.

That I was dating a cop truly thrilled Mr. DuBois. For a short time, Eric had stayed with me while he recuperated from an accident. Mr. DuBois had waited on him hand and foot, serving incredible meals, and reveling in the company of Eric's police friends who came by to visit. When Eric moved back to his apartment, the meals had come to an abrupt halt. I didn't mind, but found it mildly amusing.

"I knocked at the kitchen door of the mansion," Eric said. "No one answered. I thought I might find Mr. DuBois over here."

Mr. DuBois rose to his feet. "Thank you for coming. I knew I could count on you."

Mr. DuBois fetched the covered plate from my oven and lifted the top. "Won't you join us?" He deftly set the additional plate of eggs Benedict at the table.

He had clearly been prepared for Eric's visit.

Eric greeted Veronica. "Has Jacquie turned up yet?"

"Not a sign of her."

We settled at the table again and Veronica whined in a stressed tone, "The professor said we should give her a couple of hours, but people will be arriving soon to set up."

"Do you have any reason to think she didn't go of her own free will?" asked Eric.

Mr. DuBois shook his head. "No. I suppose we should be thankful for that."

"Does she still have an apartment somewhere? Maybe she went there for some reason."

Mr. DuBois sighed. "She moved into the mansion months ago. I believe she still owns her condo but has rented it to someone, so it's unlikely that she would have gone there."

"What about the underground passage between the carriage house and the mansion?" I asked.

"Maxwell checked it this morning," said Mr. DuBois. "She's not hiding there, either."

Veronica's phone rang. She almost dropped it in her haste to answer the call. The rest of us watched her expectantly.

Chapter 2

"That's the stupidest thing I've ever heard," Veronica said into her phone. "She hadn't even been born then. . . . Yes, I can prove that." She disconnected the call and said to us, "It's a shame there isn't a way to slam a cell phone down when you hang up on a person. There was something satisfying about that. Kind of like punching someone in the face but without the violence. Disconnecting a call doesn't have the same impact."

"What was that about?" asked Mr. DuBois.

"Some news editor was calling to confirm that Florrie is the Maxwells' missing daughter."

I recoiled and then laughed. "People get the strangest ideas. At least they were smart enough to confirm it before blabbing about it."

"Preposterous!" exclaimed Mr. DuBois.

"It's crazy. I would have to be Mom's age," I protested. "I hope I don't look that old yet."

"I wouldn't say that to *her*," Veronica muttered.

Eric gazed at me. "I don't understand. People think you're related to the Maxwells just because you live in the carriage house?"

"You can't imagine the preposterous things people have suggested about Miss Caroline over the years," said Mr. DuBois. "That she was hidden in Europe. That the Maxwells kept her in their attic. That she grew up in another family and has finally come home. It's ridiculous. Just the other day someone asked me if Florrie's mother was Miss Caroline."

"Mom?" Veronica sputtered. "I wouldn't mind that. We'd be heiresses!"

"At least Mom is closer to Caroline's age," I pointed out.

"This is all because the Maxwells are wealthy?" Eric winced.

"It's that social media gone amok," said Mr. DuBois. "Did you know that perfect strangers post their absurd speculations about Miss Caroline? Some people claim to have seen her."

"Really?" asked Veronica.

"That's what they *claim*. It has always been this way. The Maxwells are a famous family with a good bit of scandal in their history. Miss Caroline's disappearance is one more tragedy in their checkered past. And that, my dear Florrie, is why people want to believe that your mother could be Caroline Maxwell, keeping a low profile. Especially now that you live here and you run the bookstore. The Maxwells treat you like family."

Veronica shot me a sideways glance. "They are very nice to us."

"We're not Maxwells!" I laughed. "We're plain old everyday Foxes."

"If I didn't know better," said Mr. DuBois thoughtfully, "I would presume that Maxwell's sister, Miss Liddy, chased Miss Jacqueline off. She is remarkably adept at finagling her way into matters that don't concern her."

I had just raised a bit of croissant to my lips but stopped midair. Of course she was coming to the wedding. I had forgotten about her and now shuddered at the mere thought.

Liddy, possibly the most despicable, pretentious, demanding woman I had ever met, blamed me for the death of her son.

I had nothing to do with his death, except for the great misfortune of finding his body. Liddy knew what her son was like and how many people he had conned. His father, a decent man, had been more realistic about his son's devious behavior that led to his demise. Liddy, on the other hand, wanted desperately to place blame elsewhere and had irrationally landed on me as a scapegoat.

I placed the bit of croissant on my plate and gulped coffee. Five hundred people would be in attendance, I reminded myself. Chances were good that at the most I would only have to smile or nod and pretend to be busy. But then a truly horrific thought sprang to mind. "She's not staying here, is she?"

Mr. DuBois grimaced. "I confess I am not thrilled about her visit; however, it *is* her childhood home. Maxwell felt compelled to invite her and Miss Jacqueline encouraged him to do so." A sly smile crossed Mr. DuBois's lips. "I recall the fuss Miss Liddy made about your presence on the estate. I can only hope she will be less agitated and more gracious this time."

I doubted that. Mr. DuBois had been so kind, defending me and throwing her out of the house.

"Just keep your distance," Mr. DuBois advised. "And if she gives you any trouble, come to me. I've known Miss Liddy since she was a girl. It's funny how different she is from Maxwell. They have the same parents and were raised the same way in the same household, yet they aren't a bit similar."

"Her husband was nice," I mused. I hadn't spent much time with him, but he clearly felt the death of his son deeply and had briefly reminisced about his son's life and how he had become an odious man.

"Walter," DuBois said softly. "Miss Liddy doesn't deserve him. He was engaged to marry a friend of Miss Liddy's,

Annabelle Constantine, probably the most beautiful woman I have ever had the pleasure of meeting. Rich dark hair, ruby lips, and mischievous eyes. But Miss Liddy had set her sights on Walter, probably to irritate her father, as Walter did not come from money and had no particular plans to make a living. Well, Miss Liddy paid another young fellow to court Annabelle and made sure Walter saw them together. Liddy was standing by to comfort the brokenhearted Walter and promptly swept him off to the altar. That wedding took place so fast that people thought she was pregnant. Which she wasn't. Her daddy took young Walter in hand and made sure he had a well-paying position at a local brokerage firm. Luckily, Walter was a good man, and he had a knack for the stock market."

"So it all ended well," said Eric.

"For everyone except poor Walter, who has had to put up with Miss Liddy for most of his life. He is the true image of a long-suffering man," said Mr. DuBois.

"I didn't know any of that," I said. "It makes me feel much better about the way Liddy treated me. I'm lucky she didn't do anything worse."

After breakfast, Veronica changed into jeans and a T-shirt Jacquie had given her that said WEDDING COORDINATOR. It had been a joke gift, but Veronica took that job seriously, and as the minutes crawled by, she was in no mood for jesting.

"I have made a list," she announced. "The chairs were set up yesterday. The florist will be here any moment now. It's far too late to stop him or the baker who will be delivering the cake."

"What about the guests?" asked Eric.

"Five hundred people are coming! I can't possibly notify everyone." Veronica winced. "Maybe they won't notice that she's not here?"

"Not notice that the bride is missing?" Eric asked. "Even I would realize that."

"Most people don't know this is the wedding," Veronica explained. "Jacquie didn't want any gifts, so she sent out invitations to a party. The wedding is, well, for lack of a better expression, part of the entertainment." Veronica gasped. "The musicians! What should I do about the musicians?"

"Look," I said in a gentle voice. "It seems to me that you have to decide whether the party will go on or not. You can't possibly cancel five hundred guests, so you might as well continue as planned. If Jacquie doesn't return, then all you really have to do is take off that T-shirt and very few guests will notice anything amiss."

The corners of Veronica's mouth twitched. "I don't like it. I can't imagine the party without Jacquie. But you're right. Completely right. Okay, everyone. The party is on, with or without a wedding!"

At that exact moment, her phone dinged. "It's a text from the bakery," she said in a soft voice. She read aloud, "'We are so sorry. Due to a power outage, your cupcake order will be delivered at seven p.m.'"

Veronica's phone thudded as it hit the floor. She clasped her hands to her head as though she thought it might explode. "Trouble comes in threes," she breathed. "First Jacquie, now the cupcakes. What's next?"

"You're having cupcakes instead of a wedding cake?" asked Eric.

Veronica turned toward him. The placid face of my mom had vanished. In an angry, yet controlled tone, she said, "They're the favors. The little gift each person gets to take home."

Eric picked up on the slight snarl in her voice and crossed his arms in front of his face, pretending to cower. "At least they'll be here in time."

"They have to be placed in boxes."

"That's not so bad. I'll help." Eric smiled at her.

"*Over five hundred!*" she squealed. "I ordered extra just to be sure we had enough."

"It's okay," I said. "All hands on deck at seven, everyone. Eric, Mr. DuBois, Mom, and I will pitch in. We can do this!"

Veronica didn't even try to hide her frustration. "I suppose that's all we *can* do. Thanks for helping out. Florrie, I'm counting on you to stay on top of the Jacquie situation. I can't imagine what she's thinking. Be sure to give me all updates. Okay?" She frowned and looked at my clocks. "Where is that man with the carpet?" She dashed outside, and the three of us who remained sighed with relief.

"Maybe being a wedding coordinator wouldn't be the best career for Miss Veronica after all." Mr. DuBois rolled his serving cart toward the door. "I hope Miss Jacquie returns soon. In any event, tea will be served at two o'clock as previously planned."

Eric opened the door for him, then closed it. "Do you think he'll ever stop calling you *Miss* Florrie?"

I held my finger up across my lips. "He's slipped a few times. I didn't think it would ever happen, but now I'm hopeful. After all, he does call the professor *Maxwell*."

Eric wrapped his arms around me. "Oooh. Maybe he'll call you Fox. That's sort of cute." He became more serious. "Do you think the professor wants to file a missing person's report on Jacquie?"

"Maybe, if she's not back soon. She has a history of running when she's in danger. But I can't understand her taking off on the day of her wedding. She wanted this and I know for certain that she loves the professor. The way she looks at him tells me that she adores him."

"Is that how you look at me?" Eric teased.

"You'll have to figure that one out for yourself."

He kissed me in a way that made my toes tingle.

"I'll be back at six, Florrie. Let me know if Jacquie turns up."

He left and I closed the door behind him, wondering anew how I had gotten so lucky. The door opened again immediately. Veronica stormed in to pour herself an ill-advised fortieth cup of coffee. I didn't dare mention that she probably didn't need more caffeine.

"I honestly thought I might want to be a professional wedding planner. I don't mind putting out fires, but this is nerve-racking. Did you see this coming? Jacquie, I mean."

"No. I don't think anyone anticipated this."

In spite of our differences, Veronica and I were close. I had hired her to work at the bookstore when she was in a pinch, even though she wasn't much of a reader. Her social media skills had proven magical, propelling the bookstore to new heights of popularity. She had taken two weeks off to focus on Jacquie's party. I knew her days at Color Me Read were probably numbered. Veronica's outgoing personality lent itself better to a job such as a wedding coordinator. But she would have to learn to cope with unexpected developments.

I had taken the day off from the bookstore. Our longtime employee, Bob Turpin, was in charge, assisted by Professor Goldblum, a regular at the store. He hung out there almost every day anyway and knew Color Me Read as well as any of the employees. I was on the verge of hiring new employees. We were open seven days a week, and the three of us were struggling to cover all the shifts. Bob and Professor Goldblum would be closing the store at five to join us. That freed me up to spend the next few hours helping Veronica with details.

At ten in the morning, Professor Maxwell popped in to inform us that he had returned from the police station, where he'd reported Jacquie missing. I noted that he hadn't waited two hours after all. He must have been sick with worry.

I had finished drawing a floral design around a seating

chart to help people find their tables for dinner and was carrying an easel to the mansion when the professor barreled out the back door and into the driveway where I was walking.

"As if it's not bad enough that I have no idea what has happened to Jacquie, now the house is overflowing with people unloading dishes and sundry for tonight's party." His gruff voice grew softer when he said, "I don't know how we'll manage to get through tonight if she doesn't come home."

I set the easel down, and despite knowing it wasn't socially acceptable to hug one's boss, I did it anyway. "She'll be back." I meant it, too. It was inconceivable to me that she would just walk away.

Professor Maxwell didn't seem offended by my hug. He forced a brave smile. "I don't know where else to look. I'm going over to my office. Maybe I can focus better at the bookstore, without all the commotion here."

"I'll be there in a little while myself," I said. "Just to check on everything."

He nodded at me and walked away, looking older than his years.

Once the easel and table diagram were arranged on the back terrace, I let Mr. DuBois know I would be at the bookstore for a brief time. "Call me if you hear from Jacquie."

"Of course, Miss Florrie. And I shan't tell your sister that you have stepped out."

I grabbed a sign that I'd made about early closing hours and headed to Color Me Read.

It was a short walk, and I was glad to leave the wedding preparations behind, however briefly. The sky, clear and blue, announced the arrival of summer. Jacquie and John couldn't have chosen a better day for their celebration. If only we knew where she was. The police would probably visit the mansion soon. Or was that only in movies? As I walked, I began to think perhaps it would be better to cancel the celebration. Even if no one noticed Jacquie's absence, it seemed in bad taste to go forward with it. But what about the people from out of town? Some of them were staying at the mansion. Oh, Jacquie! What had she done?

I was on alert for my possible stalker, stopping occasionally to pretend I was admiring a garden. I didn't see anyone following me. I hadn't told anyone yet because I wasn't absolutely certain that I was being followed. John and Jacquie were high-profile people, and I had recently been pursued by members of the press because of my association with them. Professor Maxwell had apologized to me, explaining that their daughter's disappearance was periodically dredged up in the news. This appeared to be one of those times.

Sometimes I caught a glimpse of a woman with toffee-colored hair, but that didn't mean she was after me. She probably lived in the neighborhood and our paths happened to cross. She didn't look particularly sinister, either. And there wasn't a reason in the world for anyone to want to follow me or spy on me.

The store was located on a busy street with a lot of foot traffic. The three-story-plus-basement building had once been someone's home and, as such, had a parlor with a fireplace for cozy winter gatherings and a kitchen where we sold an assortment of gift items, cards, and wrapping paper in addition to cookbooks.

When I entered the store, not a soul stood at the checkout desk by the entrance. Classical music drifted through the rooms; otherwise it was quiet. I stepped behind the desk and propped my sign up where Bob and Professor Goldblum would see it. It simply announced shorter hours than usual for that particular day so the employees could have the evening off.

Where was Bob? We occasionally left the front desk unmanned while we worked nearby. But he should have noticed me by now.

The front door opened, and a woman stepped inside. She drew my attention immediately because she stifled a gasp when she saw me.

I hadn't seen my stalker up close, but I was fairly certain it was her. I knew that toffee-colored hair.

She sped toward the parlor, gripping her phone. She pretended to be interested in the books, but I could see her angling her camera at me through the arched doorway. I swiftly stepped behind the tall pyramid display of books that I had set up at the checkout desk.

Never did I imagine that reporters would be hounding *me*. After all, Color Me Read was in Georgetown, Washington, DC. In a town full of pompous politicians, each of whom had a media-hungry entourage, I was an incredibly uninteresting bookstore manager. True, I drew adult coloring books in my spare time, but try as I might when my first coloring book hit the market, I couldn't interest a soul in the media.

Yet now they were crawling through the bookstore because of Maxwell and Jacquie. I peered at her from between the artfully stacked books. She was in her late twenties, about my age, I thought. She looked like someone I might be friends with under other circumstances. She was medium height with straight hair that hung just below her shoulders, and she wore a vivid blue shirt tucked into a black pencil skirt.

She sighed and came over to the checkout desk, her hand now holding the camera to her side. "Are you Florrie?"

My initial instinct was to lie to her, which took me by surprise because I wasn't that kind of person. It must have been some sort of defense mechanism. I didn't particularly like to be deceptive. Lies complicated life far too much and I had nothing to hide. My life was entirely too humdrum for anyone to take interest in.

She pulled a newspaper from a large bag that hung on

her shoulder, glanced at it, and passed it to me. "Of course you are."

I gazed at the photo of me in the paper. I was half-turned, gazing back over my shoulder with a look on my face as if I were being pursued by Godzilla. "Oh, that's awful!"

"You're much prettier than that." She held out her hand for me to shake. "Cara Melton."

I shook her hand. "Why am I in the paper, anyway?" I shrank at the mere thought.

She read aloud, "'Local coloring-book artist Florrie Fox resides in the Maxwell mansion but eschews publicity. We can't help seeing a Maxwell family resemblance. Is she next in line to inherit the Maxwell fortune?'"

"Resemblance?" I snorted. "What garbage!"

"You look like your mother."

My mother told everyone she met that they should shop at Color Me Read. Thanks to her enthusiasm, more than one person had mistakenly thought I owned the store.

"Really? I don't think I resemble her. My sister, Veronica, is the one who looks like mom. Where did you meet my mother?"

"Waiting on tables. I work at Grosbard's Café."

"You're not a reporter?"

"I'm working on it. So far, I haven't been able to land a paying job, but I managed to get an internship at *The DC Chatter* so I'm trying to wow them."

I knew the paper, a small local rag that avoided the gritty side of politics. It concentrated on neighborhood news and the personal lives of local superstars.

"And you thought taking a picture of me—"

Cara waved her hand and looked genuinely contrite. "That's what you thought? No, no. I was taking a photo of the store. You have to admit there's quite a story here. A missing-child mystery and now her parents are reconciling again? Mystery and romance all in one."

I understood her point, even if it made me uncomfortable. I wasn't bold and outgoing like I imagined reporters must be. But I was insatiably inquisitive, which was probably the reason I liked reading mysteries so much. Still, it bothered me that people wanted to know more about the tragedy that had come between Jacquie and the professor many years ago. The last thing they needed was for Cara to dredge up the sadness again. They were getting married. It was a time for joy.

Jacquie had agreed to some interviews. I guessed it came with the territory of being a beloved author. And business was booming at Color Me Read, so I supposed there *were* benefits to the publicity. But I was glad I wasn't in the center of the commotion.

I thought it best to treat Cara like a customer. "Is there anything I can help you with?"

"What do you know about Caroline?"

Chapter 3

That wasn't what I meant. My tone grew hard. "Probably less than you do. She was kidnapped at the birthday party of a friend. I honestly don't know any more than that."

"Who was the friend?"

"I'm sorry, I really don't have any idea." It was the truth. What had happened to Bob? He was a terrific employee. He must have gotten tangled up with a customer somewhere. To my immense relief, the front door opened and some of our regular customers entered, each of them pausing to greet me.

Cara didn't have to know they were regulars who could probably show *me* where certain scholarly tomes could be found in the bookstore. Relieved to escape her, I fell in step with Professor Zsazsa Rosca. Peering in the rooms for Bob or Professor Goldblum as we walked, I ushered her to the coffee, and offered her one of the doughnuts Bob had picked up in the morning.

"To what do I owe this kind service?" she asked with a twinkle in her eye. Zsazsa had been named after the famous Hungarian actress. Her name suited her. She colored her hair a shade of red that almost glowed and applied black eyeliner with a heavy hand. She didn't believe in wearing drab colors, either. We were alike in that way.

"I'm dodging that reporter," I whispered.

She leaned sideways and looked past me down the hallway. "Ah. The one in the blue blouse?"

"That's her."

"I don't know what they think they'll find *here*. Maxwell didn't even own this building all those years ago when Caroline vanished."

Zsazsa bit into a doughnut. "Oh! Delicious! What a lovely treat." She looked over at Cara again. "A bit of a pest, eh? I shall keep an eye on her and pretend I need your help if she persists in her quest to annoy you."

"Thanks, I won't be here long. The carriage house is party central today. I escaped for a few minutes, but I'll be heading back soon. You'll be there tonight, won't you?"

"I wouldn't miss it!"

After a quick look at the checkout desk to be sure no one was waiting for service, I went in search of Bob to tell him about the sign I made and make sure everything was running smoothly. As I crested the top of the stairs to the third floor, I caught Cara trying the door handle to Professor Maxwell's office.

I hurried in her direction to stop her. "Cara? Is there something I can do for you?"

She hastily turned the handle and swung the door open. Professor Maxwell looked up from his work.

He locked his eyes on her but didn't say a word.

Cara rushed at him. "Professor Maxwell! What good luck to find you here." She pulled a pen and a lined yellow pad from her bag. "How do you feel about your daughter's abduction all these years later?"

His shoulders and face tightened. I could feel anger rippling out from him in waves. He stood up, towering over

Cara, raised one hand, and pointed his forefinger at the door. "Out!" he bellowed.

"I know it must be very emotional for you . . . ," she blathered.

His eyes widened at her impudence.

I rushed toward Cara and wedged my way between her and the professor's desk. "It's time to leave," I stated firmly.

She looked at me like I was an annoying gnat.

"Professor Maxwell only gives interviews by appointment, and those are precious few. I'm afraid I have to ask you to leave the store."

"You're awfully protective of the old geezer," Cara said with a simper.

"You have been asked nicely. Do I need to call the police?" I asked.

"I haven't done anything wrong," she whined, stepping sideways.

I whirled around, grabbed the phone on the desk, and punched in 911.

"All right! You don't have to do that."

I turned to face her, the phone in my hand. She didn't have to know that I had disconnected the call.

Cara scowled at me and finally took a step backward.

I hung up the phone.

Cara smiled coyly at the professor. "Won't you please grant me a few minutes of your time? I've heard about the things you did for your students to help them with their careers. It would be such a boost for me to get an interview with you."

Professor Maxwell sat down. "In that case, I suggest you reflect on what happened here today and learn from it." His tone was dismissive. Any sensible person would have known she had been sent away.

I made a point of not touching her. She was just the sort to twist things around and accuse me of assault. But I maintained my position between her and the professor and continued to step forward, thus forcing her to back up and out the door.

"Does that mean he'll give me an interview?"

I closed the door behind me and studied her. Could she really be that dense? I would have crawled away in shame by now. I tried to sound official. "Professor Maxwell will not be giving any interviews in the foreseeable future."

Her mouth twitched to the side. "I went for the wrong one, didn't I?"

I knew exactly what she meant. If I had been a nicer person, perhaps I would have shrugged it off or laughed. But I was angry. This woman didn't know or care about Jacquie and the professor and she was doing her level best to bring up the worst thing that had ever happened to them. How dare she impose on them like that? And it was all the worse because she was ignoring their pain in the interest of advancing her own desires in life.

I probably sounded testy when I said, "Jacquie is very busy."

I gestured toward the stairs. As I walked down behind her, I pulled my cell phone from my pocket and opened the camera app so I would be ready.

As I expected, on the bottom floor she turned around and asked, "How would I request an interview with one of them?"

As quickly as I possibly could, I held the camera up, angled it, and snapped her picture while saying, "You would have to go through their attorney at Strickland, Wheeler, and Erba. But I can save you some time. Neither of them will be granting interviews in the next few months."

She snorted unhappily and strode toward the front of the

store. I followed her, and as luck had it, Eric walked in with a police officer in uniform.

Cara twirled toward me. "You called the police? I thought you hung up. Did you dial 911 behind my back when I was walking down the stairs and already leaving?" She turned to them. "I didn't do anything illegal. I swear." She shot me a hateful look. Her nostrils flaring and her eyes showing her outrage, she swept past them and out the door.

"Perfect timing!" I said.

Eric frowned and gazed after her. "Problems?"

"I don't think she'll return. She's a novice reporter who needs to learn when to back off."

"I'm not sure that's in their nature." He swept a hand through his loose curls and smiled at me. "They wouldn't last very long if they didn't turn up interesting stories."

His friend nodded.

"Sorry, forgot my manners. DuBois told me I could find you here. I wanted you to meet Fish Gordon. He's going to be patrolling around the mansion tonight."

Had I understood that correctly? I glanced at the name pin on his shirt. Sure enough, it said Gordon. I shuddered to think how much ribbing he had taken as a kid. Maybe it was a nickname. He was in his late twenties with hair the color of cinnamon toast. A crease had already developed between his eyebrows, giving him a serious look. A plush mustache almost covered his upper lip.

He must have been used to explaining his unusual name because he said, "It's a family name. My grandmother is a Fish. Jezebel Fish. All things considered, I'm grateful that they didn't name me Jezebel."

I smiled at the humor he had incorporated in what was undoubtedly a standard line he used. A clever icebreaker that said a lot about him. "It's nice to meet you, Fish. Do you anticipate problems tonight?"

Eric shook his head. "There haven't been any threats, if that's what you mean. But there will be a lot of locally high-profile types in attendance. Traffic will probably get tied up in the neighborhood."

"I seem to recall Veronica saying something about a valet service, so maybe it won't be too bad," I said. I hadn't thought much about it at the time, but I could see how a couple hundred cars might clog up the residential street. Where would they all park? I smiled at Fish. "I hope you'll come inside for your break and have some dinner."

"That's nice of you, but"—he wrinkled his nose—"the bride might not like a uniformed cop wandering around."

"I don't think Jacquie would mind one bit," said Eric. "Any word from her yet?"

I shook my head.

"And I can assure you that the butler, Mr. DuBois, will be thrilled to see you," said Eric.

Fish looked surprised. "Okay. Thanks for the invite, Florrie."

Professor Maxwell appeared. "Is she gone?"

"Eric's fortuitous arrival put a scare in her and she took off."

"I loathe being locked into my own office just to keep the public out. I can't concentrate. It's like a scene in a horror movie. I can't tell what will be on the other side when the door opens."

I spied Zsazsa in the parlor and excused myself. Trying to act casual, I strode in and motioned to her to join me on the far side of the room, where the professor wouldn't see us.

I whispered, "We have a problem. No one can find Jacquie. Professor Maxwell has tried to be calm, but I think he could use a distraction. Or maybe a friend to talk to? I'd ask Professor Goldblum, but he's pitching in here today and we're short-handed as it is."

Zsazsa frowned. "That's terrible! Did they have a fight?"

"Not that I know. Maybe you can get information out of him."

Zsazsa nodded vigorously. "I'll take care of Maxwell. Don't worry about him."

"Thanks, Zsazsa." I returned to Eric and Fish, who were explaining the missing-person process to Professor Maxwell.

"She's not a person in need, not a child or disabled in some way. They get priority treatment, but I expect someone will be around to have a look at the house and ask questions this afternoon or tomorrow morning," said Eric.

"I thought I heard your voice," said Zsazsa, as she emerged from the parlor. "I'm on my way over to see a former student who just returned from Chengdu, Sichuan province—"

Maxwell's eyes opened wide. "He saw the newly uncovered tombs?"

"He has even brought back exclusive photos."

Professor Maxwell appeared torn.

Before he could object, I said, "Go with her. You have your phone, so you will be the first to know when Jacquie comes home. I'll make her call you. And if she doesn't, then I promise I will phone you."

He shot me a tired look but finally nodded and followed Zsazsa out the door. Eric and Fish left the store right behind them.

I watched them go, unable to stop smiling. Unlike Veronica, who'd had a steady stream of beaux, I had only dated a few guys. I had plenty of male friends, but there hadn't been a spark. Eric treasured books as much as I did. I appreciated his calm, thoughtful approach to crises. I never thought I would find a guy like him and was astounded that things were still going well between us.

When they left the bookstore, I noticed that the professor paused on the landing outside the door and looked around as if making sure Cara wasn't lurking nearby.

I found Bob and explained about the sign. "Should I stick around a while?"

"Nah, I've got it covered. A customer needed my help on the second floor and it took a while. You go on."

"I don't suppose you have any friends who would like to work here?"

"I can ask around, but I won't be holding my breath."

I left the store before he changed his mind about my offer to stay. Jacquie's disappearance weighed heavily on me. If she had gone somewhere, surely she would have returned or called us by now. I imagined her on a train gazing out the window, weighing her abrupt decision to leave. Everything had been going so well between Jacquie and the professor. At least it had seemed that way to me. One never knew what was really going on behind closed doors.

As I ambled along the sidewalk, a cocker spaniel barked in his yard. A squirrel had likely eluded him, I thought. He remained intent on his prey. The squirrel was undoubtedly taunting him from the safety of a tree.

But the next sound I heard was unfamiliar. Definitely not the chatter of an angry squirrel. I stopped to listen.

Was someone moaning?

I peered at the beautifully landscaped lawn. Short brick retaining walls kept the lush gardens at bay. "What is it, fellow?" I asked the dog.

He wagged his tail briefly but commenced barking again.

The moan grew louder. I glanced at the house, wondering if the owner would think I was trespassing. I probably was. I inched along the sidewalk toward the house.

I braced myself in anticipation of an angry voice yelling at me from a window. Well into the brush on my right, the sun filtering through the trees reflected on something shiny. As I drew closer, I realized it was a glittering half-moon.

Chapter 4

My heart pounded so loud I could hear it in my ears. I had seen Jacquie wearing a similar moon on a necklace. She favored white shirts open at the neck, usually with a necklace inside the collar. As I drew closer, I could see flesh and the collar of a shirt.

"Jacquie?" I inquired tentatively.

"Mhhh."

I jumped onto the short wall and parted plants. Jacquie lay on her back, her eyes open, her hands reaching toward me.

"Jacquie!" I kneeled next to her and smiled.

Her faux-blond hair bushed out, wildly askew. "Floor. Floor." She repeated an attempt at my name over and over.

"I'll call an ambulance."

But her fingers wrapped around my wrist. "No! No, no, no. Up."

I clutched her hands and pulled her forward into a sitting position. "Jacquie, you need help."

She shook her head. "Jus' de-hy-dray . . . Stand."

I wasn't sure she could stand. But if not, that was all the more reason to call an ambulance, I reasoned. She wrapped her arms around my neck, and I did my best to pull her upright.

She proved me wrong and held her own, not even leaning on me for balance. She licked her lips. "Let's . . . go . . . home."

She had to sit down and swing her legs over the little brick retaining wall, but she managed, appearing stronger with each passing minute.

I pulled out my phone, but she placed her hand over it. "Where is Maxwell?" She still spaced her words and her voice was tentative.

"He's with Goldblum. I promised him I would call with news about you."

"And so you shall. As soon as I clean up a bit. Don't want him to see me like this."

The little cocker spaniel had stopped barking and came to us for petting. Jacquie smiled and caressed his head. "Thanks for waking me, little guy."

We walked back to the mansion, Jacquie gaining strength rapidly. The color had returned to her face.

"What happened?"

"I'm not sure," Jacquie said in little more than a whisper. She sounded a bit befuddled.

"Were you mugged?"

Jacquie stopped walking and patted her jeans pockets. "My phone and wallet . . . gone. Maybe so."

"You don't remember?"

She placed one hand on her forehead. "I was so groggy when you found me. But I'm feeling much better now."

"Jacquie, you must have hit your head. I really think you should go to the emergency room and get checked out."

"You're . . . sweet. I'm fine, honey. Just fine." She began to walk again.

"Jacquie! I don't understand. You must have gotten out of bed and gone outside."

She spoke with more vigor. "I went for a walk and got mugged. End of story."

I didn't believe her. There was more to it than that. There had to be! And even if that was true, had it happened to me, I would have been hysterical.

"Jacquie, no one is going to believe that."

She stopped again and gazed at me. "Florrie, are there people in your life whom you will always go to if they need help? Even in the middle of the night?"

I didn't have to think long about that. My parents, Veronica, Eric, Bob, the professor, and a few more. "Yes. And you are one of them."

She smiled. "Same here, darlin'. But I'm not saying anything more about last night. As far as I'm concerned, I went for a walk, was mugged, and now it's over."

She marched toward the mansion determinedly. I had to move fast to keep up.

"All I need is a shower and a nap. Oh, look! Everything is underway."

It was almost one in the afternoon but the street in front of the mansion was already packed with cars. Catering trucks lined the circular driveway in front of the house. People scurried in and out carting boxes of champagne, glasses, and plates.

Jacquie disappeared into the mansion, and I pulled out my phone to call the professor. I had promised to call him. What Jacquie chose to tell him was her problem. "Professor Maxwell? Great news. Jacquie is home and apparently quite fine."

"Where was she?"

"I'm not sure." That was the truth. "Will you notify the police that she has returned home?"

"Yes. Thank you, Florrie."

I hung up and went in search of Mr. DuBois and Veronica. They asked the same questions I had put to Jacquie. I simply said they would have to ask her.

An hour later, Jacquie, carrying a bottle of water, found us outside where Veronica was directing the florist on the placement of giant floral arrangements. They overflowed with blooms and were far too heavy for us to move later on should they be in the wrong places.

The yard behind the mansion was the size of a small park, yet Jacquie's mere presence filled it with warmth. She exuded an effervescence that drew people to her. I had never met anyone else with her ability to walk into a room or situation and immediately become the center of attention.

"Veronica!" she cried. "I'm so sorry to have worried you. Will you forgive me?" Without waiting for a response, she hugged Veronica and me, then surveyed the property. "It's wonderful!"

White wood folding chairs had been placed in perfect rows with an aisle cutting through the middle. A gentleman was unrolling a soft coral carpet down the aisle toward the hundreds of azaleas, rhododendrons, and lilacs that bloomed at the edge of towering oaks, sugar maples, and tulip poplars. The heavenly scent of lilacs wafted to us.

"It's simply beautiful. I was worried about the coral being too pink, too girlish for a woman my age, but I think it's just right. And the azalea bushes steal the show."

I had to agree with Jacquie. They were worth seeing, even without a wedding or a party.

We returned to the carriage house, where Peaches roamed among us, rubbing our ankles. Veronica had the moxie to ask Jacquie, "What happened last night?"

I was slightly aghast at her boldness, but I was curious, too.

Jacquie didn't seem to mind. "I couldn't sleep, so I went for a stroll. The stars and the moon were so beautiful. And then someone mugged me. I guess I hit my head when I fell, and the next thing I knew it was daylight, a little dog was barking at me, and Florrie was helping me up."

Leaving no time for questions, she deftly changed the topic. "I needed to feel Caroline yesterday afternoon. You know how upset Maxwell gets when I mention any psychic connection to her. I thought I would slip over there and he'd never be the wiser."

"Slip over where?" I asked. Caroline had never been found. What was Jacquie talking about?

"The Sorellos' house, where she was last seen. I walk by sometimes, but yesterday Grady and Celeste came out and chatted with me. I hadn't spoken to them in decades. We've all aged so much. I don't think I'd have recognized them if I had seen them on the street. Veronica, I hope it won't upset the plans, but I invited them to come to the party tonight. We can squeeze in two more seats, can't we?"

Jacquie didn't wait for an answer, but Veronica didn't seem put out. Jacquie picked up Peaches and sat down on the sofa, stroking her fur. "It was their little girl's birthday party. You can imagine how guilty they still feel. Caroline and another little girl were snatched from under their noses. They were responsible for all the children at the party."

Jacquie didn't say it in an accusatory tone, but I could imagine that she faulted them for allowing someone to take her child.

She forced a sad smile. "I never meant to stay so long. But I couldn't pass up a chance to talk about that day. I thought perhaps there was something that came to their minds later on. Years later, even. You know how that goes. You relive an event in your mind over and over. Sometimes a tiny detail can come to light."

"Did that happen?" asked Veronica.

"Nooo." Jacquie dragged the word out as if she was musing. "But they speculated that the police may not have been thorough with the other children present."

"What do you mean?" I asked.

Jacquie sighed. "We've come so far with investigations. DNA changed everything. And child witnesses are handled differently today. Back then, the focus was on getting the children back to their parents and trying to protect them from the tragic side of life. They were very young. But children can be amazingly observant. You know what I mean. Out of the blue they'll ask something like 'Why doesn't Daddy like Mr. Bluenose?' And you think, 'Now how did she pick up on that?' We treat them like they don't know what's going on, but they do."

"Did you warn the professor that the Sorellos are coming?" I dared ask. He was a reasonable person, but each of them had coped with the loss of their daughter in a different way. The professor was often quite gruff about it.

"Yes. I think he'll be all right."

Someone knocked at the door. I peered out the tiny window in the door at a group of women. When I opened the door, my mother burst in first, all smiles. She held out her arms, bypassed Veronica and me, and made a beeline to Jacquie.

Jacquie's hairdresser and manicurist were right behind Mom. Roxie, Jacquie's assistant, brought up the rear.

Greetings and hugs were exchanged, followed by a brief discussion about what should be done first. They were just getting down to business when Veronica shrieked, "The tables for the favors! They have to be set up in the foyer."

I held up my palms to stop her as she leaped from her chair. "Relax. I'll go check on them."

To tell the truth, I was happy to get out of there for a few minutes. I let myself into the mansion through the back door.

The caterers were at work in the kitchen. I darted through, staying out of their way, and headed to the foyer.

Veronica was correct. The tables had not been set up. I spied them outside, where they had been forgotten. A truck with the name of the event-furnishings company idled in the circular drive. I hurried to it and asked about the tables. The driver moaned and called, "Everybody out."

It took them all of ten minutes to set up the tables. Had Mr. DuBois and I been left with that job, it would have taken an hour, so I was relieved that I had caught them before they left. I stood on the front stoop and watched them pull out onto the street. A tall lean man stood there, gazing around as if unsure of himself.

Chapter 5

He had the tanned skin of a golfer. His lush white mustache matched a full head of wavy silver hair. Bushy coffee-colored eyebrows rose in peaks, giving him a rascally look. The perfect fit of his well-tailored tuxedo suggested it had been custom-made. He was far too early for a guest, though. And surely the minister wouldn't be wearing a tux.

I walked toward him and went with the completely neutral phrase "May I help you?"

He turned and quite literally looked down at me with brown eyes. The expression on his face was somewhat annoyed, as though I were a pesky child. In that moment, I recognized the heavily lidded sensual brown eyes. Arthur Bedlingham! I wondered how he had looked when he was young. I did my best not to stutter or say something stupid to the brilliant author.

In a cultured southern voice he said, "I am lookin' for Jacqueline Liebhaber. I fear the bossy woman in the front wearing an abhorrent T-shirt declaring her the wedding coordinator shooed me away. Is there a wedding goin' on today?"

Ouch. I held out my hand. "I apologize, Mr. Bedlingham. I'm Florrie Fox. I manage John Maxwell's bookstore."

His eyebrows rose. "I must do a signin' for you some-time."

I faked a smile to disguise my panic. I didn't think it would be a success. One reviewer had called his most recent book "abstruse" *and* "impenetrable." I quickly switched the subject, hoping he would forget. Besides, maybe he'd just offered that to be nice. "Jacquie is in the carriage house getting ready for the party."

"Wonderful. Would you show me the way?"

He followed me to the carriage house, where I knocked on the door, opened it, and poked my head inside. "Is everyone decent? Jacquie has a visitor."

There was a chorus of "Bring him in. Anyone except John!"

I opened the door and stepped aside to allow him in.

"Jacqueline, sweetheart!" He held out his arms and kissed her on both cheeks. "How do you do it? Honestly, you look even more beautiful each time I see you."

Despite Jacquie's graciousness, I thought I detected a hint of discomfort, a barely perceptible second of hesitation before she introduced him to my mother, who to my complete surprise appeared to recognize his name. "Mr. Bedlingham!" she tittered, bashful as a schoolgirl. "What an honor to meet you."

"The honor is mine, ma'am." He bowed to kiss her hand.

Mom giggled like a ten-year-old and I winced.

He nodded politely at the hairdresser and manicurist as they were introduced. They were both engaged in their tasks and nodded back at him, probably thrilled they didn't have to have their hands kissed.

"Darlin', have you redecorated since the last time I was here?"

I quaked a little bit as he eyed the long wall of book-shelves, which were loaded with books, my artwork, and my clock collection. Would he notice that not a single recent copy of his books was on my shelves? All I had was *The Death of Mrs. Grimkill*, Arthur's last hit, published ten years before. It was the heartbreaking story of a young woman who had attached herself to a man who didn't love her. She clung to him, trying to please him. He wasn't harsh or vicious; his true cruelty lay in his complete indifference to her. When I read it, I almost wished he would be horrid so she would finally leave him and live a happy life of her own.

I kicked myself mentally for not lining my shelves with the books of the authors who were invited to the party. Then again, I never dreamed one of them would be in my home.

"Florrie lives here now. We're planning to build a small addition to the mansion so I can have a private office of my own again."

"After all you went through, you're back together again." He took Jacquie's hands into his.

"Incredible, isn't it?" Was it my imagination or was Jacquie gritting her teeth and pulling away from him? "Could I see you for a moment outside?"

"Of course!"

Jacquie excused herself and Arthur followed her into my garden. We could see them through the French doors, one of which Arthur had left open just a crack, enough for Peaches to sneak out if she tried.

While she often lounged in the sun or prowled in the walled garden, I didn't want her out there on her own. Although the wall had thoughtfully been designed with an inward-slanting top to prevent cats from escaping, they were clever, and the last thing I needed was for Peaches to choose today to figure out how to scale the garden wall.

Trying to be discreet, I walked slowly toward the open door, while watching Peaches, who had already noticed the escape route.

I picked up speed and so did she.

She beat me to the door by seconds, but paused briefly, halfway out. Just enough time for me to grab her. I promptly fell but did not release my grip on Peaches. In the few moments it took me to get on my feet without using my hands, which were full of squirming cat, I overheard Jacquie and Arthur.

"Just what do you think you're doing, Arthur?" Jacquie didn't hold back. She was angry.

"What do you mean?" At least he sounded sincere.

Jacquie let loose a loud guffaw. "You never change. But I have. I'm no longer the girl who was willing to put up with your nonsense. Is it money? Is that what you want?"

"All I need is you."

"So help me, Arthur, if you do anything to ruin my relationship with John, you *will* regret it."

I scrambled to my feet and pushed the door closed, still clinging to Peaches, who let out a bloodcurdling yowl of protest. She sprang from my arms and ran halfway up the stairs, where she sat in a huff.

Mom launched into a story about a rambunctious kitten we had when I was a child. But I was thinking about Jacquie.

I had feared Jacquie would want the carriage house back when she married John. I loved living here. I could walk to the bookstore in minutes, instead of driving in from northern Virginia, where the rent was more affordable. Plus occasionally I'd needed to respond to a crisis at the bookstore in the middle of the night, not to mention how helpful it was to be close by when it snowed. Living in the carriage house allowed me to open the bookstore for all the people strolling about in the snow looking for a good book to curl up with. Happily, Jacquie was excited about designing a new space in which she could write. At the moment, it looked like I would be staying put.

As it was her third marriage and the groom's fourth, they

had dispensed with such matters as bridal showers and bachelor parties. No ball-gown-style wedding dress for her, and no bridesmaids, flower girls, or wedding gifts. After all, they had been wed before—to each other.

Everyone was happy for them. But none more so than Mr. DuBois, who I suspected might be a romantic at heart since he had told Jacqueline she was his favorite of John's three wives and that the two of them were meant to be together. At that moment, there was a knock on the door and he pushed a serving cart into the carriage house. It was laden with a silver tea samovar, and all the makings of a proper British afternoon tea.

Jacquie and Arthur returned from their private chat.

Wizened little DuBois maintained proper protocol, but I knew him well enough to note that he stiffened. He nodded his head and murmured, "Mr. Bedlingham," in a polite, if unenthusiastic, greeting.

"This can't be Mr. DuBois!" exclaimed Bedlingham. "I thought you'd have forsaken Maxwell by now. Haven't you earned a retirement?"

Mr. DuBois set about transforming my small dining table into a wondrous tea. He whisked a pristine pink tablecloth over it, laid out napkins, plates, forks, and fine porcelain teacups. The silver stand he placed in the center of the table nearly overflowed with tiny triangular sandwiches, scones, petits fours, and miniature tarts and éclairs.

"DuBois," said Jacquie, "this is marvelous. Just what we need to keep up our strength until dinner."

Mr. DuBois smiled at her like a doting uncle. "My pleasure, Miss Jacqueline."

Mr. DuBois had been with the Maxwell family for decades. I thought of him as very much a part of the Maxwell family. He had been overjoyed when Professor Maxwell asked him to be his best man.

"Well then, I must be off," said Arthur. "I shall leave you delightful ladies to your tea. Jacquie, perhaps the two of us can find time for a little chat at your party this evening." Bedlingham kissed Jacquie again. "Florrie, darlin', we must chat about a signin' tonight."

I nodded my head and said as sweetly as I could, "I look forward to it." Another lie! What was going on with me? Of course, I couldn't exactly tell him we didn't carry his books. I saw him to the door and closed it behind him. Maybe I was wrong. Would people come to buy his books if it gave them an opportunity to meet him? After all, he must have a following. He was famous. Even my mother knew who he was.

Although there was no real wedding party, Jacquie, Mom, Veronica, and I had our nails and hair done while we enjoyed the tea goodies and helped Jacquie dress.

"Arthur Bedlingham," said Mom. "Could I borrow one of his books from you, Florrie? I always hear about him, but I've never read anything he wrote."

"Not a recent one," said Jacquie. "Arthur can be charming, but most of the time he's as tedious and boring as his last book. Linda," she said to my mom, "if you'd like to read something by one of the guests, I would recommend a book by Gabriella Archambeau or her husband, Griffin Corbyn. Gabriella's romances are simply enchanting. They will sweep you away into the lives of her characters. Griffin, on the other hand, writes thrillers that always make the bestseller lists. He's a bit of a recluse. Rumor has it that he was a spy in a prior career and he now chooses to keep to himself out of fear of retaliation."

"Nooo!" breathed my mother. "Will he be here tonight?"

"He was invited, of course, but I would be shocked if he attended. Poor Gabriella generally attends everything unescorted."

"I wouldn't like that at all." Mom frowned. "My Mike isn't as exciting as a spy, but I would hate going to everything by myself."

I walked over to my wall of books, art, and clocks and selected three books for my mom. One by Gabriella called *The Midnight Rose*, one by her husband, Griffin Corbyn, *The St. George Conspiracy,* and *The Death of Mrs. Grimkill* by Arthur Bedlingham. I handed them to her.

Jacquie exclaimed, "Great choices, Florrie. *The Death of Mrs. Grimkill* was a big hit for Arthur."

"You seem to know Arthur very well." Mom bit into a tiny lemon tart.

"We go way back. We knew one another before either of us was published. It all seems so long ago now. Like another lifetime." Jacquie laughed at herself. "It *was* a long time ago! I was a salesperson at Garfinckel's, a very lovely upscale department store—"

Mom gasped. "I remember that store. I shopped there all the time."

Jacquie grinned. "I bet our paths crossed! In those days Arthur drove a taxi. He insisted it would provide him with fodder for his stories. It probably did."

"Did I detect a bit of familiarity?" asked Mom.

Veronica gasped and I shot Mom a look.

Jacquie admired her nails. "We were young and in love. At the time, I'm sure we complained constantly, but now that I look back on it with rose-colored glasses, I think it was a wonderful period of my life. We were terribly frustrated with our failures. I'm afraid there isn't a lot of encouragement in the fiction-writing process. In the beginning, rejections are as plentiful as raindrops in a storm. And each of them feels like a personal affront. Manuscript after manuscript is abandoned in the hope that the next one will be better. And then one day, the miracle happens." She smiled broadly. "Even then we had second jobs to support ourselves. The advance on my first romance was barely enough to pay the rent for a month. Arthur's parents were quite well-off but his father refused to give him a dime unless he gave up writing and got a real job or went to graduate school. Bless his mother. She came through with a little extra cash every month so we could make ends meet."

"What happened to you and Arthur?" asked Veronica.

"I'm afraid Arthur didn't think much of my romance books. He put them down every chance he got. He was envious, of course. How could *I* possibly have a contract to write romances when he couldn't sell his"—her tone changed to sarcasm—"vastly superior books? That was the end for me. I understood his pain and bitterness, but I couldn't take his constant belittling and I left. He consoled himself by drinking." She shook her head. "He would call me in the middle of the night, and every time, I went to pick him up at a bar and drove him home."

She looked at us with sadness. "Well, I couldn't let him stagger through the streets!"

"How did you meet the professor?" asked Veronica.

"At a dinner party. Finding Maxwell was the best thing that ever happened to me." Jacquie's eyes widened. "Florrie, have you got a pen and a scrap of paper?"

I handed her a pen and a notepad.

"Perfect." She scribbled a note. "*Finding Maxwell* should be the title of my next book. Anyway, I married Maxwell and pretty much cut off communication with Arthur. And then one day, he left a manuscript on our doorstep called *Isle of Lament*. I read it and wept. And then I picked up the phone and called my agent. She thought it was wonderful, too. It went to auction with several publishing houses bidding on it, and when it came out, *Isle of Lament* was an instant sensation. Truly his best book in my opinion. He reveled in his fame.

But the book that followed wasn't as wonderful. It happens. He went back to the bottle and there was a long succession of books that received some degree of acclaim but didn't sell well. This business can be such a roller-coaster ride. And then there was another bomb. When his money ran out, Arthur started teaching writing classes, which was how he eventually met Gabriella. She was one of his students. Happily, *The Death of Mrs. Grimkill* brought kudos again. He desperately needed help managing everything, and Gabriella was tired of waiting on tables, so he hired her as his assistant. His cycle of brilliant success and dismal failure continues to this day."

"Your fiancé doesn't mind that you invited a former boyfriend to your wedding?" asked the hairdresser.

Jacquie had just selected a pink-iced petit four from the tray. She held it in her fingers and froze momentarily. "Veronica, would you check the guest list? I don't believe Arthur was invited."

Veronica checked her iPad. "He's not on here." Veronica snapped her fingers. "Gabriella asked us if she could bring someone else since her husband doesn't attend parties. I bet she's the one who invited Arthur."

"I'm sure you're right," Jacquie agreed. "Gabriella has no idea this is a wedding."

"She's one of your best friends and you didn't tell her?" I asked.

"Gabriella is wonderful, but she *cannot* keep a secret. Sometimes I wonder if that's a writer's affliction. We spend so much time by ourselves that once we start talking, we just don't know when to stop. No matter. John won't care if Arthur is in attendance. After all, John is the one I'm marrying. He doesn't know that my first book to be published, *Sparks in the Stars*, was based on Arthur. He doesn't *need* to know that. It's all ancient history."

Someone rapped on the door. I looked out the window at

a woman I didn't recognize. I opened the door. "Yes? May I help you?"

Jacquie called out, "Mia? Is that you?"

"Oh! I *am* in the right place. You must be Florrie. Jacquie has told me all about you. I'm an artist, too."

Veronica hurried over to her and introduced herself. She turned to the rest of us. "Mia will be sketching guests today, and they'll be able to take their sketches home with them. Isn't that fun?"

I poured Mia a cup of tea. It seemed to me she had arrived early, but she was dressed for the party. She wore a most curious dress. It looked as though she had painted abstract peonies and roses around the waist in broad strokes and splattered the vibrant reds, pinks, and purples on the top and the bottom. It made me want to try my hand at painting on a dress.

Veronica tapped her watch. "Ladies, enough about books. It's time for Jacquie to get dressed."

We took that not-so-subtle hint, and as Mom and I walked upstairs to dress, I heard Veronica whisper to Jacquie, "I'm enjoying being the boss. I snap my fingers and they do what they're told. That has never happened before!"

When I returned, I joined Mia for a cup a tea and a mini lemon tart.

"Jacquie has been encouraging me to try my hand at a coloring book," she said. "How did you go about getting it published?" She pushed orangey-blond bangs out of her face. They were a color I had come to associate with brunettes who colored their hair. Indeed, her eyebrows were several shades darker, with two deep wrinkles between her eyes. She looked tired. She hadn't been able to cover up the dark circles under her eyes with makeup, and her lids hung heavy.

"You can go directly to a publisher or through an agent. In my case, Jacquie suggested I contact her agent, who took me on. She'll be here tonight. Make sure I introduce you. Either way, if they're interested, they'll want to see a full collection of finished drawings for a book before they'll take you on as a client."

"That would be great. I love being an artist, but sometimes it's hard to get a steady flow of income. You know?"

"Absolutely. I manage a bookstore and sketch on the side."

At that moment, Veronica shooed us out of the carriage house. I led Mia outside. She carried a bag with her. Drawing paper peeked out and we had a short conversation about which papers we preferred for sketching.

She excused herself, walked to the first row of the seats, and began to draw.

Chapter 6

Just as the musicians started to play "Clair de Lune," I slid into the empty chair between my mom and Eric. My dad peered past my mom and flashed a grin at me. We watched Jacquie walk down the aisle by herself, surrounded by five hundred friends. She carried a simple bouquet of coral and white roses and wore a dazzling floor-length white dress. It featured a tasteful V-neck and was adorned with Swarovski crystals and small pearls. It really could be worn to a gala. Only the white color suggested a wedding. Jacquie had considered a cream dress, but everyone had agreed that white went better with her complexion and silvery-blond hair. She wanted to keep it simple and had insisted there would be no train or veil.

Jacquie came to a halt in front of the minister. The groom, John Maxwell, smiled at her as though he was glad this day had finally come. In his youth, Professor Maxwell had been quite handsome. Even now, he was a remarkably stunning man with a face that was both aristocratic and rugged.

His bronzed skin was as creased as the ancient maps he continually studied and compared in his quest to uncover treasures lost to history. His upper eyelids drooped over kind violet eyes. The effect was enchanting. Like a wizard who had seen too much and knew the wisdom of the ages.

Mr. DuBois stood beside him as the best man, the only member of the wedding party.

Jacquie, Maxwell, Mr. DuBois, and the minister gathered in front of hundreds of azaleas and rhododendrons in full bloom. Jacquie had said the riot of color from the flowers was all she needed in decor. She had been right. Even the most talented florist couldn't have made anything that would have rivaled the gorgeous display of color behind them.

Gasps rose as a precious little pink pig trotted down the aisle toward them. She wore a diamond collar, clearly dressed for the occasion. When she sat down in front of John and Jacquie, the gasps turned to laughter.

Mom leaned over and whispered, "Was that planned?"

"I don't think so." I looked around for Veronica.

She stood in the back, her mouth open and her hands clasped to the sides of her face.

Fortunately, Professor Maxwell and Jacquie laughed, too. They ignored the little pig and continued. A wise move, I thought. If anyone had tried to catch the little pig, she would undoubtedly have run, creating mayhem.

Maxwell took Jacquie's hand into his as they recited their vows. In an odd quirk, at that moment my mom reached out for my right hand and Eric took my left hand into his.

The couple's masses of friends oohed sentimentally, few of them having known that Jacquie and John would be wed at the party. The newlyweds were at an age where they were most certainly not in need of vases, silver, or china. They truly did not want gifts, and Jacquie had claimed that suggesting people make donations to their favorite charities was too much like when a death occurred. Nor did the couple want their celebration to become a means of collecting funds to support some cause. They thought the best idea would be to throw a grand party and surprise their friends. Jacquie wanted as little fuss as possible. "It should be fun," she'd said, "with a lovely dinner and dancing under the stars."

I scanned the guests in search of my stalker and guessed from the beaming faces that Jacquie and John had accomplished their mission of surprising their friends.

Jacquie had invited a good number of her author friends. Nevertheless, it was a bit of a shock to see Buzz Powers among the guests. A retired FBI agent, he was the hottest new and upcoming author. If I could get him to come to the bookstore for a signing, there would be a line out the door. Would it be gauche to approach him about a signing tonight? Probably. I could make a point of meeting him tonight and call him next week about a signing.

The musicians struck up a lively rendition of "When the Saints Go Marching In." All smiles, Jacquie and John returned down the aisle, officially married again. As they walked, the guests formed a conga line behind them, and the party was on. I had no idea where the pig had gone.

My mom turned to me. "When you and Veronica were born, I never imagined that the two of you would involve your dad and me in high-society celebrations." Dad seized her hand and off they went, with Eric and me right behind them.

Silly as it seemed, it was fun. Everyone danced, even the minister and Mr. DuBois.

Waiters made an entrance and walked among the guests with trays of raw oysters, prosciutto-wrapped mangoes with goat cheese, caviar and sour-cream mini-tarts, savory Parmesan palmiers, and olive crostadas.

Veronica rounded up our mom, Mr. DuBois, Eric, and me and ushered us into the mansion foyer where dozens of boxes filled with cupcakes were stacked in neat rows. In short order, Veronica had us all hard at work filling favor boxes with cupcakes.

Jacquie and John were so adamant about no gifts that they'd written a little note to be tucked into each favor. It read:

> We are so pleased that you could join us for our party and nuptials. As you can imagine, we really don't want any gifts. Mr. DuBois requests that you not increase his chores by sending gifts, because they will be returned. Your presence is a gift to us. We are grateful that you have honored us by sharing our special day.
>
>   Jacquie Liebhaber and John Maxwell

Unfortunately, we could hear an angry discussion. I recognized the voices of Professor Maxwell and Mr. DuBois, but who was the woman?

"What could possibly have possessed you to bring a pig to our party?" demanded the professor.

"I don't know what you're so upset about. Rosie behaved like a perfect angel and she livened up your dull little ceremony. Everyone loves my Rosie!" said the woman.

"I hope you don't plan to have that filthy animal stay here with you!" Mr. DuBois sounded angry.

"Of course I do. And by the way, pigs are not filthy. They are amazingly clean. Did you know that they have hair instead of fur? She's nonallergenic! Besides, it's far too late to book a sitter. Pigs are very much like dogs, you know, and she's my 'ittle bitty baby. Yes, she is!" the woman cooed.

A moment of silence followed. All the cupcake workers paused and looked at the others.

"Liddy, it would be a shame if she got lost in Washington. It's a big town with lots of traffic and dangerous situations for a pig."

"That's Jacquie!" hissed Veronica.

"Wait, Liddy. I'm not done yet," Jacquie continued. "You will keep your pig on a leash while you are visiting. We have not pig-proofed the house for her, and I wouldn't want her to encounter anything harmful. You will take her out as needed. You will not burden Mr. DuBois with additional cleaning. You will sanitize any messes she makes. Is that clear?"

"I don't know why you're being so mean to Rosie and me. My son is gone. All I have is my little Rosie."

"For pity's sake, Liddy," growled the professor. "Put that animal on a leash before it gets out in the street."

The next thing we heard was a squeal, which undoubtedly came from little Rosie, followed by the sound of hurried footsteps and people calling her name.

With five of us working, our project went fast. The boxes were soon displayed on the tables, waiting for guests to pick them up on their way out.

We returned to the festivities. I hadn't seen Cara, the woman who was following me, and assumed she hadn't been able to get past the guards in front, who were diligently checking the guest list as people arrived. I relaxed and enjoyed myself.

I spied Jacquie motioning to me and hurried over, imagining that she needed me to fetch comfortable shoes or some such.

A full-figured woman stood next to her, holding a cocktail in her hand. Her mahogany hair had been swept up in a formal French twist, and she wore a dress that looked remarkably like a bathrobe made of black fabric with horizontal streaks of gold shooting through it. The collar, cuffs, and tied belt appeared to be a shiny black satin. But something about her demeanor, the stiff way she held her head and her cocktail, screamed, *I am better than you.* Her cold brown eyes appraised me as I approached, suddenly feeling young and fussy in the bold candy–apple-red Halston that Mom and Veronica had talked me into buying. Its high neck left my shoulders bare, but the rest was simple, except for a leg slit designed so a person could walk in it.

My love of bright colors conflicted with my instinctive desire to remain discreetly unnoticed and go about my life quietly. It was Veronica who craved the limelight and ironically leaned to black clothes.

"Florrie, I've been telling my friend Margarite Herbert-Grant all about you and the bookstore," said Jacquie.

I drew in a sharp breath at the mention of Margarite's name. I hoped my reaction hadn't been too obvious. Countless authors who had visited Color Me Read had told me they lived in fear of her. A book review from Margarite could make or break a book and the author. She presented herself as a priggish upper-crust type, but she delighted in writing crushing reviews that could only be described as cruel.

"How nice to meet you," I said. "I've heard a lot about you."

The hint of a smile twitched at the corners of her mouth. "It's all true, I assure you."

"Florrie does such a wonderful job running the bookstore. I don't know what we would do without her," said Jacquie.

Margarite gazed at me. "I really should stop by. I so seldom see books in their natural habitats. I receive far more books than I could ever read. A frightful number of unsolicited ones, so I'm afraid I am a bookstore's worst nightmare. I have always been fond of bookstores. There's something about the atmosphere. Like one has entered another realm in which anything is possible."

I hadn't heard a bookstore described quite that way before, but I supposed there was some truth to what she said. "We would be very pleased to have you pay us a visit. Color

Me Read has a wonderful parlor where the professor and his friends often gather for fascinating discussions."

"Jacquie, my love!" Arthur Bedlingham descended upon us and kissed Jacquie on both cheeks. "I am crushed to my core. If you were in desperate need to marry a former paramour, you should have rung me up. How I long to wish you a happy marriage, but I simply cannot, having lost you to Maxwell once again."

"Thank you, Arthur," said Jacquie with sarcasm.

My heart pounded in my chest. Jacquie had invited authors to her celebration because they were friends. But for me, it was as if celebrities were coming for a personal visit. Arthur was an odd mixture of elegant southern graciousness and rustic western cowboy. There was something mischievous about him. Perhaps the long dimples imparted an impish look, almost as though he were up to mischief. I sought something nice to say to him.

"Mr. Bedlingham, I so enjoyed *The Scent of Time*." It was an exaggeration, but after all, he was *Arthur Bedlingham*!

He eyed me with a sly grin. "So you're the one who bought it."

Everyone laughed at his old joke. One of my customers had told me that chic people mentioned Bedlingham's books to impress friends, but no one had actually bothered to read them.

"Dear Florrie!" He smiled broadly. "We shall become fast friends, I'm sure."

His gaze then fell upon Margarite. "How lovely to see you, Margarite," he said without enthusiasm. He leaned toward her for a double over-the-shoulder air kiss, but she remained stiff and stoic, like a cat tolerating a slavering dog.

She muttered, "Arthur," as if his name were enough in the

way of a greeting. "Rumor has it that you have another dreadful manuscript in the works. If you can't pull off literary novels, then I suggest you include a plot."

Ouch! I hoped this was some kind of friendly banter, but from the shocked looks on Jacquie's and Arthur's faces, it must not have been.

"Oh, but I have," said Arthur. "It's about the murder of a book reviewer. A dreadful old biddy who pretends to haute monde but is actually in the business of self-aggrandizement when in truth she comes from swinish beginnings."

Chapter 7

Swinish? Had Arthur Bedlingham just called snooty Margarite Herbert-Grant a pig?

To her credit, Jacquie forced a laugh and said, "Oh, you two! If you don't mind, I'm going to borrow Arthur. There's someone he simply must meet."

I was left with the daunting Margarite, whose complexion blazed right through her expertly applied makeup, giving away her annoyance. She glanced at me slyly. "He's angry with me. In my review of *The Scent of Time*, I wrote, 'Only a true master of the English language could write a six-hundred-page book in which absolutely nothing transpires.'"

I didn't know what to say to that. There was some truth in it, but it was so rude!

"He had great talent once," she said. "But now he scribbles any kind of garbage, and they fawn over him like a child who has finally learned to tie his shoelaces. A pity really. Hand a man a couple of awards and he becomes a self-important fool."

I tried to get her off the subject of Arthur. "Which authors do you recommend?"

"Griffin Corbyn. His writing is merely adequate. When

he's writing at his best, he doesn't have Arthur's talent. However, Griffin has an ability to draw the reader into his stories. I didn't even look up until I finished his last book. It was breathtaking! A wonderful tale, and, of course, that's really what fiction is all about, isn't it? Telling a grand story."

"I liked that one, too. They sell quite well at the store." I looked around in hope of seeing someone who might rescue me from Margarite.

"You won't find him here. He's alluringly elusive. Hates publicity. Have you noticed that the photo of him on the dust jacket doesn't reveal his face, only a fedora, tilted at a rakish angle. A man of mystery, one might say."

I had heard that about him. "That's unusual. Most authors are clamoring for publicity. Have you met him?"

"Of course. I have met everyone worth meeting. You are quite right about authors. Too many are positively cheap and vulgar about promotion. There is no genteelness left in the rush for publicity. Take that one." She pointed at a woman who reminded me of myself.

Unlike the many guests who had clearly had their hair done for the party, her dark brown hair hung lank, as if she had stepped out of the shower and run a comb through it but hadn't bothered styling it. Long bangs hung over her forehead. My mom had always said that meant the person was hiding something. I thought it might be a fashion choice, but there could be some truth in Mom's theory. The woman wore an off-the-shoulder lapis-blue dress with sequins all over it, and a short necklace of three hearts with pavé diamonds. If I had to pick out the romantic in the crowd, I would probably have zeroed in on her. She drank a pink-colored cocktail and nodded at something a woman said to her.

"Gabriella Archambeau, a pen name if I ever heard one," sneered Margarite. "She writes romances, but she doesn't have Jacquie's flair for it. They always miss the mark. She never fails to send me one of her books to review. Jacquie says I should take pity and open my mind to the possibility that she may have grown as a writer, therefore Gabriella's tenth book may be vastly superior to her first."

"That's probably true," I murmured, totally intimidated by Margarite.

"Only in her dreams. I read so many books that's it easy to tell. I have seen everything. Every plot, every character, every tedious hero's journey. There is nothing new under the sun, only creative ways of presenting it."

I wondered if she should retire or find another job. I couldn't that say to her, of course. I delighted in reading books, always intrigued by what might lie between the covers and whom I might meet inside. Margarite was burned-out. No wonder she found satisfaction in publishing scorching words that devastated authors and tanked books.

"Which other authors do you like?" I asked.

"I must admit that I had no hope whatsoever for a writer with a name like Buzz Powers. Turns out that's his real name if you can imagine that. What *was* his mother thinking? What ever happened to men named Grant and Robert? But the man can spin an exciting tale. I will be the first to say that I generally find the entire subgenre of government-agent thrillers to be shallow and commonplace. Still, he pulled off a rather intriguing story in his first book. The test will be to see if he can do it again. He claims it's mostly biographical. The emphasis is on *mostly*, I'm sure. He can't have lived through dangerous assignments like that on a regular basis. *Second-book slump* isn't just a saying. Sadly, it is a reality for authors. A successful second book is proof, one might say, that the first book was not a fluke."

I was relieved when Professor Maxwell motioned to me to join him and my literary agent, Sloan Rogers. Her whitish-blond locks flared out in messy curls. She wore glasses the color of seaweed that made her look chic and bookish. The arms attached at the top, causing her to peer through them rather high in the lens. The round bottoms grazed her prominent cheekbones. Her pewter gown was elegant in its simplicity, adorned only by a silver belt dotted with seaweed-colored beads.

Sloan gave me a perfunctory hug. "Maxwell has been raving about you. I'd love to drop by to see the bookstore tomorrow before I leave town." Her eyebrows raised when she added, "I always like to see which of my authors' books are in bookstores."

Oh no! Hadn't Jacquie said Arthur was one of Sloan's authors? "We carry all of Jacquie's books."

"Gabriella's, too, I hope."

Whew! She didn't mention Arthur. "We keep them in stock. She has fans who always order her books when a new one comes out."

"That's what I like to hear." Sloan focused on something behind me.

"Do you suppose he *missed* the nuptials an hour ago?" asked the professor. "I have never quite understood the attraction."

"He's almost as handsome and debonair as you are, Maxwell," said Sloan. "He can be charming and has a surprisingly wicked sense of humor."

I turned around to see whom they were talking about. Arthur had slung a possessive arm around Jacquie. He gazed at her adoringly while a small crowd of women appeared to be swooning over him.

"And he has the celebrity thing going on for him," I added. "Some people find money and fame irresistible."

"If that were the case, I would also have a doting entourage," joked the professor.

Sloan chuckled. "Arthur could do with a good dose of your self-deprecation."

"Has he ever been married?" I asked.

Sloan shook her head. "He doesn't believe in marriage. He has had an endless parade of admirers. There was one years ago, much younger than Arthur, who I thought might stick it out. But she bit the dust like the rest. Frankly, I think it may be because he would miss catting around."

"If you ladies will be so kind as to excuse me, I believe my first act as Jacquie's husband will be to rescue her from the evil grip of Sir Arthur." The professor gave us a nod, and we watched as he strode toward his new wife and managed in one swift and barely noticeable move to insert himself between Arthur and Jacquie.

"I'm so happy for her," said Sloan dreamily. "We should all be lucky enough to find a man like Maxwell. He will never let her down."

I thought she might be speaking from experience, that perhaps she had been let down by a man, but it would have been rude to ask. Luckily, we were called to dinner.

I fervently hoped that I would not be seated next to Margarite.

Veronica had done a great job. While the rest of us were gabbing and snacking on hors d'oeuvres, long narrow tables had magically appeared and the chairs that had been neatly lined up in rows had been moved to tables. A sea of lanterns glowed in the dark. I heard cameras clicking and hoped I could reconstruct the scene in my mind and draw it later. I longed to sketch it. I spied Veronica directing someone to a table and hurried up to her.

"Do you have a pen?"

Without a word, she flicked a grass-green–colored pencil at me. I stared at it as I took it. "Is this mine?"

In an I-don't-have-time-for-this tone, she snapped, "Of course. I couldn't find a plain old normal ballpoint pen in your house this morning."

Leaving her to her job, I found a paper napkin and sketched the lanterns as quickly as possible. It wasn't much, but it would be enough to remind me of the atmosphere. Jacquie's wedding plans had prompted me to draw a wedding coloring book. This image had to go in it. It was positively magical.

As I drew, voices nearby caught my attention.

"Rumor has it that his new book is about me."

"Relax. I have read it and it's clearly fiction."

"You are familiar with libel laws . . ."

A laugh. "Don't be silly. He's toying with you. You know what he's like. Anything to generate an outrage."

"How can you stand working with him?"

"He's not that bad. I have worse authors."

"I shudder to think!"

"Florrie! Did you hear me?"

I looked up at Veronica. "What?"

"Have you had too much to drink already?"

"No!" In a whisper I asked, "Did you hear them?"

"Hear who?"

"Never mind. What did you want?"

"The pencil, please."

I handed it to her. "Did you come up with this lantern idea?"

"I didn't think we could pull it off. There are so many lanterns! But Jacquie loved the concept. You know what a romantic she is. By the way, I hope you like lanterns because you're getting a bunch of these tomorrow." Veronica lowered her voice. "I put you at my table. And pulled a fast switcheroo at the last minute. Wait until you see who is seated with us!"

I was pretty sure she didn't mean Mom and Dad. Please, I thought to myself, please don't let it be Margarite. I decided to hold back a little so I could wangle a seat away from Margarite if she was seated with us. Veronica continued directing people to their tables. I spied Eric waving at me and assumed he had found ours. I hurried over, and bless him, he actually pulled my chair out for me. I didn't know men still did that.

When I sat down, I found myself facing Buzz Powers. He was as stunningly handsome up close as he was in photos. He wore his brown hair short and was clean-shaven. Even in the romantically dim light, I caught a flash of white teeth when he smiled at me. Introductions were made and it turned out I was sitting beside Gabriella Archambeau, the romance writer whom Margarite had pitied.

When she said her name, Buzz suddenly took interest. "You're married to Griffin Corbyn! He's a fantastic author. Is he here tonight? I'd love to meet him."

"I'm afraid Griffin loathes crowds and parties. He's at home, writing and probably eating tortilla chips and salsa for dinner. He loved *your* book." In a slightly coy voice, she added, "And so did I."

"I heard something about him turning down public appearances," said Buzz. "It's amazing he can do that and still be a successful author. I feel like I have been on a media Tilt-A-Whirl going from one thing to the next."

Sitting on the other side of Gabriella, Arthur Bedlingham piped up, "Griffin is a delightful fellow. I suspect the two of you would have a good deal to talk about."

"Oh? Was also he in the FBI?" asked Buzz.

"He has never told me. He keeps that part of his life to himself," said Arthur.

Buzz eyed Gabriella. "I presume you know."

Gabriella flushed. "I am sworn to secrecy."

"I'd like to meet him sometime," said Buzz.

"Email me," said Gabriella. "I'll see what I can arrange."

I glanced at Eric, who was so amiable. I was a fairly private person myself and didn't enjoy massive groups of people in most cases. I hoped I wasn't a pill about it like Griffin appeared to be. I wondered if it was a thorn in his relationship with Gabriella.

Veronica slid into the seat next to Buzz and smiled at us all. She sat quietly for a moment as if she expected something to happen.

The gentle background music suddenly rose to a crescendo and tiny fairy lights appeared all around us, even overhead, where they looked like fireflies in the sky.

Applause broke out and the musicians played classical music softly. I wasn't enough of an expert to identify the exact melody, but it was soothing and added an elegant ambience.

The other couple within speaking distance at our table introduced themselves as Grady and Celeste Sorello. I guessed them to be in their sixties. Grady had lost most of his hair and had the slim physique of a runner. Celeste seemed sweet. Tiny and delicate, she spoke in a gentle, tentative voice as though she was afraid of the world. I sensed a sadness in her. She dressed conservatively in a plain, long midnight-blue sheath as if she hoped to fade into the background as night fell. On her thin wrist, she carried a sizable bag in azalea pink that stood out against her dark dress.

Waiters arrived with a small bruschetta, topped with piped avocado and a spiced shrimp standing up. That was followed by a colorful salad of roasted red peppers, corn, grape tomatoes, and onions on a bed of butter lettuce, all topped by a lemon garlic vinaigrette. The main course was beef Wellington with buttery gnocchi and roasted spring asparagus.

We chatted while we ate, but when Buzz asked Grady and Celeste how they knew Jacquie and John, there was a conspicuous silence. It felt as if all the guests had stopped eating to listen. I knew that wasn't the case, but the Sorellos seemed paralyzed by the question. Finally Grady said, "We knew them many years ago during their previous marriage."

I wanted to add, *And their daughter was attending a birthday party at your house when she disappeared.* But they didn't go there. I couldn't blame them. As horrific as it was for John and Jacquie, the Sorellos must have suffered as well.

Grady went on to say that he was now semiretired, which prompted Celeste to suggest jokingly that she had anticipated cruises and vacations but Grady kept so busy that their lives weren't very different than before.

In the pause between dinner and dessert, a man with curly ebony hair stopped by our table. His mustache and beard were immaculately trimmed, though I thought his tuxedo couldn't be comfortable because it fit him far too snugly. His plump face was positively endearing, but his mannerisms were those of an insecure person. "Gabby? I thought that was you."

She stood up to hug him. "Evan McDowell! It's been ages!"

He grinned at her. "Romance isn't really my thing, but I always buy your books."

"You're so sweet. We have to catch up. Where are you sitting?"

Evan pointed toward a table. "Find me after. We'll have champagne and toast to your success."

He returned to his table and Gabriella sat down, looking uneasy.

"Is everything okay?" I whispered.

She turned toward me. In a low voice, she said, "I feel terrible. We met in a class we took from Arthur. Bless Evan, he's a wonderful writer, but he's painfully shy and I don't think he has published anything yet. He was working on something the last time I heard from him. I just feel for him. He probably thinks I'm some kind of star, which I'm not. Jacquie and

Arthur are big names. I just struggle along trying my best. He's such an introvert. It's hard for Evan to put himself or his writing out there. It takes guts, with all the rejection we writers face. It wouldn't surprise me if he had finished his book and had spent years revising it."

Arthur must have overheard. "He has done exactly that. I hired him on in your position when you left me, Gabriella. He's excellent at his job but lacks the courage to be an author."

The waitstaff whisked away our dinner plates and began circulating with coffee, tea, and champagne. Since wedding cake would be served, it seemed silly to eat dessert, but I loved sweets and had never turned down chocolate mousse!

While Buzz entertained us with tales of daring from his time in the FBI, I noticed my parents posing for a photographer. They were smiling and having a good time. At first, I thought it sweet, but as I watched, I realized that the photographer was taking their picture with a *cell phone*!

Alarmed, I leaned toward Veronica. "Did you hire someone to take candid photos?"

"Yes. He's . . . right over there where Mr. DuBois is standing with that blond woman."

"Then who is taking pictures of our parents?" I didn't wait for her response.

Eric was watching me. "Trouble?" he mouthed.

I nodded and beckoned to him. He joined Veronica and me quietly. I explained as we hurried toward Mom and Dad.

I was a lousy runner, but between guests and servers, we couldn't make our way to Mom and Dad fast anyway. When we reached them, I recognized Cara and seized the phone from her hand.

Luckily, she hadn't been prepared for that and wasn't holding onto it tightly.

"Give me my phone!" she cried.

I looked at it and scrolled back through the most recent photos. They were of the guests at the party. There must have been two dozen of my mother. And another dozen or more of the brief wedding ceremony. As fast as I could, I hit DELETE on photo after photo.

Cara began clawing at me, shrieking for me to return her phone. I turned my back to her and kept deleting. I could hear Eric's soothing voice behind me, asking what was going on. The clawing stopped, but my parents had rounded the table. I had a bad feeling we were drawing a lot of attention, but I kept deleting because sooner or later someone was going to make me give Cara's iPhone back to her.

When I reached a photo of me in the bookstore that she had clearly taken when I brought the sign in, I knew she had lied to me. I deleted it and found half a dozen more of me walking the streets of Georgetown. I deleted those, too, and turned around. "What do you want from us?"

Chapter 8

She snatched the phone out of my hand with the speed of a striking snake. "The story." She slipped her telephone inside her bra and walked away.

Eric said, "I'll see that she leaves."

I was right behind him.

Mia, the artist, waved at me. "Don't forget to come over to where I'm drawing. I'm looking forward to sketching you!"

I nodded, looking for Cara, who had fled through the crowd. I glanced around, mostly grateful that our little scene hadn't been widely noticed. I had been so focused on getting rid of the photographs that I hadn't really considered why she wanted them. She'd said she wanted "the story." What story? For a second the notion of something dramatic in my parents' past flicked through my head. It was preposterous. I supposed they had more adventurous lives before they settled down and Veronica and I came along, but if there was anything significant, surely there would have been a whisper or hint of it before now.

At the front door of the mansion, I stood next to Eric, who said to his pal Fish, "Don't let her back in. She's some kind of reporter and was taking photos of Florrie's parents."

We watched her run out to the road. She looked back when she reached the sidewalk. I was glad the three of us were standing there so she could see we were serious.

"Is that the same woman who rushed out of the book-store?" asked Fish.

"Yes." I sounded a bit snarkier than I'd intended. "I can't imagine what she wants with us."

"I'm wondering how she got in," said Fish. "We've been checking the invitations. Mr. DuBois has been very helpful in that regard when people have forgotten to bring them. He knows everyone!"

"One of the guests who would not have been invited showed up as a plus-one. Maybe that's what she did, too."

Eric slung his arm around my shoulders. "She's gone now. Let's see if they've cut the cake yet."

When we returned, the newlyweds were indeed cutting a four-tier cake. Jacquie, ever the romantic, in spite of her insistence on forgoing some of the traditions, had told me the top layer would be removed before serving. Mr. DuBois was to wrap it and place it in the freezer to be consumed on their first anniversary.

Mia, the artist, had set up a tabletop easel on the patio where the light was better. A little line had formed behind the bench where a smiling couple sat, proving that guests loved having their portraits drawn.

We watched as she completed the sketch and handed it to the couple, who appeared delighted.

"We should do that!" said Eric.

I nodded. "Maybe a little later when the line isn't quite so long."

The musicians were playing a waltz, and my parents, apparently none the worse for the incident with Cara, were effortlessly gliding around the dance floor that had been installed just for the occasion.

"They're pretty good," said Eric.

"I had no idea they could dance like that."

"Shall we?" Eric held his hand out to me.

The two of us had never danced together. I was surprised by how well it went. It wasn't long before the musicians picked up the pace and encouraged people to sing along with tunes from the sixties and seventies.

At one point, Buzz and Eric were conversing while I watched John and Jacquie dance.

Arthur sidled up next to me. "When I was a young lad, there was a song we used to sing. I didn't understand it at the time, but I do now." He sang it softly.

> On top of ole Smokey,
> All covered in snow
> I lost my true love
> By courting too slow.

"I used to think a person would have to be a dolt to court that slow. But now I see I lost my chance. I should have shown up a year ago when she left her last husband."

"If it's any consolation," I said, "when she needed help, she came looking for Professor Maxwell."

Arthur sighed. "There was a time when she came lookin' for me."

In an effort to take his mind off Jacquie, I asked, "Is your next book really about Margarite?"

He glanced at me. "She's a piece of work. Margarite, my aunt Fanny! Her real name is Ada Bubnick. You see, her big mistake was overlookin' the fact that writers are great at makin' things up, but we're also pros at research. Up until my last book, I was a gentleman and kept what I knew to myself. It may not have been my best book, but it wasn't packed with 'indiscriminate triviality.' Nor was it 'painfully tedious.' I don't write cheap thrillers designed to titillate. I write for the thinkin' reader. The ones who cherish novels and appreciate clever exposition on the human condition. People like you."

I didn't know quite what to say. "You're not the only writer who has suffered the wrath of her reviews. Margarite has a tendency to be harsh. No one is spared."

"Hmpff," he grunted. "After her scathing review, I did some nosin' around into her background. I'll share a little secret with you. She's a high school dropout."

I couldn't help looking for her. She stood not too far away, looking prim and sour, which I suspected was the norm for her. She held a glass of champagne in her hand and was the picture of elegance in her bathrobe-style dress.

"She's very articulate and certainly has an amazing vocabulary." I stopped short of questioning his information.

"People wouldn't bother reading her reviews if they weren't so nasty. They take some sort of perverse pleasure in her criticism, even while she's ruinin' a writer's reputation."

I was more than a little uncomfortable with the conversation, so I said brightly, "I can't wait to read your new book. What's it called?"

"I wanted to call it *The Death of Medusa*."

My skin crawled. I wasn't up on my Greek mythology, but I didn't need a refresher course to recall the woman with the head of snakes who had been on the cover of a book my parents owned when I was a child. I had been afraid to look at it because she turned people to stone when they looked into her eyes.

"But the publisher didn't like that and switched it to *As the Shrew Turns*."

My agent, Sloan, swept up beside Arthur. "I have been looking for you everywhere! They told me you were here, but it's a rather large crowd."

"Sloan! You look splendid," Arthur gushed. "Have you met Florrie? She manages Maxwell's bookstore."

"I know her well, darling. Who do you think represents her coloring books?" Sloan winked at me. "Maybe we can arrange for a signing when Arthur's book comes out."

I tried my best to smile graciously. "He's been telling me about it."

"You'll love it. It's a departure from his previous books and so intriguing."

"Evan!" Arthur motioned to Gabriella's friend to join us.

Sloan's expression changed ever so slightly as Evan approached us, staggering slightly. He carried an old-fashioned glass in his right hand and held it out to a passing server. "Bring me another one of these, please." Evan smiled at us. "What a party!"

Arthur introduced us, saying, "Not only does Evan keep me organized, but he has an eagle eye for proofreading."

With a twinkle in his eyes, Evan said, "I used to be impressed by Arthur, but I just met Buzz Powers!"

We all laughed, including Arthur.

"But I'm disappointed that our beautiful Gabriella's husband, Griffin, isn't here. I bet he would have some great advice for me."

Arthur scowled. "Had I only known that the road to writing success was to hide from the public, I'd have done that years ago."

"A bit of mystery never hurts. But how do you know Griffin isn't here?" asked Sloan. "Maybe he mingles with people under another name."

"Hey! It's not too late for me to do that," said Evan.

"What do you write?" I asked.

"Science fiction. Fantasy. Adventure. I don't like to commit myself to a specific genre."

I was confused and revised my question. "Where would I place your book in Color Me Read bookstore?"

"Oh!" Evan thought for a moment. "In the front with the bestsellers."

This wonderful response brought on laughter. "I hope I can do that one day."

"I'd like to be like Grisham, you know? He writes thrillers and sports books and what interests him. I'm a huge sports fan. Arthur says I need to get out more, meet people and hear about their lives. What should I know about you, Florrie? What secrets do you hide?"

At that moment, the musicians struck up lively swing music and Eric seized my hand. "Excuse me! It was nice meeting you," I said, dashing for the dance floor, relieved that I didn't have to answer that silly question.

When the musicians went back to a waltz, my dad sweetly cut in and I felt like a little girl again, except this time my feet weren't on my dad's shoes when we danced. Well, not most of the time anyway. Even Professor Goldblum asked me to dance. He wasn't much taller than me and had the roundest head I had ever seen. His face showed his every emotion, and tonight he smiled with delight.

I was breathless by the time Eric and I made our way to Mia's bench for our sketch. "Don't you need a break?" I asked her.

"I've taken a few. And one of the servers keeps bringing me iced tea and little snacks."

"Is this a side gig for you?" asked Eric.

"I do these on a regular basis. And I teach art classes. I'll never be a Picasso. But at least I'm doing what I love. Right, Florrie?"

"I know how you feel. Drawing my coloring books is a joy and so satisfying."

Mia handed us our sketch.

I was in awe. "I can't believe you can do this so fast."

Mia smiled. "They can't be as precise and detailed as I would like, but time just doesn't permit that."

We thanked her, and after securing our sketch, we returned to the dance floor.

I was certain that some guests left after dinner, but the bulk of them stayed until midnight, when coffee and tea were served along with tiny egg-salad and chicken-salad sandwiches. Fresh sugar-dipped strawberries and cream appeared for those who craved a little sweet before driving home. By one in the morning the musicians had packed up and left, and my parents had gone home, as had most of the guests. I was bushed and wanted nothing more than to slip away to the carriage house and upstairs to bed but felt obligated to help Veronica.

Mr. DuBois packed up leftovers for Eric and Fish to take home, and they departed, too.

The cake had disappeared, the tables and chairs were empty, the newlyweds had vanished into the mansion, and only Mr. DuBois, Veronica, and I were left.

When Veronica shut down all the little lights, Mr. DuBois said to her, "A job well done, Miss Veronica. People will be talking about this party for years, and it will be hard to top. A delightful blend of celebration and gaiety without being stuffy."

"Thank you, Mr. DuBois," she said. "We didn't do anything very original. Jacquie wouldn't even let me arrange for fireworks because she thought it would upset dogs."

"You made everyone feel welcome and they all had a good time. That's far more important."

He was probably right.

He looked at his watch. "I'm glad we decided on a bridal brunch instead of an early breakfast for the out-of-town guests."

I had forgotten all about that and groaned aloud.

"Miss Florrie, I took the liberty of placing some leftovers in your refrigerator. I can't abide throwing out perfectly good food," said Mr. DuBois. "I suggest you freeze a good deal of it."

We walked together to the back door of the mansion and waited until Mr. DuBois closed the door and we heard the bolt click into place.

"I, for one, had a wonderful time." I smiled at Veronica even though she couldn't see me well in the dark.

"Me, too. What do you know about that guy Buzz?" she asked.

"That he's at least twenty or more years older than you."

I unlocked my door and Peaches ran to us meowing. I swung her up into my arms while Veronica locked the door behind us. I gazed at my clock collection. It was eighteen minutes past one in the morning.

"You don't think he's cute?" she asked.

"He's very good-looking. But he's old enough to be your father."

She curled her upper lip at me in a mock snarl. "He's so interesting. I mean, FBI! That's just so exciting."

Veronica had a history of choosing the wrong men. She'd decided not to date for a while, but there were lots of signs that she was ready to reenter the dating game. I had Eric, so I could hardly criticize that desire. "I guess you wouldn't be the first May-December romance."

"It's not like I'm marrying him."

She was right. As her big sister, I was used to being bossy. I wouldn't have worried if she just hadn't made such terrible decisions about the men she had dated in the past. A guy who had been in the FBI had to be on the up-and-up. And he *had* been nice. I'd let Mom deal with the issue of the difference in their ages. I bet she'd have a thing or two to say about that!

"Did you notice Celeste's purse?" asked Veronica.

"Hmm? Not really. It was big."

"They must be rolling in money. That was a real Hermès Birkin."

I ignored her and brushed my teeth.

"Do you know what they sell for?"

"Not a clue," I burbled through toothpaste.

"Try thirty thousand dollars."

Toothpaste hit the mirror. "What?" I grabbed a washcloth and made a big mess cleaning it up.

"I know! Can you even imagine? You could buy a car for that kind of money!"

"Do people take out loans to buy them?"

Veronica laughed. "Probably!"

I fell into bed utterly exhausted. Luckily, the following day was Sunday, when the store was closed until noon. Veronica would probably expect my help at the brunch, but I would have to leave early to open the store.

Chapter 9

As luck had it, my plans to sleep in were dashed at eleven minutes past six in the morning. Screams broke through my dreams. I sat up, still groggy. Had I imagined them?

Veronica, who was sleeping on the trundle bed, grunted and turned over.

I thought I heard someone yell, *Help!* Followed by the most outrageous high-pitched squeal. Had Rosie gotten stuck somewhere? I pulled my plum bathrobe over my oversize T-shirt and stumbled down the stairs. Peaches already waited by the door, which led me to think it hadn't been my imagination.

I stepped outside and heard it much clearer. "Help! Maxwell, help!" DuBois's cries were followed by more ear-splitting pig screams.

I pulled the door closed behind me and pushed my way through the bushes that provided privacy for the mansion's backyard, where the party had taken place.

Mr. DuBois stood by the pool, his face ashen. Rosie was next to him, safely on the edge of the pool, staring at the water.

And there, in the middle of the swimming pool at the bottom, was a large black blob. A scream escaped me as I realized that it was a human. The person was facedown with the black fabric of his clothing around the body. I couldn't tell who it was. "Call 911," I shouted at Mr. DuBois. I dropped my robe and dove into the pool.

I seized the man under his arm, but the weight of his waterlogged clothes hindered any progression. I swam to the top for a fresh breath of air and tried again. He was so heavy that I began to think I might not be able to bring him up. I placed my feet on the bottom of the pool and pulled. Suddenly, his body moved, and I was able to tug him to the top. I flipped him over and wrapped my arm under his chin like I had been taught. Dragging him to the side of the pool was easier. But I was worried. I had a bad feeling he had been underwater for quite some time.

I was almost certain that it was too late to revive him. Two minutes of slipping and sliding and trying to wrangle him out of the pool was enough to let me know that I didn't have the strength to shove him out of the water unless I could touch the bottom.

I pulled him to the shallowest part of the pool. Once I was standing, it was easier for me. It was then that I recognized his face and dark curls.

He was Evan McDowell, Arthur's assistant and a friend of Gabriella's. They had arranged to chat last night after dinner. I didn't know much about him, except that he was a writer who hadn't been published yet, but seemed to think he had bestsellers in his future.

I tried to raise his head and the upper part of his body to roll him onto the concrete surrounding the pool, but it felt like he weighed three thousand pounds.

Thankfully, large hands reached down and latched on to Evan's tuxedo. I looked up at Professor Maxwell, who strained to pull Evan out of the water.

Forgoing all politeness and civility, I muttered, "Sorry, Evan," and struggled to roll his body, holding on to his hips and pushing them upward.

"Evan! No!" Jacquie loomed above us, her hands tented over her nose and mouth.

As we struggled, Jacquie's beautifully manicured hands reached for his legs. Rosie's snout wedged beside her, sniffing.

The three of us heaved and pushed. Jacquie fell backward onto her bottom and Evan was finally poolside.

He lay on his back and the professor was about to start CPR.

"Wait!" I cried.

I rolled Evan's body to the side in an effort to help water leave his mouth and nose. It poured out.

We let him roll onto his back just as the emergency medical technicians raced in. They began CPR immediately.

Not until that moment did I realize my T-shirt clung to me like I was in a wet T-shirt contest. Thanking my lucky stars that it was purple and not white, I seized my robe and pulled it on, feeling the flush of embarrassment flood my face.

I caught my breath and swiped my long, wet hair out of my face and onto my back.

Mr. DuBois hurried over to me and wrapped a giant towel around me.

"Thank you," I whispered, using one corner of the fluffy towel to dry my face.

Professor Maxwell placed his arms around his crying wife. Her sobs were the only sound as we watched the EMTs try to resuscitate Evan. Even Rosie looked on somberly. From an elevated porch, overnight guests began to trickle out to watch, undoubtedly awakened by the commotion.

Sadly, Evan could not be revived. The police arrived and the medical examiner was called.

I slipped away to dress in dry clothes. I didn't think anyone noticed me leave. Even though the temperature outside wasn't cold, it was a little bit premature for swimming. My teeth chattered and I shivered.

Back at the carriage house, Peaches mewed and rubbed my ankles until she realized I was wet. She retreated in a horrified pout to lick her fur. I hurried upstairs, woke Veronica, and told her what had happened.

She blinked at me. "Did you say dead? Why are you wet?"

I repeated the story.

"Evan? Which one was he?"

"Arthur Bedlingham's assistant. I understand he was a writer, too."

"I don't understand. Didn't he leave with everyone else?"

"I imagine the police will be asking the same question."

"Police?" She swung her legs over the bed, completely alert now. "The police can't come. We're having a brunch."

I shot her a look.

"Noooo! That does it! I do not want to be a wedding planner. No way. How could this have happened? Is there any chance the police will depart before our guests arrive?"

"I doubt it. The police are already here whether you like it or not. And most of the people who stayed over at the mansion are awake and watching."

She rubbed her face. Her shoulders sagged. "I don't suppose we could pass it off as entertainment?"

"Not funny, Veronica."

She glanced at the time. "Here's the plan. You warm up and get some dry clothes on while I make coffee. Then I'll hop in the shower. And then the two of us will answer all the questions the police have, and maybe, just maybe, they'll be gone by the time our other guests arrive."

I took a hot shower to warm up, then pulled on a sleeveless periwinkle dress that I hoped would be appropriate for being questioned by the police, having brunch, and working at the store. I knew it wouldn't be cold, but I didn't seem to be able to warm up. I added a white cotton sweater over the dress. Feeling better, I took the time to add a thin gold necklace and slipped on comfortable white sandals.

The scent of coffee wafted up the stairs. My hair was still damp, but I had a feeling the police would be knocking on my door soon and I needed hot coffee more than I wanted dry hair. One of the advantages of long hair was that it could dry on its own without looking too terrible.

I walked down the circular stairs.

Still wearing a bathrobe, Veronica handed me a mug of steaming coffee.

"Exactly what I needed. Thanks."

"I wasn't completely awake upstairs. Did you really say that it was Arthur Bedlingham who drowned?"

"No. Evan McDowell, his assistant. I don't know if he drowned by accident or was killed and then pushed into the pool, but from the amount of water that came out of his mouth, I'd bet on drowning as the cause of death."

"Ugh. I did *not* need to know all that. I don't know if I even met him."

"I didn't know him, either."

"How could this have happened?" asked Veronica. "I can't say I looked in the pool before we went to bed, but I think we would have noticed if someone was in there. Not to mention the splash when he fell in." Scowling, Veronica rushed up the stairs to shower, and I fed chicken cat food to

Peaches. For all of three minutes, I relaxed, drank my coffee, and watched Peaches eat her breakfast.

The knock I had expected came early. I peered out the tiny window in the door. I didn't know the man who stood outside. A detective perhaps, because he was dressed in plain clothes.

I opened the door tentatively.

The man flipped a badge at me. "Sergeant Bridges. Are you Florrie Fox?"

I invited him in and asked to see the badge again. It looked official. But I didn't know enough to discern if it was a fake. I was expecting the police, in any event. He was medium height, with a slender build, dark skin, and intelligent eyes. He was too young to be bald, so it was my guess that he shaved his head.

We sat down at the kitchen table, and I offered him coffee.

"Have you got some ready? I could use caffeine."

I poured him a mug and refreshed my own. I brought them to the table with napkins, spoons, cream, and sugar.

"Thanks!" He smiled at me and stirred cream into his coffee. "So tell me what happened."

I explained about being awakened, seeing someone in the water, and trying to pull him out.

"Was anyone else there?"

"Mr. DuBois, the Maxwells' butler and Rosie, the pig. Then Professor Maxwell and Jacquie Liebhaber, his wife, joined us and helped. They live in the mansion."

He smiled again. "I've met Mr. DuBois. He's fond of the police. Did you know the man in the pool?"

"Evan McDowell. I met him for the first time yesterday. We spoke briefly. I wouldn't say I knew him well. 'In passing' would be more accurate."

"I hear he was Arthur Bedlingham's assistant. My mom is a big reader. I tried one of Bedlingham's books once. I think I'm more of a science fiction and thriller kind of guy."

"Bedlingham's books can be a little long-winded."

"Mr. DuBois tells me you and your sister were the last to leave. What time was that?"

"One eighteen."

"You sound very certain of that."

I made a little circle with my finger in the air. "Turn around."

He twisted and looked at the shelves that ran along the wall. He couldn't miss my clock collection.

"I hate to be late. Time is one of my quirks."

He checked his own watch. "And they're right on time. We're synchronized. As habits go, being precise about time isn't such a bad one. Last I heard there was no rehab for the time obsessed," he teased. "Did you look around? Check to make sure no one else lingered outside?"

"You could probably tell that it's a wide-open space. The tables and chairs were still there, of course, and I think they turned on spotlights when they brought out the coffee at midnight. I suppose it could have been possible for someone to hide under a table and have gone unnoticed, but if I had wanted to hide until everything was dark and everyone had left, I would have waited among the trees. Some of the lilacs and rhododendrons are large enough to conceal a person, too."

His eyes narrowed. "You've given this some thought."

"Actually, I hadn't given it any thought until now. But the mansion and grounds are situated for maximum privacy. The gardens are lush and full at the moment. I take it you think Evan hid and remained behind when the rest of the guests departed?"

"It's a possibility. What do you think happened?"

"I haven't the first clue. Why would he do that?"

Bridges tilted his head. "You're the one who knew him."

"Not really!" I protested. "I don't know. Because he had too much to drink? Maybe he was sleeping it off somewhere and stumbled into the pool?"

"Or maybe he planned to meet up with a pretty girl?"

I caught his ridiculous implication. A distasteful suggestion at the very least. Though I reluctantly supposed that could have happened, I pointedly denied any involvement. "If that was the case, I don't know about it and the girl was not me."

Bridges narrowed his eyes and rubbed his thumb against his forefinger. "Did he make plans to meet with you? Or to come here?"

I could be just as direct. "He did *not*."

"When did you last see Evan alive?"

I thought it was time to mention Eric, just in case Bridges didn't know that I dated a cop. "We were chatting near the dance floor when the musicians started playing swing music and my boyfriend, Sergeant Eric Jonquille, invited me to dance."

"I've heard about you. You have some kind of weird artsy job."

"I am a coloring-book artist." My tone had grown hostile. Weird artsy job? Really?

He frowned. "You color coloring books?"

I tried not to roll my eyes or let him see my impatience. "I draw them. When you were a child, you probably colored—"

"Trains. I was a nut for trains."

"Well, someone had to draw the trains so you could color them."

His eyebrows rose. "Oh, I get it now. I understand your sister spent the night here?"

I saw what he was getting at. "She did. Veronica and I were together from the time we cleaned up after the party until I heard Mr. DuBois calling for help."

"The whole time?"

"Yes. We even slept in the same bedroom."

"Would you have heard her if she got up and slipped out of the house?"

No one could answer that question and he knew it. I chose to protect my sister, who was more exhausted than I was last night. "Yes. I'm sure I would have heard her leave the house."

"Did you see or hear anything last night, during the party or afterward, that was out of the ordinary?"

I shrugged. "There was no love lost between Arthur Bedlingham and a book reviewer who unmercifully shredded his last book. Her name is Margarite Herbert-Grant. They were hateful to each other in their taunts, but I can't imagine how that would have anything to do with Evan's death."

He made note of Margarite's name. "Thank you. I'd like to speak to your sister if she's still here."

I called up the stairs and knew instantly that she had been eavesdropping. Veronica walked down wearing three-inch heels and an elegant light slate sheath. She subtly squeezed my hand as she walked by me.

Sergeant Bridges stood up and shook her hand. He glanced at me. "I'd like to speak with her privately."

"Of course." I left the carriage house and headed for the pool. Police tape kept the pool and most of the yard off-limits. Guests who had stayed at the mansion overnight still watched from the back porch, some of them in bathrobes.

Mr. DuBois busied himself among them, refilling mugs with coffee.

I was about to make my way around to them when Professor Maxwell gently touched my elbow and whispered, "In your garden."

Chapter 10

I looked up at the professor quizzically.

He tilted his head in the direction of the carriage house.

Following him across the driveway to the wooden gate with an arched top, I wondered why he was being secretive.

I closed the gate behind me, and Professor Maxwell held a finger up to his lips and retreated farther into the little forest behind my home. It had been an unusually rainy spring, which had encouraged lush growth everywhere. My walled garden seemed like a hideaway in a storybook, miles from Washington, DC, crowds, and traffic.

We stood among the trees near the rear and Professor Maxwell whispered, "I need your help."

I nodded. "Of course." He had been my boss for years. I admired and respected him, in awe of his vast knowledge about the world and its history.

Speaking so softly that I could barely hear him, he said, "Jacquie went out last night."

He didn't need to say more. I felt like someone had knocked the air out of me.

"They're going to figure that out," he said. "You have to help me find the real killer."

"How do you know she left?"

He shot me an incredulous look. "We were sleeping in the same bed. I thought she got up to use the bathroom, but then she didn't return right away as one would have expected."

"Did you look for her?"

He appeared pained when he said, "In retrospect I wish I had. But I was beat and fell asleep."

As far as I knew, Jacquie had no reason to be upset with Evan. I wondered why he had been on the guest list. Had he come as someone's plus-one? I had to ask, "Do you think—"

"That she pushed him into the pool? Absolutely not. But our guest rooms were filled to the rafters last night. Chances are good that she met with someone or one of them saw her up and about. If they mention that to the police, she'll be targeted as his killer."

"That doesn't sound so terrible. Unless there was bad blood between them that I don't know about?"

"Arthur is involved in this somehow. I know he is, but I can't piece it together." The professor scowled. "Jacquie and Arthur were an item once, decades ago. I don't know what she saw in him. They shared a passion for writing, but in my eyes, the man is a lush, feckless and madcap. From what Jacquie has told me and what I have observed over the years, he spent his life being foolhardy. I believe he came to Jacquie for money recently, which is saying a lot because he hailed from a wealthy family. I imagine he has run through that fortune."

"Jacquie said he drove a taxi."

"Precisely. The man took on jobs that he hoped would bring him in touch with a variety of people. Fodder for his books. Experiencing life through the eyes of others, that sort of thing." The professor rubbed his brow. "Please do not misunderstand me. I'm telling you these things to help you search for Evan's killer. My sole interest is to protect Jacquie."

"Relax. First of all, Jacquie may have gone downstairs to have a cup of chamomile tea with her agent or another guest. Second, we don't know yet that Evan didn't die of natural causes. It may just have been an accident."

The professor fixed his eyes on mine. "An accident is falling into the pool in front of everyone at a party, not drowning in one after everyone leaves. His death was neither accidental nor from natural causes."

Chapter 11

Professor Maxwell was probably correct. "But why would Jacquie kill him?" I whispered. "It was a lovely party and all she wanted was to be married to you again. Neither Arthur nor Evan made a scene or created any problems that I noticed. She had no reason to want Evan dead."

"Arthur collected information on people. He was a walking time bomb."

I thought back to what Arthur had told me about Margarite. He hadn't hesitated to reveal facts about her to me, a relative stranger. "Are you saying Arthur may have told Evan some dirt about Jacquie?" I shook my head, unwilling to believe that Jacquie would kill anyone. "Professor Maxwell, I appreciate your noble desire to protect Jacquie. But everything you have told me has been about Arthur, not Evan. I don't think you have anything to worry about."

"Mark my words, Florrie. Evan's death has something to do with Arthur." The professor winced. "And that means Jacquie is involved."

Our return through the garden gate went unnoticed. The two of us continued to the mansion, where a small staff prepared brunch. The unmistakable scent of bacon mingled with cinnamon and coffee. I ventured onto the patio, where the first person I saw was Liddy, the professor's sister. Rosie ran around off leash among the guests, most of whom seemed amused by her.

Liddy smiled at me, which sent shivers to my very core. Hers was no smile of warmth or even friendliness. It was the smile of a snake, its cold eyes appraising me before striking.

Her husband, Walter, approached me with his hand outstretched. "How nice to see you again, Florrie. I'm so sorry that Evan's death has put a big damper on the celebration. Please forgive my wife. I'm afraid she is experiencing flashbacks to the death of our son."

"Of course. That's completely understandable." Eager to change the subject, I asked, "Is this a buffet or will we be sitting at tables?"

"I see place cards. Don't worry, you're not sitting with my wife." Walter winked at me. "Did you know this Evan?"

"Not really. We met briefly at the party."

"They say he was quite a talented writer. A bit too emotional, perhaps. He struggled with rejections."

"He drank heavily to cope." That news came from a woman's voice.

I turned to find Sloan Rogers, Arthur's and Jacquie's agent, as well as mine.

"I'm not making that up about Evan," she said. "Because he worked for Arthur, he had access to my phone number. I'm sorry to say that he called me around the clock, with no regard whatsoever for the fact that some of us keep regular hours and might prefer to sleep at two in the morning."

"Oh, that's awful!" I said. "He looked so sweet."

"Arthur insisted that he was a lovely man. But you know how it is when people drink too much. They lose their inhibitions and act out in ways that they later regret. Where is Arthur anyway?"

Jacquie, looking teary, joined our conversation. "I didn't invite Arthur. Only houseguests and out-of-town guests are coming for the brunch."

"He'll be lost without Evan," said Sloan, "though I always thought Gabriella was a far better assistant. Not to mention that she didn't wake me up in the middle of the night, crying about a book that hadn't been written yet."

Macabre was the only word that came to my mind as we took our seats. Evan's body had been removed, but police still searched the lawn, and we were watching like they were a floor show! No matter how hard I tried to change the subject, it always came back to Evan.

Sloan sat at my table and, as far as I could tell, knew Evan better than anyone else present. "His father wanted him to be a doctor. Arthur thought Evan had the smarts to do it, but he simply wasn't interested in the sciences. Last night, after too much to drink, he was rambling about an alternate universe in which everything was reversed. Shy men were sought-after. Being overweight was sexually attractive. In other words, nerds ruled. I told him I thought the nerds and their revenge had been done many times in the movies, but he insisted his take on the subject was fresh and different."

The chatter turned to other topics, but I felt sad for Evan. It sounded to me that he had been carrying a lot of insecurities about himself, and now he wouldn't live to find out that he was a great guy. Although he did need to stop drinking since that was clearly a big problem for him.

I was worried about Mr. DuBois, since he had found Evan. But he showed no signs of panic or stress. He held his head high and went about his duties as if nothing had happened.

As tempting as it was to stick around and gab, especially after the horrible events, I finished my delicious Belgian waffles with glistening fresh berries and bowed out to go to work.

I paused in the kitchen and nabbed some fresh-from-the-oven blueberry coffee cake for Bob, then hustled to the carriage house. Peaches mewed when I entered, probably thinking I was home for the rest of the day.

I found it difficult to leave for the bookstore. Every fiber of my being longed to remain at the mansion, but duty called. It would be a short day, so I took Peaches with me. She would enjoy prowling the bookstore and being petted by visitors. When we arrived, I took off her walking harness and she shot to the window display at the front of the store, where the sun shone brightly. I switched off the alarm and turned the CLOSED sign on the door to OPEN. Next, I put on classical music, which played softly. I inhaled the scent of books, realizing that I was glad to be here after all. The store felt like an oasis far away from troubles.

The room that had once been a kitchen was in the back, overlooking what was now basically an alley. I measured Summertime Blend coffee into the coffee machine and added water. It gurgled at me, and the delicious scent of vanilla flavored the air.

The bell rang at the front door, letting me know someone had entered the store. I hurried to the checkout desk. Bob had arrived, looking bleary and tired. He munched on a calzone.

"Hi. There's some blueberry coffee cake for you in the back."

The bell rang again as Celeste Sorello darted in. "Good morning, Florrie, Bob. We certainly enjoyed the party last night and the wedding came as a wonderful surprise."

"I'm glad you enjoyed it. Is there something I can help you with?" I asked.

"I need a book for my brother-in-law. A gift for his birthday. He likes thrillers, that sort of thing, and I haven't the first notion what might be good. Except . . ."

"Yes?"

"That nice woman Gabriella, doesn't her husband write that kind of book?"

"He does. Come with me." I led her to our extensive mystery and thriller section and pointed out the books by Griffin Corbyn.

She thanked me profusely. "We had a lovely time last night. I haven't danced that much since my daughter's wedding. What time did it wrap up?"

"Everyone was gone by one in the morning."

"You must be exhausted. Where are Arthur's books? I'm ashamed to say that even though I love to read, I have never read one of his books."

I hated to tell her that we didn't carry most of them. "I could order one for you. Did you have a particular book in mind?"

"How about the most recent one?"

At that exact moment, Bob raced up to us, his eyes wide. "Did you hear? Arthur's assistant is dead!"

Celeste swallowed hard. "Arthur Bedlingham's assistant? Evan? We met him last night."

"Apparently he drowned," said Bob. "It's all over the news."

Celeste nervously twisted a button on her blouse. "How awful! He seemed like such a nice young man."

Bob stared at me. "Florrie? Do you know about this?"

I nodded. "Mr. DuBois found him dead in the pool at the mansion this morning. I pulled his body out of the water."

Celeste gasped. "And you came to work? I would be sobbing in my bedroom."

"Someone had to work and I'm the manager. Besides, it's still a bit of a commotion at the mansion right now."

Celeste sat down. "I can't believe it. Was he staying there overnight?"

"Not that I know of. I don't think he was in the pool when the party ended. I can't imagine what happened."

Celeste handed me two books. "I'll take these. And please order one of Arthur's books. Poor Evan! I just can't believe that he's dead."

I rang up the books and Celeste left in a hurry. I wasn't sure what was going on with her, but she seemed terribly distressed by the news of Evan's death. Then again, she impressed me as delicate, easily distressed by bad news. As the day went on, we had several requests for Arthur's books, so I quickly placed an order.

Shortly before closing, Peter Rudigan walked into the store. One of our regulars, he most often bought nonfiction books for himself. "Hi, Florrie. My wife sprained her ankle and will be off her feet for a while. Could you put together a stack of cozy mysteries for me?"

"Sure!" I left him to wander the store and picked out six new cozies, which I brought back to the checkout desk. I found him smiling as he looked through a copy of Buzz Powers's book.

"Have you read Buzz's book?"

He snorted. "Quite a name, isn't it?"

"I hear it's his real name."

"It is." He tapped his credit card on the machine.

"Do you know him?" I tied our ribbon around the stack of books.

"I'm an FBI agent."

"You're friends!"

"Nah. I barely know the guy." He leaned toward me. "Want to hear something funny?"

"Always."

"He's in HR, human resources."

I slid the books into a bag to make them easier to carry. "I thought the book was based on his adventures."

Peter laughed out loud. "I'd say it's based on his imagination. Thanks, Florrie!"

When the door closed behind him, I picked up Buzz's book and took a closer look. It didn't claim to be nonfiction. I guessed human resources employees were entitled to write fiction as much as anyone else.

When I returned to the cottage that evening around six thirty, I found Professor Maxwell, Jacquie, Mr. DuBois, and Veronica in my living room. Everyone held a mug, which clued me in that something serious had happened during my absence. Serious enough that not even one of them was indulging in cocktail hour.

I took off Peaches's harness, picked her up, and walked toward them. "What's going on?"

Professor Maxwell said, "Sit down, Florrie. There has been a development."

Feeling like the comfort of my home and job might slip away from me, I perched on the edge of a chair with Peaches in my lap.

"The police have been able to put a few bits of evidence together. They discovered someone's regurgitated dinner in the woods behind the azaleas and rhododendrons. Those contents reveal a large quantity of alcohol as well as brownies laced with high-potency THC, the effective part of marijuana. Remains of the same THC and brownies have been found in Evan's stomach contents."

"How can they possibly know that already?" I asked.

Professor Maxwell somberly replied, "When the police discovered the, er, stomach contents, Eric informed them that no brownies were served at the party. They tested for pot right away." He tsked. "Brownies are such a marijuana cliché. Apparently, marijuana can be detected in a matter of minutes. The official toxicology report won't be back for a while, but they expedited the autopsy to make sure nothing was in the food that might cause other guests to be sick."

I blinked hard. "You're saying Evan ate brownies with pot in them and threw up?"

"Exactly." Jacquie dabbed her nose with a tissue.

"So, Evan got high, fell into the pool, and drowned?" I felt relieved because although it was a tragedy, it wasn't murder. "Isn't that good news? Not because he died, but because no one killed him."

"Not exactly," said Veronica. "There's this thing called greening out. It's kind of like blacking out, I guess, but with pot. It happens when you've had a lot to drink and then you ingest high-potency pot. In his case, the brownies were laced with it. According to the medical examiner, it would have taken longer to get into his system because it was an edible, which would have had a delayed effect. It would have taken two hours or so before he felt sick."

I was trying to follow. "He ate the pot, partied on, continued to drink, and then when everyone went home, he was sick?"

"And likely psychotic," Veronica added.

"I shudder to imagine," said Mr. DuBois. "The poor man had a heart condition. At his age! The effects of greening out caused him to have a heart attack, and then he fell into the pool and was unable to get out." Mr. DuBois leaned forward toward me. "The problem is that the THC-laced brownies came from one of our favor boxes."

Chapter 12

"That points at one of us," said Veronica, her voice small and frightened.

"That can't be," I said. "I know we put the cupcakes in the boxes fast, but one of us would surely have noticed if someone was stuffing brownies into the boxes instead of cupcakes."

"Then how did they get into the box?" asked Veronica.

I looked around. "Really? You think Mom or Eric would stuff brownies into the boxes when the rest of us were filling them with cupcakes?"

Mr. DuBois faked a cough.

"Or Mr. DuBois," I added. "None of us would have done that."

No one said a word.

"Oh, come on. We barely even knew the man." I looked around at their expressions. Had one of them known him better than I thought? "Besides, I have never bought pot in my life." I felt a little guilty for saying that, because I had a feeling Veronica could not say the same. "Did anyone else get sick?"

"Not that we know of," said Jacquie. "Evan appears to be the only one so far."

"Then someone brought the brownies with them," I said. "That's the only possibility. And it wasn't one of us!"

Peaches leaped to the table, causing a book to fall off.

The four of them jumped at the thud.

"Why are you so nervous?"

"We're not supposed to be here," said Jacquie. "The police are searching the mansion and the four of us slipped over here through the underground tunnel."

"Searching? What for?"

"*Someone* brought the pot," Veronica said. "We didn't serve it!"

"Maybe Evan brought it with him. If the rumors about him were true, then he was a lush. Maybe he regularly ingested pot, too." I looked to Jacquie. "You knew him best."

She ran one fingertip along her eyebrow. "I didn't know him. I knew *of* him. He had a problem with alcohol."

Professor Maxwell interjected, "A rather public problem. Seems a lot of people knew about it. Apparently, he was an ugly drunk, making scenes in bars and belittling people."

Jacquie winced. "That sounds just like Arthur. I didn't spend much time with him in recent years, so I honestly don't know the extent of his drug use, if any. When we were young, Arthur drank moderately, but with the years and the highs and disappointments, it got away from him."

"You're saying Arthur was a bad influence on Evan?" Another thought hammered at me. "If you didn't know Evan, then why did you invite him to the party?"

"We didn't," moaned Jacquie. "I am never ever inviting people with a plus-one again. Apparently, Arthur was trying to wheedle Sloan and Gabriella into inviting him with their plus-ones, so when Gabriella agreed to bring Arthur, he arranged for Sloan to bring Evan."

"Sloan didn't seem very broken up about his death," I said, thinking of her attitude at breakfast.

"He was a thorn in her side." Jacquie winced. "It can be very difficult to land an agent. Evan treated her like she was his personal publishing fairy and could wave a magic wand to make it all happen for him."

"Did anyone know he had a heart problem?" asked Veronica.

As they shook their heads, I counted. Before last night, only Jacquie knew that Evan McDowell existed. And it was beginning to sound like most of what she knew about him came from Sloan.

"I believe our Mr. McDowell bought the tainted goodies and did himself in by accident," said Mr. DuBois. "We know that none of us, Eric, or your mother had anything to do with his death. Perhaps he simply ate the cupcake and then transferred his own THC brownies into the container. I'm terribly sorry that he died, but I fear the police are chasing their tails here."

"I would have to agree," said Professor Maxwell, stretching his legs and getting to his feet. He offered his hand to his wife. "It's a pity he chose the night of our wedding to pursue his ruinous behavior to the end, but his death was surely an accident."

Jacquie stood up and lightly kissed Maxwell on the lips. "I suppose you think we should return to the mansion to see what mayhem they have left us?"

Professor Maxwell strode to the small opening hidden in a column in my living room. "DuBois? Are you coming?"

The three of them disappeared, leaving me alone with Veronica.

"You must be bushed," I said.

"A little. I'm glad that it's behind me."

"Still considering a career as a wedding planner?"

"Good heavens, no! I think I'll stick with social media. It's not as dependent on other people. I can control what I post and when."

I was thrilled. She would move on eventually, but for now, she would continue to boost the bookstore with fun social media, and I wouldn't be looking for a dependable employee to replace her. Not yet anyway.

Even better, when the police realized that Evan had bought the brownies himself, no one except Professor Maxwell would have to worry about why Jacquie had left their bedroom two nights in a row all by herself.

Veronica stretched and headed for the stairs.

"Are you staying for dinner?" I asked.

"Not today. I have plans. Is it okay if I sleep here one more night?"

"Sure. No problem."

I put on the kettle and opened the refrigerator door. Oof! There was no shortage of food. Leftovers from the party filled every nook and cranny. I would have to freeze some. I couldn't possibly eat all of it before it spoiled.

When someone knocked on the door, I had a hunch it would be the police, asking me to review the details I had already told them.

I peeked out the window, surprised to see Buzz Powers on my doorstep. I swung the door open. "Hello."

He gazed at me, looking as surprised as I was to see him. "Florrie, right?"

"Yes." I stepped aside so he could walk in. Six feet tall, he had a long oval face with gray eyes. He could easily have been the leading man in an action movie. "What can I do for you?"

"Is Veronica ready?"

I had not seen that coming. But now that I thought about it, the signs had been there.

Veronica trotted down the stairs, her short skirt showing off her legs. "Perfect timing." She shot him a dazzling smile and said to me, "Don't wait up."

They talked about where to go for dinner as they walked out the door. It was Sunday night. She would be home early. Even though Georgetown had a lively nighttime scene, Sunday evenings were slow, with many businesses closing early or closed all day.

Not that it mattered to me. All I wanted was some dinner and a blissfully quiet night with my sketchbook. Although I longed to change into pajamas, I thought the couple might return early, and I didn't want to be caught in my nightclothes. I pulled on soft skorts and a T-shirt, returned downstairs, and examined the contents of the refrigerator more closely.

While Peaches snarfed her kitty tuna dinner, I dined on rare roast beef, asparagus, and the delicious salad. When I finished, I took my iced tea over to the couch and eagerly sat down with my sketch pad and pencils.

I drew the beautiful lanterns from the night before, relying on my memory and the green sketch. It was harder than I expected because the lanterns didn't have the same impact without the dark of night around them. But as I added stars and the moon, and a close-up table, the image came to life.

I flipped the page and drew the cute display of favor boxes and cupcakes, which unfortunately took my thoughts to Evan McDowell.

Why would anyone bring THC brownies to a party? I supposed some people would plan to share them with friends. That seemed plausible with so many people in attendance. I presumed that someone who ate them to cope with pain might carry some along everywhere in case he needed them, sort of like carrying aspirin, though not nearly as handy. But in that case, wouldn't one prefer to carry THC gummies, which could easily be stashed in a pocket or a purse? Brownies, while delicious, don't lend themselves to being tucked away as easily. Where had they been before they landed in the favor box?

I sketched Evan as I had seen him in the pool. Had he known about the dangers of greening out? Of the potential of a heart attack? Of the dangers of drinking too much and then eating high-potency THC? Was he hoping for a high? If he had purchased the brownies for his own consumption, then he had brought on his own demise.

If someone else had offered them to him, and he didn't know they were laced with THC, then it would have been a horrific series of events that led to his death. But would that person be responsible? Was it foreseeable that Evan would have an adverse reaction and a heart attack? Probably not. How many people would have known?

Maybe I was just out of the loop because I was oblivious to the possible repercussions. Veronica knew about greening out. Maybe people who used THC knew not to take it after drinking heavily. In my own life, when pot-laced brownies were mentioned, people giggled like it was something silly and fun. And harmless.

I sketched a platter of brownies as I thought about it. And then a favor box, open to show the brownies inside.

Had someone replaced the cupcake with the brownies as a gag? And Evan had been the unknowing recipient? Had he eaten them not realizing that they contained THC?

A knock at my door made me glad I wasn't in my jammies. I hoped it would be Eric. I hadn't heard from him all day. But when I peeked out the window in the door, I saw police. Lots of them.

I admit that a chill went through me. Still, I opened the door. Sergeant Bridges did not smile this time. "Miss Fox, I have a warrant to search your premises." He handed me a sheet of paper and stepped aside, allowing people in white hazmat-type suits to run amok through the carriage house.

Tucking the paper under my arm, I scooped up Peaches and put her halter on her so she wouldn't run outside in the commotion. Still holding her, I read the document. I wouldn't know a fake warrant if I saw one, which made me feel totally helpless.

One of the crime-scene investigators pulled package after package from my refrigerator and peered inside them. The investigators reminded me of huge white ants crawling all over my dwelling.

"Sergeant Bridges! What exactly are you looking for? Maybe I can help."

He gave me a look that sent chills up my spine. What happened to the nice guy from this morning? "We'll find it on our own." He looked away and watched the person at the refrigerator.

"I don't have brownies, with THC or otherwise."

Bridges snapped around and stared at me. "What do you know about brownies?"

I was pretty sure that if I told him how to bake brownies, he would think I was a wise guy. "Apparently Evan ate some."

"I see. You've been talking to Eric."

"I haven't seen or spoken to him all day." I became uneasy. I hoped Veronica didn't have brownies or pot in her belongings. I knew I didn't, but now that it was semilegal, she might have some. The laws were in flux. We were in DC. But over the bridge in Virginia, a person could have an ounce or less. I honestly didn't know what could happen if they found pot among Veronica's possessions. But I did know one thing. It was time for me to stop talking. I had nothing to do with Evan's death, and I suspected he had brought it on himself. But something must have led the police to suspect a crime had occurred.

I had absolutely nothing to hide, but Bridges made me nervous, and I did not like the way he was eyeing me and the carriage house. Moving slowly so I wouldn't draw his attention, I inched away from him and stood in front of the fireplace, out of the way.

Three white-clad individuals walked down the stairs. I heard one of them say, "Nothing. Not even prescription meds."

A wave of relief swept over me.

The three of them stepped outside, leaving Bridges and the one who'd examined the contents of my fridge.

Peaches grew antsy and mewed for me to set her down. As I was doing that, I heard a shout outside. Bridges and his friend bolted out of the door.

I picked up Peaches and followed them.

Chapter 13

Professor Maxwell stood on the pavement between the mansion and the carriage house, his cheeks ablaze. Jacquie, clearly aghast, held a hand over her mouth. Mr. DuBois was shaking his head.

One of the white-clad people held a garbage bag in one hand, and a food container in another.

I rushed up to Jacquie and whispered, "What happened?"

"They found packaging for THC brownies in the trash," she murmured.

I peered at the package. A simple plastic clamshell, it was empty, save for a few crumbs. The top bore a label that clearly stated BROWNIES THC 1000.

A familiar woman's voice broke through the chatter with authority. "Five hundred people were on this property yesterday evening. That empty clamshell doesn't mean a thing."

I looked around for her. Either the professor or Jacquie had had the good sense to call their attorney, Ms. Strickland. I'd dealt with her when the professor was arrested a while back. She was only a few inches taller than me. Her light brown hair had been streaked blond. She wore it in a traditional pageboy cut, now pushed back by oversize sunglasses on top of her head. She carried her head high, her well-defined jaw and steely eyes letting everyone know she was no push-over.

Bridges scoffed aloud. "We'll see what you have to say after it has been fingerprinted." He gave a nod, and the white-clad ants stripped off their costumes and became people again. They headed to the street, where I imagined their cars were parked.

Bridges didn't have the decency to say a word to those of us whose possessions had been rifled through. He followed the others, talking about fingerprints.

We heard the engines starting and the dull roar as they drove away. And suddenly, we stood in the calm silence of a Sunday evening in early summer.

Professor Maxwell turned to me. "Do you know who brought those?"

"Not a clue. I can assure you that it wasn't me."

He tried hard to hide a smile.

"I'm still hopeful that the only fingerprints will belong to Evan," I said.

Ms. Strickland scowled at us. "It strains credulity a bit to imagine a guest bringing a clamshell like that to a party."

"It had to be a woman," said Jacquie. "That clamshell would have fit into a purse. Not a teensy clutch, of course, but I have several purses that it could easily slide into. No one would have been the wiser."

Ms. Strickland nodded. "The perpetrator could have grabbed a favor box and made a quick trip to a bathroom where she swapped the cupcake for the brownies."

"Don't be so quick to eliminate male guests," said Mr. DuBois. "The favors were in the foyer near the front door. It would have been equally easy to leave the brownies in a car and nab a favor box on the way out. Perhaps he even ate the cupcake. Then he filled the box with brownies and returned carrying a favor box. To borrow your phrase, no one would have been the wiser."

"Well then, we wait for the results," said Ms. Strickland. "With just a little bit of luck, the only fingerprints will be those of the deceased, Mr. McDowell. I imagine the police have made a right mess of your homes. I'll leave you to restoring order. I'm available whenever you need me, Maxwell."

She turned toward me and held out her hand. "How are you, Florrie?"

I shook her hand. "A little shaken."

"What a beautiful cat." She reached out and stroked Peaches. "I'm a cat person myself. After a trying day, all I want to do is snuggle up with them."

Peaches yowled, letting me know she wanted to run free. Ms. Strickland and I laughed about it and said goodbye. I returned to the carriage house, where the biggest chore I faced was putting away the contents of the refrigerator.

As soon as I took off her harness, Peaches scampered over to the French doors and embarked on a major grooming session.

I pulled out freezer bags and began dividing the food into portions. It didn't take as long as I expected. When I finished, I went up to the bedroom, where clothes lay scattered all over. It was truly annoying. Why did they have to be so messy about it? I certainly hadn't planned on spending the rest of the evening tidying everything. Why didn't I share Marie Kondo's joy in organizing?

That finally done, I returned downstairs, made a mug of hot tea, and returned to my sketchbook. Brownies on my mind, I drew the clamshell the police had discovered in the trash. The label had been artsy. The baker probably paid someone to design it.

The front door swung open. I looked over my shoulder at Veronica. "You're home early. How was your date?"

The bolt clanked in place as she locked the door. "Awful." She poured herself a glass of white wine and plopped into the armchair opposite me. "You no longer have to worry about me dating someone Dad's age. Buzz should be named Snoozy. There is no buzz in Buzzville."

"That's too bad."

She swirled her wine. "To be honest, I find it very hard to believe that he could ever have had the gumption to participate in the kinds of daring and dangerous adventures that he describes in his book."

I looked at her in surprise. "You read his book?"

"Parts of it. Like when he was tracking this criminal in the jungle, and all of a sudden he's surrounded by natives carrying spears. It's totally Indiana Jones. But the guy I had dinner with tonight was totally boring. Like the Spratts' son, Norman."

I groaned at the thought. I went out with the son of our parents' friends once, but that was enough to convince him that he loved me. "No one could be as tedious as Norman. You have not experienced boredom until you have listened to someone describe grass maintenance for two hours. He doesn't hold himself out as a former FBI agent who lived to tell about his exciting adventures, though. No false advertising. Norman is as boring as he looks."

"I can't figure it out," said Veronica. "Dad is more interesting than Buzz, and we both know Dad isn't exactly the life of the party."

"Maybe he can't talk about his work?"

"He *wrote* about it! It's already out there. I thought he would be interesting to talk to, but I'm done with him."

"Veronica, have you ever eaten brownies laced with pot?"

She snorted and laughed. "In college. One of the girls on my hall baked brownies that were supposed to have grass in them. I think she called them Magic Brownies. For all I know she baked them with dried parsley. As I recall, they weren't very good."

"Did you get high?"

"No. But we giggled a lot. Are you asking because of Evan?"

I told her what had happened. "If your clothes aren't where you left them, it's because the police took everything out of your bags, and I put it all back."

"Whoa! They must have some clue that leads them to think he was murdered."

"Maybe. If the person who gave him the brownies didn't know about his heart condition, then was it murder?"

"Good question. I think you had a more interesting evening than I did!"

Even though I knew the doors were locked, I double-checked them all before we went up to bed.

When I had moved to the carriage house, Veronica hadn't hesitated to stay over, especially on nights when she had been out partying in Georgetown. I finally got wise and replaced my old bed with a new one. A massive trundle hid underneath it and only needed to be pulled out when Veronica visited. She'd been staying over a lot as the party date neared.

A few months before, poor Eric slept on my sofa when he had a broken leg, so I had added a large Murphy bed down-stairs. When closed, it looked like a modern cabinet. But it opened to a comfortable bed, large enough for two. Even my parents had slept over a couple of times.

When I woke on Monday morning, Veronica was pack-ing her bags. Had I been in her shoes, I would have been eager to go home and get back into my regular routine.

On the way to the bookstore, we made a detour to stop at one of my favorite bakeries. I stayed outside with Peaches while Veronica darted in to buy two large lattes and sinfully delicious croissants, some plain and some filled with chocolate, ham, or Asiago cheese. She emerged with a giant box. When we rounded the corner we stopped dead in our tracks.

People had created a remembrance to Evan, with flowers surrounding a photo of him in front of a sports bar.

"Okay, this is weird. That's Evan, right?" asked Veronica.

It caught me unaware. Even though I had dragged him up from the bottom of the pool, I must have compartmentalized it somehow, and now, seeing his photo, emotion overwhelmed me. "Yes."

Veronica whispered, "At a bar?"

It *was* odd. "Excuse me." I addressed a man who was entering the bar.

"We're not open yet." He appraised Veronica and me. "Did you know Evan?"

"We did," said Veronica firmly. "Why is a memorial here?"

"Evan was a regular. There's even talk of putting his name on his favorite bar chair. He loved sports and liked to drink. Man, we're going to miss that guy." He nodded and hurried inside.

"Do you think someone meant to kill him?"

I couldn't look at her. Tears welled in my eyes. "I hope not."

We turned and silently walked the few blocks to Color Me Read. I unlocked the door and dashed inside to turn off the burglar alarm.

A tear spilled over onto my cheek. I barely knew the man, but I felt as though I did. He wasn't too much older than me. It wasn't his time yet. But for the brownies, would he have died? Would he have had a heart attack or been sick? Would he have fallen into the pool?

A fury rose in me at the injustice, the unfairness of his

demise. He might not have been perfect, but who was? He might have provided us with great books, and now his voice had been stilled for eternity.

Veronica bustled past me. "Here's your latte. I'll put on the coffee and set out the croissants."

Her attention to the details of daily life helped me shift my focus. I flipped the CLOSED sign to OPEN on the door and switched on the background music.

To my surprise, Celeste Sorello was our first customer of the day. She sidled in, as though she didn't want to open the door all the way. Like she meant to cause the least amount of disturbance by her presence.

"Good morning," I said.

Wringing her thin hands, she asked, "Is it true?"

She had heard of Evan's death the day before, so I wasn't certain what she meant. "I'm not sure what you're asking."

She leaned toward me over the checkout desk. "The poison. Was Evan poisoned?"

"I don't think it's considered poison. I don't really know. It's all a little bit confusing. Sort of a very unfortunate string of events."

"I don't understand."

"He ate brownies laced with a high amount of marijuana. That probably made him ill and might have caused the heart attack. And then he fell into the pool."

Her face grew pale and the muscles in her jaw twitched. "Isn't that murder? It would be if someone put the same drug in his drink and he died because it gave him a heart attack."

Chapter 14

I hadn't thought about it quite that way. "It's sort of like serving shellfish to someone who is allergic to it and doesn't know there is shrimp in the dish."

"That could be accidental," she said. "Would it still be murder?"

I didn't have any answers for her. The door opened. Professor Goldblum and other members of the Monday Morning Coloring Club flooded into the bookstore. I could hear them making a fuss over the croissants.

Poor Celeste looked distraught. She toyed with the pretty gold chain she wore.

"Would you like to join one of our coloring clubs? I think you might enjoy it."

"Coloring? That's for children."

Goldblum overheard her. He carried a croissant on a napkin. One bite was missing. "Pardon me, but I do some of my best thinking when I color. You see, it reduces stress and cortisol, while stimulating the amygdala."

She gazed at him with doubt. Ever so politely she murmured, "Thank you."

He smiled. "You don't believe me? The amygdala processes emotions, particularly those associated with fear. You've heard of fight or flight? That's the part of your brain that determines whether you will fight or flee!"

"Celeste Sorello, this is Professor Goldblum," I said. "He's one of the smartest people I know."

She reached out to shake his hand. "So you color, Professor Goldblum?"

I caught a tinge of satisfaction in his tone when he responded, "Every Monday morning and sometimes during the week, too. It clears my mind and soothes me."

"Perhaps I *should* give it a try. My husband tells me I'm high-strung and that I worry too much."

A delighted smile broke on Goldblum's face. "Come with me, Celeste. I'll introduce you to everyone and get you started."

Celeste returned to the checkout desk half an hour later with more coloring books, pencils, and coloring pens than she needed. "I think this could be good for me. It seems like a very nice group of people. They were so helpful about their preferences regarding these items." She paid, took her bags, and stepped cautiously into the parlor. I could hear members of the group greeting her.

Veronica rushed through the hallway and sidled up to me. "Jacquie and the professor have canceled their honeymoon," she whispered.

"Because of Evan?"

"I don't know. I called Jacquie to wish her bon voyage and DuBois answered her phone. He didn't say much, just that they weren't going."

I didn't like the sound of that. Not at all. I tried to reason. Maybe there was an innocent explanation. "Maybe they think it would look bad if they left right after Evan died on their premises. Especially given the rather bizarre way he died."

"You're probably right. They wouldn't want to be seen having fun in Hawaii." Veronica was quiet for a moment. "I must have phoned Jacquie a million times before the wedding to get details right. Never once did Mr. DuBois answer her phone."

Our eyes met.

"This is going to get worse, isn't it?" asked Veronica.

I winced when I said what I truly suspected. "I hope the medical examiner declares it an accident, but I don't think we'll be that lucky."

Veronica went to check on the coloring group, and I picked up a stack of books to change the window display in the parlor. As I removed the current display from the window, I felt someone looking at me. My skin crawled.

I turned and gazed around. The friendly chatter of the coloring club eased my tension. But then I spotted him.

Norman Spratt, the son of my parents' friends, stood on the other side of the room, watching me. I hated to be critical about him because I wasn't a model by a long shot. But at thirty, Norman had lost most of his hair, and gained a paunch. Those things wouldn't have bothered me if he'd only had a sparkling personality. Great wit, for instance. But Norman was as boring as he looked.

He crossed the room. "Hi, Florrie."

I tried to sound happy to see him. "Hi, Norman! Can I help you with something?"

"No."

Then why was he here? I chatted to be polite. Even if I wasn't interested in Norman, what I said and did would get back to my mom. I couldn't embarrass her. His mother was her dear friend. "How's it going in the police academy?" And why wasn't he there right now?

"I dropped out after one week."

"You didn't like it?"

"My mom insisted on it. I'm their only child. If I die, then our family line will end."

"I see. It would be very hard on them if something happened to you. Have you gone back to taking care of grass at golf courses?"

"No." His chest puffed up. "I'm a private investigator."

I almost fell over. Norman, while as boring as the grass he used to talk about, wasn't a dolt. He held a master's degree in some subject related to grass. I stared at him unabashedly. Maybe that job would suit him. After all, most PI work fell in the category of painfully tedious, not unlike watching grass grow. And if Norman was on a stakeout, everyone would overlook him. No one would ever suspect him of being a detective. "Congratulations! Wow. I never thought you would be interested in being a PI."

He beamed. "See you later, Florrie."

I watched him leave. What an odd encounter. Thankfully, he hadn't asked me out on a date. I made a mental note to ask my mom to remind his mom that I was dating Eric. His mother would be delighted. She had banned Norman from having anything to do with Veronica or me because we were too dangerous. I laughed aloud at the thought.

Jacquie's wedding inspired my window selections. Books on wedding gowns, wedding ideas, wedding checklists, how to organize a wedding, and my favorites, tons of books with photos, recipes, and ideas of food for weddings. I would have bought the books for the covers alone.

When I finished, I returned to the checkout desk and was perusing information on upcoming releases when the phone rang.

"Meet me at Book Hill Park." The phone clicked and the dial tone buzzed in my ear. That was all. Almost a command, a directive at the very least, from Professor Maxwell.

I found Veronica and told her I was stepping out to pick up some lunch.

"If you're going by Good Greens, I'd love a chicken salad. Not the mayonnaisey kind you put on sandwiches, but an actual salad with lettuce and bits of chicken in it."

"Will do."

My route took me right by Good Greens, but I didn't know what the professor had in mind and thought it better to pick up the salad on my way back lest it spoil. The sun shone, but the temperature wasn't yet unbearably hot. Still, food spoiled easily.

I spotted the professor right away. He cut an impressive figure, standing at the top of the hill, looking down. That was a good sign, I guessed. He certainly wasn't trying to hide from anyone.

"Hi!" I smiled at him.

"Hello, Florrie."

He gazed at me. Either he didn't know where to begin or he was reconsidering the reason he had called me there. "I need you to be completely honest with me."

"I don't think I've ever been otherwise."

He nodded. "On occasion, we wish to protect those we love. This is not the time for such kindnesses."

"All right." Did he think Veronica was the source of the brownies?

"What exactly happened on the day of the party when Jacquie disappeared and you found her?"

Uh-oh. "I happened upon her in a state of grogginess. As though she had been asleep or unconscious. She was well hidden in a garden. I helped her to her feet and walked home with her. She gained strength as we proceeded, sort of like she was recuperating from something."

"Was anyone with her?"

Ah! Now I was beginning to understand. He thought she had met up with someone. Arthur, maybe? "No. She was alone."

"What did she say to you?"

"Not much. I was under the impression that she either did not wish to tell me about her experience or she didn't remember it. I didn't push her to reveal what happened."

"Did she say anything about Arthur or meeting Arthur?"

Now we were getting to the crux of his questions. Was he jealous? She married the professor, not Arthur. "She didn't say a word about him. She asked me if there were people in my life whom I would go to help in the middle of the night."

He nodded. "She woke me to say Arthur was in trouble. I was half-asleep. Since her return, she has been elusive with me, clearly trying to avoid the subject. But now . . ." He slid his hands into his pockets and gazed out over the hill and the Federal-style buildings below. "The plastic brownie box shows a couple of very clear fingerprints. They belong to Jacquie."

A shiver ran through me. I tried to rationalize. Maybe there was a good reason. "Does she take medicinal THC? For joint pain? Arthritis, maybe?" I had never heard her complain about that sort of pain, but maybe she controlled it with THC.

"No. If she's buying edibles for some reason, neither DuBois nor I are aware of it. She could easily hide it from me, though I don't know why she would. But you can't get anything past DuBois."

"You think she met Arthur that night?"

The professor turned his gaze to me. "I would bet on it. Arthur is an unusual character. That's the kindest way to say it."

"In what way?"

"Ambitious people usually judge their success in two ways: money and power. He is reckless with money. He treats it as though he assumes there will always be more. He doesn't care about it a whit, though I suppose he might if he runs out of it. Arthur has a need to feel superior. He wants to wield power over people. Usually that means a career in politics or being the best at some sport. But Arthur's father was a thug in custom-tailored Savile Row suits. At his knee, Arthur learned to manipulate people by getting the goods on them. Knowing their weaknesses and learning their secrets. He tried that on me when Jacquie and I married the first time and again a few days ago."

He smiled at me. "I am not so blind as to have delusions of self-grandeur. I have as many flaws as the average man, perhaps more. Jacquie claims my biggest fault by far is the absence of fear for my own safety. An emotion she feels acutely. But I digress. My point is that while I have a good many vices and weaknesses, they are not of the sort one can use against me as blackmail. I am an open book."

"I suppose he resents you for that?"

"Quite. Jacquie left him because of his brusque domination. She couldn't take it anymore. I don't think he ever recovered from losing her. He thought he could control her, but Jacquie is a strong woman and a free spirit. She walked out. I imagine he thought it would be easy to replace her. But our Jacquie is one of a kind."

"Then why would she be willing to meet him in the middle of the night?"

"She is a very loyal friend. And she likely has sentimental memories of a first love. She wouldn't tolerate the way he treats people, but he was a part of her life once. Like most of us, Arthur is not without some degree of charm."

I squinted at the professor, trying to put it all together. "You're saying Jacquie met with him the night before the wedding. She was somehow incapacitated but refused to report anything to the police. She married you, fed Evan brownies during the party, and then slipped out at night to make sure he had died?" I shook my head. "I don't buy that. Jacquie wouldn't murder Evan. All she had to do was cut Arthur out of her life. Unless she had some other connection to Evan that I don't know about. But when would she have acquired the brownies? I don't think she left the property from the time she came home until the wedding."

Still, her fingerprints were conclusive evidence. . . .

"Jacquie claims she must have touched the box when she was helping DuBois clean up the following day."

"Didn't the caterers do that before they left?"

"It was after that. After Evan's body had been found. We had all those houseguests, and I understand there was a bit of chaos in the kitchen as they woke and discovered the police on the property. DuBois did his best to accommodate everyone, but there was quite a mess in the kitchen, and Jacquie helped him clean up before the brunch chefs arrived."

"Are the guests gone now?"

"They left yesterday afternoon after they were interviewed by the police."

I pulled out my phone and called Mr. DuBois on speaker. "Hi, Mr. DuBois. It's Florrie. Can you do me a huge favor and not clean the mansion until I have a chance to look around? I'm especially interested in the guest rooms."

"I can't do that!"

"Yes, you can, DuBois," said Professor Maxwell. "Cease all cleaning activities until I say you may resume."

Mr. DuBois sputtered, "But, Maxwell—"

"It's important, DuBois."

"Very well, but don't come to me complaining about dust bunnies and spiderwebs." He clicked off.

And in that moment, as I tucked away my phone, I saw something curious and disturbing. The sun glinted off two blue spheres. Unmistakably binoculars.

Chapter 15

I darted toward the tree where I had seen them. A figure in khaki green loped away. The person wore a hat and shapeless clothing.

"Florrie!" called the professor. "What's going on?"

When I arrived at the tree, I looked around, turning in a full circle, but no one appeared to be watching. A mom pushed a little boy in a stroller, and two teenaged girls eating popcorn giggled as they walked a good distance away.

Professor Maxwell caught up to me. "What was it?"

"Binoculars. I'm certain of it."

He turned in a complete circle, much as I had. "Perhaps it was merely a bird-watcher."

"Then why run?"

"Did you tell anyone you were meeting me here?" he asked.

"Not a soul."

"He must have followed one of us."

I gazed at him in horror. "What's going on?"

"I don't know, Florrie."

"Do you think Jacquie has something to do with this?"

To my surprise, his face showed no fury when he nodded. "Jacquie and her crew of writing friends. We have to figure out what happened to Evan." He sighed. "All right then, my job is to get to the bottom of things with Jacquie. You see what you can find out from the rest of them. I'll fill in for you at the store for a couple of hours. Go see what you can find at the mansion."

I agreed, but that raised another problem. The professor wasn't much help at the store. When we each went our own way, I phoned Bob to see if he could fill in for a couple of hours. I had to bribe him with an entire extra day off. I really had to hire more help.

As I walked, I darted behind trees and paused to look in shop windows in the hope I might see who was following me.

I hurried around the mansion to the back door, watching over my shoulder, and knocked. If anyone was tailing me, he was likely to come around the corner on the pavement, where he would be seen.

Mr. DuBois didn't answer the door. I knocked again, a bit nervously, as I continued to keep an eye on the driveway.

Even though I knew it would be locked, I tried the handle, and the door opened.

That worried me.

Thanks to all the true-crime shows Mr. DuBois watched on TV, he kept exterior doors locked at all times. I reminded myself that Jacquie and the professor might not be as conscientious. "Mr. DuBois?" I shouted. I stepped inside. The house was cool and quiet. "Mr. DuBois?" I closed the door behind me and listened. If he was upstairs, he probably couldn't hear me coming in. But the unlocked door and Mr. DuBois's not running to see who'd entered the house were highly unusual. In addition to his scelerophobia, the fear of burglars, I had long suspected that he suffered from a fear of leaving the property. He gossiped endlessly with the staff of houses nearby, and I gathered that he sometimes had coffee with them, though I wasn't certain whether it was an over-the-fence sort of thing or he went to their houses. Nevertheless, the current situation left me feeling wary. I stared at the door. If I didn't lock it, anyone who might be following me could come inside. On the other hand, what if I needed to make a quick exit? Common sense won. I locked the door because chances were good that elderly Mr. DuBois had simply forgotten or that Jacquie was outside somewhere. We all expected so much of Mr. DuBois, but forgetfulness might be setting in.

I tiptoed through the kitchen and into the foyer. Suddenly, I heard faint shouting and banging. "Mr. DuBois?" I called again. I thought the sound came from the second floor. I raced upstairs and stopped. "Where are you?"

The banging and his voice were much louder now. To the left, I thought, and called out to him one more time. Had he fallen? Gotten trapped somewhere?

"Miss Florrie! In here! In the blue room!"

I thought I heard something rattle. I dashed along the hallway, peering in doorways and looking for anything blue. I spied soft blue walls in a room that faced the rear of the house. Blue toile curtains matched the coverlet on the bed. The double closet doors rattled. A chair had been angled on its back legs, the top propped under the door handles of the closet, holding it closed. Even though I was in a hurry to get Mr. DuBois out of his prison, I took one moment to snap a quick photograph with my phone as proof.

As I removed the chair, the front door slammed closed.

Mr. DuBois burst from the closet, his face scarlet. He pointed a finger. "See who that was!"

I hurried across the hall and looked out a bedroom window. Leafy trees prevented me from seeing anyone who might be running along the sidewalk. I cranked the window open to listen. An engine started. The car did not pass in front of the mansion as its engine droned away. With a start, I realized I had probably passed that car on my way here. But I had paid no attention whatsoever to the cars parked along the street.

I returned to poor Mr. DuBois, who sat in the chair that had held him prisoner in the closet. I perched on the edge of the bed. "Are you all right?"

"I wasn't harmed, if that is what you mean."

I rose to inspect the closet, a walk-in with two white louvered doors. They didn't lock. "What happened?"

"I was putting away extra blankets when someone slammed the doors."

"Did you see who it was?"

"Don't you think I would have been calling out that person's name if I had?" he grumbled. "What I don't understand is how the person got into the house. This is most disturbing."

"The back door wasn't locked."

He looked at me in horror. "It was so. I locked it myself before coming upstairs to clean."

I thought it better not to remind him that he had promised not to clean the guest rooms. What was done was done. "Would you like to go to the emergency room?"

"Miss Florrie! I am not so frail that I wither like a vine at the slightest bit of discomfort."

"Have you cleaned all the rooms?"

"I cannot imagine what would have possessed Maxwell to expect that I would leave the guest rooms in their morning-after state for an extended period of time."

"Meaning you cleaned them yesterday?"

"Naturally. I stripped the beds and washed the linens."

"Have you vacuumed?"

He seemed pained. "No. Nor have I scrubbed the bathrooms yet."

"Great!" I smiled at him. "Who stayed in this room?"

"Sloan, your literary agent. She's very tidy and well-mannered, which I can't say for all his guests. Both of her husbands ditched her for a younger model, which has made her quite sensitive about her appearance. I think she looks fine, personally. It's rather sad because she's not old but she thinks that love has passed her by."

I peered in the bathroom. The towels were missing. "Does 'linens' include towels?"

I heard his sigh. "I collected the towels. They have all been laundered."

So much for that. "Did anyone have sopping towels? Like they'd been for a swim?" I pulled open drawers in the vanity. Nothing of interest. The toile-covered wastebasket gleamed inside. "You emptied the trash?"

"Jacqueline did that. I believe there were a few damp towels, but nothing so remarkable that I took note."

I returned to the bedroom, knelt on the hardwood floor, and lifted the dust ruffle to look under the bed. Something poked me from behind.

"Perhaps this would be useful." Mr. DuBois handed me a floor duster. I shoved it under the bed, and it captured a scrap of paper.

Mr. DuBois picked it up. It looked like part of a peanut–butter-cup wrapper. Hardly what we had hoped for.

Mr. DuBois followed me as I went from room to room. Although he criticized people for gossiping, it didn't prevent him from giving me a running commentary on each of the houseguests as we checked the rooms.

"I can't help thinking that Walter must regret having married Liddy. Do you suppose a divorce is on the horizon? Surely he doesn't feel obligated to stay with her because her father set him up in business."

Once again, I knelt on the floor and swept the cleaning device under the bed.

"They've lost their only child," he continued, "so it's not as though they would need to stay together for the children's sake. I must say that I admire him. I can't imagine anyone else putting up with Liddy all these years."

"You'd better hope she doesn't leave him. She might be inclined to move back here."

Mr. DuBois gasped. "A pox on that! The day she moves in is the day I retire. Imagine the nerve of bringing a pig to an elegant party. I will not be manipulated by that she-devil."

I tried not to laugh. "Gee, Mr. DuBois, it sounds as if you don't like Liddy."

Something clunked on the floor as though it had been caught between the headboard and the mattress. I aimed the sweeper for it.

"You jest. But you would leave, too. Imagine if she were on the property every day. I couldn't bear it. What's that you've got?"

I reached for the little object. It was a small translucent green pig with inset diamond eyes.

Mr. DuBois reached for it. "Oh my. This is quite valuable. Jadeite, I believe. See how translucent it is? And it glistens, almost as though it were liquid. Quite beautiful."

"You're certain this was the room Liddy and Walter stayed in?"

"Positive. Liddy phoned before the party to demand this room. She never asks for anything, she always demands. The most annoying thing about her rudeness is that it works. She always gets what she wants. I thought she desired this room because of the size or the location at the end of the hall. But now I wonder what she could have been up to. Maybe she wanted to be closer to the back stairs."

"*If* it was Liddy who just ran out of the mansion, I wouldn't blame her for coming back to look for this little piggy. But why not just ask if you found it? There wasn't any need to lock you into a closet."

"Why, indeed?" His eyebrows cocked up.

"Are you going to call her?"

"Not so fast. First, I think I'll have a chat with Maxwell. Just to be sure this isn't some exquisite family heirloom that has been locked away for safekeeping. Besides, we don't know it doesn't belong to her husband. No, I believe a bit of due diligence is warranted here."

"Promise me you'll tell Professor Maxwell about it."

His eyes widened and he muttered indignantly, "That goes without saying! Perhaps she stole this from Jacquie."

"I thought you said she and her husband are well-off."

"They are. I'm sorry to say I don't trust Liddy."

We worked our way through the other rooms, but the rest of the guests had been tidier, and we found nothing of interest, except a purple eyeliner pencil.

I handed it to Mr. DuBois, who took it with disinterest. "I'd better get back to the store."

"Thank you for rescuing me. I would have been locked in that closet until Jacquie or Maxwell came home!"

I took the long route back to the bookstore so I could pick up Veronica's chicken salad. While I was paying for it, Buzz Powers strode up to the takeout counter.

"Hi!" I said. "Florrie Fox. We met at the Maxwells' party."

"Veronica's sister! I remember you. How is Veronica?"

"Bossy," I joked. "I'm picking up lunch for her."

"Not back on her feet yet?" He made a sad face. "Maybe I should stop by. Brighten her day while she's recuperating."

Chapter 16

I'd put my foot in it now! Yikes! What on earth had she told him? Trying to sound like I was confiding, I said, "I think she'd rather be made up and looking pretty. I'll tell her you asked about her. Sorry, I'm in a bit of a hurry today." And I took off as fast as I could without looking like I was running away from him. I was, of course. I didn't want to have to answer any more questions.

I hurried straight to the bookstore. "Veronica!"

She emerged from the parlor. "It's about time."

"I ran into Buzz."

"Oh," she said dully. She took her salad and popped open the top. "You've been with him all this time?"

"No, the professor had some errands he wanted me to do." That was my second lie in less than ten minutes. Guilt washed over me. "Buzz sends his best and wanted to drop by to see you."

Veronica froze, wide-eyed. "I forgot about that. I never imagined he would come by."

"With flowers and chocolates from the sound of it."

Veronica grimaced. "He's been calling and sending me texts. I really don't want to go out with him again, but I didn't want to hurt his feelings, so I said I was out sick, and I'd call him when I was better. I figured a month would go by and he would have gotten the message."

I tried to hide a smile, but I couldn't. "He's your Norman! At least he's good-looking and far more interesting than lawn care."

"Oh, sure. You haven't had to sit down and talk to him for an hour one-on-one. You'd change your tune quick." She frowned at me. "Does he know I'm working?"

"No."

"Great! He doesn't have my address. I'll text him and say the doctor recommends bed rest." She pulled out her phone and began a message.

"It's wiser to come clean, Veronica," I said as I walked away.

She followed me along the hallway muttering, "I can't tell him I'm not interested. Besides, it's not like we had a torrid affair. We went out on one date!"

I located Bob in the kitchen making a fresh pot of coffee. "Thanks for filling in."

"No problem. Jacquie was here looking for you a few minutes ago."

"Thanks." I found her upstairs in John's office.

"Florrie! I've had the most brilliant idea. John loves it."

I glanced at him. He *was* beaming.

"Let's have a big signing event with Gabriella; her husband, Griffin Corbyn; Arthur; Buzz Powers; and me, of course."

"You realize that Griffin won't attend."

She smiled broadly, a twinkle in her eye. "I have worked that out. Come with me."

I followed her to the checkout desk, where she handed me a stack of books wrapped with a wide ribbon of fine burlap imprinted with the store's name.

"I want you to deliver these to Griffin at home. He won't be able to turn you down face-to-face."

I did not share her confidence. "You're the one who knows him. Maybe the invitation should come from you."

"I have had no luck at all with him." She nodded at me. "You give it a try."

Veronica walked up with a flyer and handed it to Jacquie. "How's this?"

I peered at it.

COLOR ME READ announces
Old Friends
An evening with the authors
Jacquie Liebhaber
Griffin Corbyn
Buzz Powers
Gabriella Archambeau
And Arthur Bedlingham
Friday 6–9 PM

"Not that I mean to be a spoilsport, but don't you think we'd better make sure we have Griffin on board before we move forward with advertising his presence?" I asked.

"Absolutely!" said Jacquie. "And that is why I shall stay here and assist Veronica while you are off procuring his assurances."

"I honestly don't know why you think I can work that miracle. He's probably a bigger agoraphobe than Mr. DuBois."

Jacquie looked at me, startled. "I've been telling Maxwell that DuBois is afraid to leave the estate. I'm so glad you noticed, too. Maxwell holds you in the highest regard. Now maybe he'll believe me. I think DuBois should see someone about it."

"Good luck. I expect Mr. DuBois will be as receptive to that as Griffin will be to a signing," I said.

Veronica snorted. "You're so much like Gabriella."

"You hardly know her," I snapped back.

"The long hair, the shyness, bookish, petite. I don't have to know more."

Jacquie shooed me out the door. "Get going already!"

I walked away, looking at the address. I knew the general neighborhood. It wasn't far.

Gabriella and Griffin lived in a Federal-style red brick house. Three tall windows with black shutters ran along the front so low that they seemed only a foot or two off the ground. A shallow bed of hostas and ivy ran along in front of them. The front door was actually on the side of the house. I swung open a black iron gate and followed an old uneven brick walk to the door. Ivy grew on the house, all the way up to the second floor.

Taking a deep breath and bracing myself, I knocked on the black door.

Gabriella swung it open. "Florrie!"

I held out the package of books I was supposed to deliver. "Jacquie sent these over for you and Griffin."

She took them and looked at the top one. "We were talking about this book at her party. That was so thoughtful of her. Won't you come in?"

I stepped inside and gazed around. Gabriella didn't just write romance books, she lived in a romantic cottage. A ruffled cream-colored pillow sat on a farmhouse bench. Above it coat hooks held a Stetson and a red hat with the Washington Nationals baseball team logo. A pair of well-worn green men's running shoes lay underneath the bench. They seemed large to me and were distinctive because of the matching interior and laces in a neon lime green.

Gabriella moved over whitewashed candlesticks and a bowl of lush pink peonies on a white coffee table to make room for the books. The sofa was upholstered in a pinkish tan, the perfect backdrop for her English country-style floral cushions.

"Is Griffin home? Some of the books are for him."

"Sorry, Florrie. He's off at a cabin on the Chesapeake Bay. He goes there at some point during every book. He just has to get away to write without any distractions. It's only the two of us, but it's easy to break concentration when someone else is breathing in the same room," she joked.

"That must be hard on you."

"I think it might be if I weren't a writer, too, but I love the time alone. No cooking, no obligations, and precious few errands. When he leaves, I stock up on white wine, Georgetown Cupcakes, and orange Milano cookies. I fill the house with pink flowers and rose potpourri, and then I step into my world of romance. Most husbands wouldn't understand that."

"No, I suppose they wouldn't. That's too bad. How long will he be away?"

"Until he finishes the book."

"I suppose that would not be by this Friday?"

She giggled. "More like a month from now. But as I said, it's fine with me. I need my own writing time."

A solid-white long-haired cat slinked into the room and jumped onto the sofa. He sat regally with his tail wrapped around his front paws. His green eyes assessed me.

"This is Heathcliff."

"He's beautiful."

"Poor little guy. Well, he's not so little anymore. I found him hiding in a space under a pile of firewood when he was a kitten. I was so relieved when no one claimed him. He's my little snugglepuss."

I wasn't certain Jacquie wanted to proceed without Griffin. He would be a huge draw. But so would the others. "We thought we might have an author chat and signing at Color Me Read on Friday. The lineup would be you and Griffin, Jacquie, Arthur, and Buzz."

"I would love that. It sounds wonderful. Griffin will be sorry to miss it."

"You could call to see if he wants to come."

"I'll have to give that some thought. Probably not. We have an agreement. No calls or texts unless a trip to the hospital or emergency room is required." Gabriella laughed. "It sounds so dire, but the whole point is to be away from all the little diversions of everyday life. Kind of like being on a working vacation. But it works for us."

Oh no. I realized that I had interrupted her writing. "I'm sorry, Gabriella. I didn't mean to disturb you."

"No! I didn't mean that. I'm glad you came. I haven't been able to focus on anything. Not since Evan's death." She looked down at her hands. "We went way back. I hadn't seen him in ages. I'm so grateful we had a chance to catch up at Jacquie's party. I still can't believe he's gone. I heard that he drowned in the Maxwells' pool."

I nodded. "Do you know if he was into eating pot edibles?"

Gabriella burst into laughter. "Not Evan. I know people who are very excited about it, but Evan preferred alcohol. He loved to eat, too, but alcohol was his undoing. He turned to it with every rejection and every writer's block. He could write! But not under the influence. I know they say a lot of classic authors were heavy drinkers. But I don't think it was the booze that made them successful."

"Did he like brownies?"

Gabriella snorted a laugh. "They were his favorite. Cupcakes ran a close second, but he could not resist brownies."

That would have been easy, then. He probably didn't

know they were laced with high-potency pot. "Did you know he had a heart problem?"

She nodded. "QT syndrome. His heart would beat super-fast."

"Was that something most people knew about, or did he keep it quiet?"

"He talked about it on social media, so I guess he wasn't hiding it. Why do you ask?"

"His death is a bit of a mystery. No one knows if it was intentional or accidental."

"Intentional?" Gabriella blanched. "Why? Why would anyone murder Evan? A more harmless person never lived!"

It was beginning to sound that way.

"He wouldn't hurt a fly, he—" She shrieked and stood up abruptly. "Chewie!"

"Chewie?"

"His name is really Chewbacca—you know, from *Star Wars*." Gabriella rushed across the room and opened a decorative box on the wall. "Get a grip, Gabby," she muttered. Keys clinked against one another as she ran her fingers over them. "Here it is! Come on. Poor Chewie probably hasn't been fed since Saturday night!"

"You have a key to Evan's house?"

"Sure. I used to go over to feed his cat when he was out of town. Chewie is a newer cat, though. Evan was telling me about him at the party."

I hesitated briefly. It would take me away from the store much longer than I had anticipated. Jacquie was probably waiting for my return. On the other hand, Jacquie would be the first in line to help an animal in need. Not to mention that I probably wouldn't get another chance to snoop around Evan's apartment.

"Of course," I said, following her out the door.

Evan had lived on Wisconsin Avenue in an apartment over a local restaurant. Gabriella turned the key in the lock and the front door opened easily.

"Shouldn't we knock or ring a bell?"

"He's dead, Florrie. I don't think he'll hear, or care, for that matter."

I closed the door behind us and locked it, just in case someone was watching.

Chapter 17

"Chewie!" Gabriella called. "Chewie kitty!"

Pitiful, anxious mewing could be heard in another room. Gabriella hurried in that direction.

The apartment could only be described as grad-student digs. A giant TV screen overwhelmed everything else in the living room. A worn black leather sofa was shoved up against the wall. If I'd had to guess, Evan's favorite spot was probably in the recliner that faced the TV. A few movie posters had been taped on the walls that weren't covered with bookshelves. I recognized *The Hobbit* and *Star Wars*. A generous window overlooked Wisconsin Avenue. I'd never seen it from this perspective before. On one side, he overlooked a hodgepodge of rooftops, and on the other, the fronts of three-story buildings with stores and restaurants on the street level. If I lived here, I would have spent countless hours watching strangers go about their business on the sidewalks below.

A laptop lay closed on a desk that was covered with scraps of paper. I peered at them without touching anything. Some contained a single word. *Survival* knocked me for a loop. I guessed survival was a primary theme in a lot of science fiction, but it still spooked me. Was he worried about surviving? I glanced at others. *Wizard. Omen. Sugarcane.* That was different.

A trash bin nearby sported a miniature basketball hoop atop it. Wadded balls of paper filled it halfway. More crumpled paper lay around the bottom.

I walked into the kitchen, where Gabriella held a fluffy tabby with tufts on the tops of its ears.

"Maine coon?"

"That's what Evan thought. Apparently, he was the tiniest kitten you can imagine. You must be so hungry, Chewie!" she cooed as she opened a cabinet with one hand.

The kitchen was barely big enough for two people and a cat. Clearly designed by someone who had never cooked anything. It could have used some updating, but from the looks of things, Evan didn't cook, so he probably didn't care.

I opened the refrigerator.

"Hungry?" asked Gabriella.

"No. Just learning more about Evan."

"Like what?"

"Leftover pizza, and Chinese takeout. Looks like mayo and baloney for sandwiches. No fruit. No salad. No veggies or yogurt. Lots of beer."

"What does that tell you?"

I swung a cabinet door open. "Instant coffee and bottles of vodka. He did not have a girlfriend and he didn't cook. He ate takeout whenever he could, but on lazy days when he didn't go to work, he dined on baloney sandwiches."

I made a quick trip through the messy bedroom, where clothes had been strewn over the floor and furniture. A half-empty bag of chips lay on the bed, along with Saturday's newspaper, open to the sports section. Bits of clothing hung out of not-quite-closed drawers in an old dresser. An open can of beer rested on top beside a baseball cap and a T-shirt that said BE NICE TO ME OR I'LL PUT YOU IN MY BOOK. I didn't see any photos of him, friends, or family. I tried to peer into his closet, but clothes and worn running shoes fell out of it haphazardly. In the back of it, I could see a baseball bat and a catcher's mitt.

Gabriella joined me, holding a cat carrier and the laptop.

"What's the deal with Evan's family?" I asked. "I don't see any pictures."

"He's a guy. And a messy one at that. There are probably photos around here somewhere."

"There's no bolt on the only exit and no baseball bat by the door or his bed. He wasn't afraid. He didn't expect anyone to break in. If he was murdered, it wasn't for something he had in his possession."

Gabriella wiped her teary eyes. "Poor Evan. It had to be an accident. No one had anything against him. He was like an overgrown puppy, just bumbling around."

I remembered Professor Maxwell's words about something going on among Jacquie's writer friends. I liked Gabriella. And so did Chewie. He wound around her ankles, purring. Animals had a special sense about people, didn't they?

"Is there a chance that he stole someone's idea for a book?"

"I doubt it. But I haven't been in touch with him over the last few years. I don't know what might have been going on in his life. Arthur probably has a better feel for that than I do."

She was probably right about that. I hadn't known Evan, but looking around his apartment sent a tidal wave of sadness through me. So he was messy and he drank too much. He seemed like a nice guy.

Gabriella placed Chewie in the carrier. "Maybe I should leave a note. His parents or someone will be coming to get his belongings. They'll wonder what happened to Chewie." She scribbled a quick note with her phone number and propped it up on his desk. "I'm taking his laptop to see if I can find a phone number for his parents."

"Is that legal? Won't the police want it?"

She looked around. "I don't see any crime-scene tape, do you?"

I didn't. It made me wonder if the police had closed the case as an accidental death.

I helped her carry the heavy cat down the stairs. The carrier was a bit unwieldy. "I'll give you a hand carrying him home."

"Thanks! It's not that far. If I keep him, I'll need to get one of those cat carriers with wheels."

Now I was worried about Chewie. "*If* you keep him?"

"I'd love to have him, but what if Evan's mom wants him? I couldn't deny her that."

I smiled at her. Gabriella's heart was in the right place.

When we reached her house, I said, "Six o'clock on Friday, then? Veronica will send over some memes to share on social media."

"I'll be there!"

We parted ways and I strolled back to the bookstore, thinking that Evan probably didn't have a clue that he was eating pot brownies. Would he have turned them down if he knew? We would never know.

When I reached the store, I informed everyone I had returned. Then I checked our inventory of books by Gabriella, Griffin, Jacquie, Arthur, and Buzz. I ordered a few more, just to be on the safe side.

As I completed the order, Buzz walked into the store. I wished I could give Veronica a warning, a heads-up that he was here.

"Hi, Florrie." He picked up a book and read the cover copy. I took that moment to text Veronica, *Buzz just arrived*.

"Hi, Buzz. I'm glad to see you. Jacquie is putting together

an author signing here on Friday. It will be you, Jacquie, Arthur, and Gabriella."

"Count me in!" Buzz grinned as if I had handed him a gift. "But what about Griffin?"

"He's out of town."

"That's too bad. I, uh, I was hoping to see Veronica. Is she around?"

A great sister would have fibbed for her. A super sister would have said something clever designed to discourage his interest. Only a dolt of a sister would fudge. Yet I was about to do that because nothing more clever came to mind. "Possibly. I just returned a few minutes ago." Well, at least it wasn't an outright lie.

"Buzz!" I heard Jacquie's voice before she made an appearance. She approached him with her arms out and gave him a hug. "Thank you for coming to our little party. I hope you had a good time?"

"It was great! I sure didn't expect a wedding! And Maxwell! What a guy. I'm thinking about basing a character on him in my next book. Do you think he'd agree to that?"

"Agree? He would be flattered!"

She walked him toward the door so subtly, so smoothly, that he probably didn't realize what she was doing. I could learn a thing or two from her. She held the door open for Buzz, saying, "Friday night we're having an author signing."

"Florrie just told me about it."

"Wonderful! We'll see you then." She waved her hand, dismissing him, and walked inside.

"That was the slickest removal of a person I have ever seen. He's probably walking away feeling good about himself."

She had the decency to blush. "Awful, wasn't it? I bet he

doesn't even remember that he came to see Veronica." She sidled over to the checkout desk. "Why doesn't she like him?"

"Apparently, he's a bore."

Jacquie's brow wrinkled. "That's strange. His books are so exciting. Good imagination, I guess. How did your meeting with Griffin go?"

I filled her in about his writing retreat. "But Gabriella will be here."

"Pity. He'd have been a big draw. I'm heading home then." She left in a flash, leaving behind the scents of rose and jasmine from her J'adore perfume.

Shortly before six, Margarite Herbert-Grant phoned. "Florrie, dear, we met at Jacquie's wedding."

"I remember." Boy, did I!

"I understand that you deliver books."

"That's correct. What with all the next-day deliveries available now, we try to compete by delivering to our customers in Georgetown."

"Oh. I'm a bit out of your area, but not too far. Would you make an exception and deliver to Foggy Bottom? I will be buying quite a few books, so it would be worth your while."

Wasn't this the woman who said she received so many books for free that she couldn't read them all? I considered. I would have to drive over. But business was business. Besides this woman had clout. I didn't want to alienate her. "All right. If we have the books you need."

"I hope so. But I must have them by seven tomorrow morning. Is that doable?"

Next she would be asking for them to be clad in gold leaf. "What is it that you need?"

"One hundred children's books, from preschool through

third grade. Preferably fun. You know the type. With animal characters, like giraffes and mice. It's all right if they are about children, too, but I do enjoy the ones with adorable animal art."

"I think we can manage that. Do they need to be wrapped?"

I heard a little intake of air. "You do that, too? Thank you for offering, but perhaps it's best if they are not wrapped. That way we can see the appropriate ages and reading levels."

"Thank you for your order. We'll pull the books and ring them up, then I'll call you back to arrange for payment."

"Thank you, Florrie. You can't imagine what a big help this is to me."

Veronica and I had fun selecting darling children's books. We piled them into boxes and carted them downstairs to the back door. I phoned Margarite and gave her a discount for buying so many books at once. She paid by credit card. I printed out her receipt and asked for her delivery address.

"Seven hundred New Hampshire Avenue."

I recognized the address. "The Watergate?"

"Yes. I'll have someone waiting for you."

I hurried home with Peaches to retrieve my car. When she had been fed, I left her happily grooming her face, and drove to the alley behind Color Me Read. Veronica and I loaded the books into my little car.

"Do you mind closing up by yourself?" I asked.

"Yes." She said it with hesitation.

"You've done it before."

"Okay, I want to see her apartment in the Watergate! I've never been inside before."

I checked the time. Considering the size of the order, I guessed it would be all right to close half an hour early just this once. We locked up the store and headed over to the Watergate.

As promised, a gentleman expected us. He came out to the car and loaded the boxes onto a dolly. "Ms. Herbert-Grant is expecting you. I'll bring the boxes up in the service elevator."

We walked through the lobby, giant round chandeliers beaming overhead. We boarded the elevator, and just as the doors were closing, a gentleman hurried in.

Chapter 18

Veronica elbowed me.

I tried to act natural but twisted just a bit to get a better look at the man.

He got off the elevator before we did. When the doors closed, Veronica hissed, "That was Senator Martin!"

"I know. He's better looking in person than on TV."

I knocked on Margarite's door.

She swung it open and invited us in. She wore baggy trousers with a white top and a loose sweater over it, sashed at the waist. Margarite led us through a formal living room with a to-die-for view of the Potomac River and continued to a smaller, more intimate room with an equally impressive view. I thought it might reflect the real Margarite in its glorious hodgepodge of colors. The things that were important to her, I thought. A large vivid turquoise rug covered most of the hardwood floor. A painting of Paris hung over the fireplace at the end of the room, and an ornate antique gold-leaf desk dominated one wall. The sofa and comfy-looking chairs were an odd mix of chintz and bold abstract patterns. Vases, porcelain tigers, and keepsake boxes filled a lighted cabinet. And the largest wall, across from the windows, was filled top to bottom with books.

We all sat down, and Margarite said, "You ladies have rescued me. You have no idea! You see, I don't really belong here among the politicians and dignitaries. I had to learn to hold my head up high."

A bell rang. Margarite rose to her feet. "That's the book delivery. I need to tip him. I'll be right back."

Veronica stretched and moseyed around the room, gazing at the items on display. I was far more interested in the paintings. Each of them was a masterpiece. Unless I was mistaken, one of them was a small Renoir. A still life of roses in a vase.

Margarite returned with a tray of cheese, crackers, and olives. She opened a small refrigerator under the bar. "May I offer you a drink? Or tea, perhaps?"

Veronica gladly accepted a glass of wine. I declined because I was driving, but happily sipped water.

We all settled again. Veronica helped herself to crackers and cheese, but I nibbled on the delicious olives.

"Kalamata?" I asked.

Margarite smiled. "You have a good palate."

"You were telling us about the books," said Veronica.

"Books saved me. It's that simple. I am donating these books to children who might not be inclined to read otherwise. They need to read early, but not all children come from homes where books are cherished."

"Saved you?" asked Veronica. "How?"

Margarite gazed at us quietly. "Arthur Bedlingham has never had much of an imagination. He steals the stories of others. Not exactly, you understand. I am not accusing him of plagiarism. But he takes their life stories and winds them into a tale. If I am correct, he is about to do that to me. He's doing it out of spite. And there's nothing I can do to stop him." She sipped fizzy water.

"I am always astonished when someone relates a childhood with two loving parents and darling siblings. They're lying, I think. No one has that storybook beginning to life. And if they do, it's surely torn asunder by age twelve. My father was shot to death in an armed robbery when I was fourteen. When I tell people, they invariably exclaim and issue sympathies. But the truth is that while he was ultimately a victim, he was not the victim of the robbery. He was the perpetrator. After that, my mother drank herself into a permanent stupor. Within two years of my father's demise, in an ironic the-apple-does-not-fall-far-from-the-tree scenario, my brother landed in prison for robbing a bank. I had a dead father, a brother in prison, and a mother who couldn't get off the couch unless it was for another drink. I did what I had to do. I dropped out of high school and I took off my clothes to support us. I danced around poles to make enough money to survive. Does that shock you?" She sucked in air. "It's true. I met my first husband, Jerry, at the club where I danced. He wasn't a genius, and he certainly wasn't wealthy. I was worried when he took me home to meet his devoutly Catholic parents. How could they possibly approve of anyone like me? He told me, 'Margy, everyone is the same. We all struggle through life the best we can, and each of us collects a fair number of bumps and bruises along the way. Be who you want to be, and they will believe it.' I couldn't imagine that was true. But I went to dinner at their sweet little Cape Cod that actually had a white picket fence. When they asked about my family, I told them my father had died and that my mother never got over it. It was a half-truth at best, but they accepted that. It was something they could understand. And when they asked what I did for a living, I told them the most wonderful thing I could imagine—that I read books." She laughed.

"The notion that anyone would pay a person to read books was as foreign to them as it was to me. I didn't know the correct terms to be believable, but they didn't, either. It was my first big lesson in being what I aspired to instead of being me. When I look back, that was the happiest time of my life. Jerry was a plumber. We were simply Jerry and Margy in a cheap little rental on the wrong side of the tracks, and to me, it was heaven. I lived in bliss for two years, and then the house three doors down caught on fire in the middle of the night. Everyone in the neighborhood gathered outside, and Jerry ran inside the burning building to rescue a little boy. He carried him to the lawn just as the fire truck pulled up. Then Jerry went back in for the boy's twin brother. A beam fell and neither Jerry nor the other child came back out. And I knew that my heaven had gone up in smoke. But Jerry had given me the gift I needed. The knowledge that no one was superior to anyone else. That I couldn't change my past, but I had power over my future. And I was determined that I was going to read books. I never finished high school. Never went to college. Did you know that many famous people who did incredible things and invented products never went to school? Never had a higher education? I made a mistake with my second husband, Arnold. I thought he was as sweet and kind as Jerry, but the scumbag was laundering money through a used-car lot. One night I was making dinner with the television news on, and there was the car lot. Everyone was being arrested for money laundering, and I saw Arnold being taken away in handcuffs. It was a big scandal involving a lot of career criminals. I divorced him and moved on. I finally landed a job in a library."

"As a librarian?" I was confused. Had she managed to get a college degree along the way?

"Cleaning. Floors, toilets, the works. But it came with a perk—all the books I could read. And read I did. Jerry might not have been brainy, but he had an innate understanding of life. Did you know what Aristotle said? 'We are what we repeatedly do. Excellence, then, is not an act, but a habit.' I am self-taught, Florrie. I have become what I made myself out to be."

"But that's wonderful!" I exclaimed. "You have so much to be proud of."

Margarite raised her eyebrows. "If Arthur goes forward with his book, people will remember two things. When they look at me, they will see a stripper who never graduated from high school."

"I don't mean to be rude," said Veronica. "But how can you afford to live here?"

"Courtesy of husband number three. Arthur will make me out to be a social climber. Though none of my husbands could be considered high society. My third husband's background wasn't that different from my own. He was a hands-on kind of man who loved woodworking. Unfortunately, he developed a degenerative disease. The poor man couldn't sleep. Nothing was comfortable, so we made a mattress for him. Other people heard about it and doctors started to recommend it, and before we knew it, we had an amazing business. But he continued to decline. I sold the company for quite a bit of money and then he passed away."

"Your life is so full of tragedy, but you always bounce back. I think you're an inspiration!" I gazed at her in awe.

"You are very kind, Florrie. I may need to call you to cheer me up when Arthur describes my life in painful detail, not even having to adhere to any semblance of truth since he will claim it is fiction."

I felt for her. That must be incredibly frustrating.

After a little more chatting about her presentation of the books to children the next morning, she thanked us again for providing the books so quickly and we left.

When we were in the elevator, Veronica asked, "Do you think she meant to kill Arthur with the brownies instead of Evan? She's smart enough to pull it off."

That was a horrifying thought. "I hope not! Surely she knows that even if Arthur were dead, they would probably continue with a book that had already been finished. If that was her goal, she would have had to kill him before he wrote the book."

"What if it was Evan who was actually writing the book about her life?"

"Do you think she's a killer?" I asked. "She said such ugly things about Arthur, yet she's giving all those books to children."

"Duh! You heard her. That woman doesn't let anything stop her."

I drove Veronica home, glad I could soon call it a day. She moaned about not having any plans for the evening, but I looked forward to a quiet night at home and the day off that would follow. Between Evan's death and the odd goings-on, I was beat.

After parking the car, I paused for a moment, listening to the calming sound of crickets. As I unlocked the front door of the carriage house, I heard Mr. DuBois call my name. I reached inside the house and turned on the lights.

"I'm so glad I caught you." He handed me a small box. "Would you mind dropping this off with Mr. Quinn at Poole's Auctions tomorrow when you go to work? He is quite knowledgeable about jade. I'd hate to make a fuss about this little pig if he's really made of plastic." Mr. DuBois slid off the cover and peered at the pig. "But I don't think so. I believe those eyes are definitely high-quality diamonds."

I was off the next day, but I knew the location of the auction house and was curious about the pig myself. "I would be happy to do that."

"Mr. Quinn is an early bird. He'll be there around six thirty, so anytime after that would be fine. He said to ring the bell." Mr. DuBois thanked me and bustled back to the mansion. I stepped inside and locked the door behind me. So I wouldn't forget the piggy in the morning, I stashed the box in a bag that I hung on the doorknob.

After changing into a cerise nightshirt, I fed Peaches salmon, and I nibbled on leftovers from the party. With a relaxing mug of tea in hand, I settled on my sofa with my sketchbook and muttered, "Hello, old friend."

Evan weighed heavily on me. I sketched him first. On the chubby side; his face and his cheeks were prominent. He probably thought his nose was too big, but it suited his face and softened it. I added his dark curls. Seeing his completed face gave me a jolt, and I couldn't help thinking of the struggle to pull him out of the pool.

I flipped the page and drew Chewie with the cute tufts at the top of his ears.

Jacquie was next. Where had she gone the night before her wedding? Had she seen Arthur? Her face was amazingly symmetrical. Blond hair going on silver. Full lips and kind eyes. Instead of drawing her wedding dress, I gave her a white shirt with the collar turned up and a half-moon pendant necklace. I had to find a way to get her to confide in me, tell me what she knew. As much as I loved and admired Jacquie, she could be at the center of what had happened to Evan.

I checked to be sure all the doors were locked, then trudged up to bed. Peaches stretched out next to me and we dozed off.

It felt like a long time since I'd had a day off. After a hearty breakfast of beef stew, Peaches sprawled in a sunbeam with the utterly content expression of a warm cat. I suspected I might have an equally content expression because I planned to meet Eric for breakfast.

After a leisurely shower, I pulled on a becoming summer dress in shades of peach and pink. I made time for a bracing cup of coffee, then set out for Poole's, carrying the bag that contained the little pig.

A CLOSED sign still hung on the door, but when I rang the bell, a debonair man with white hair opened it. I introduced myself. "Mr. DuBois sent me."

"Ah, yes. Please come in." He locked the door behind me. "It's a bit early and the rest of the staff aren't in yet."

I followed him to a counter.

"I believe you have a pig for me?"

I took the box out of my bag and opened it. The pig lay on velvet. It felt cool and smooth when I handed it to him.

Without a word, he placed a loupe on his eye and peered at it. "Excuse me, please." He disappeared in a back room for a few minutes, giving me time to gaze around at amazing paintings, stacks of Oriental carpets, and magnificent pieces of silver.

He returned and handed me the pig. "Mr. DuBois has a good eye. This is indeed very fine jadeite. At auction it would probably fetch around five thousand dollars."

No wonder someone was searching for it!

I must have shown my surprise because he added, "There are many ways that people attempt to fake jadeite, but this piece is lovely. In China, the pig is a symbol of prosperity and good luck. It would be a most cherished gift."

"I had no idea that it would be worth so much. Where would one buy something like this?"

"At auction, of course." He grinned. "Fine jewelers may carry such items. Most likely it originated in Burma or Hong Kong. I will call Mr. DuBois to discuss it with him."

I placed it carefully in the box, but this time I wedged it into my purse, which I thought might be safer than the bag. I thanked him and left, hearing the lock click behind me.

Now painfully conscious that I had a valuable pig in my purse, I strode purposefully. I considered going back to the mansion to hand it over to Mr. DuBois, but then I realized I could dart one block out of my way and stash it in the Color Me Read safe. That seemed the wisest choice, especially when I caught a glimpse of Cara, the annoying wannabe reporter, behind me.

I hurried to the store, which wasn't open yet. Once inside, I turned off the alarm and dashed upstairs to the safe. I placed the pig, box and all, inside. Feeling better, I trotted down to the second floor and into the history and philosophy room, which had large French doors and a balcony. I stepped out on the balcony and spotted Cara watching the store from the sidewalk on the other side of the street. She held up her camera and aimed it at the store entrance. She was waiting for me. How annoying!

Well, two could play that game. I trotted down to the main floor, turned on the alarm, and fled down to the basement and out the door before the alarm could go off. Feeling pleased with myself for evading Cara, I scuttled through the alley, crossed a street, and hurried through the next alley. I thought I might go through the alley on the following block as well, but a huge delivery truck was backing up and clogging everything. At that point, though, I thought it would be safe to return to the sidewalk. Cautiously peering around the corner, I took a deep breath and relaxed when I didn't see any sign of Cara.

I walked on, enjoying the day and peering into the occasional shop window. But then, out of the corner of my eye, I saw someone dart into a recessed doorway. Not again! I hoped I hadn't seen Cara and walked on, pausing intentionally to be certain. This time, when I turned to look for her, she snapped a photo of me. I'd had enough of her. I ducked into a small alley and waited for her. Minutes that felt like hours ticked by.

But she finally showed up, her face distressed as she craned her neck in an attempt to locate me. I stepped out of the alley behind her. We stood in front of a dry-cleaning establishment where a sandwich board on the street offered same-day service.

"Good morning, Cara."

She shrieked. "Oh my gosh. You scared me!"

"How do you think I feel with you tailing me? What do you want?"

Her mouth dropped open. "I, uh, I don't know what you mean. I was just on my way"—she looked down the street—"to the, um, to get some coffee." She still held her phone in her hand.

"That is such a lie. Why can't you be honest? I have no reason to be nice to you. None whatsoever. But please, just tell me what you want so you don't have to follow me. It's really creepy."

Her eyes widened. "I'm not following you."

"Baloney!" I said it louder than I'd meant to, and a few people looked at us. "I saw you outside of the store a little while ago. Was that you yesterday with the binoculars?"

Her brow furrowed. "I don't know what you're talking about."

I wanted to turn the tables on her. The notion of following her crossed my mind. How would she like that? "If you would just tell me what you want—"

"I have a theory about Caroline. I'd like to get DNA tests from the professor, Jacquie, and your mother."

Chapter 19

I was speechless. My mother? Was she insane? I found my voice. "You think my mother is Caroline, the daughter who was kidnapped?"

"So you admit it!"

She was nuts. And now she was grabbing at straws in an effort to break open a decades-old case. "I can't imagine what you think you'll gain by following me. Do you think I'm going to lead you to some great Maxwell secret? Ooo, maybe my mom and Professor Maxwell are having a big secret reunion? I'm going to breakfast. Is that okay with you? Look, I can save you a lot of time and embarrassment. I know my grandparents. My mother is not related to the Maxwells in any way. If you really want to find Caroline, then go do it. Please! A lot of people would be grateful to know what happened to her." My voice grew louder with agitation. "But leave me and my family alone! We're not related to her, nor were we involved in her disappearance."

I stalked away from her in a huff, glancing at my watch. Nine thirty-six. I had nine minutes to get to the restaurant. I could feel the flush of anger heating my face. My chest heaved as I drew in deep breaths.

Then she shrieked. I ignored her.

She called my name. "Florrie! Help me, Florrie!"

Something clattered behind me. I finally turned to look at her. She had fallen on the sidewalk, knocking over the sandwich board outside the dry cleaner's.

I ran back to her. Blood trickled along her neck. "Cara!" Kneeling beside her, I pulled out my phone and pressed 911. "What happened?"

She gazed up at me, fear in her eyes. Her fingers wrapped around my wrist.

I told the dispatcher where we were. "I don't know what happened. She's bleeding." I disconnected the call and said to Cara, "You'll be okay. Help is on the way." I didn't know what to do to help her. I leaned sideways for a better look at her neck, but there was too much blood for me to see anything. A growing pool of red had formed on the sidewalk. I looked around for something, anything to press against her neck to stop the bleeding. She'd been carrying a purse. I slid it off her shoulder and pressed it against the blood, smiling at her, hoping to reassure her.

"R . . . ," she uttered. "Faux . . ."

"You're going to be all right."

"R . . . faux . . ."

"It's okay. You don't have to speak. Conserve your energy."

Sirens howled in the distance. "Hear that? They're almost here. Just hang on."

A small crowd had gathered around us. People were asking questions and making suggestions.

Cara looked me in the eyes. Her grip tightened on my wrist. "R . . . faux . . ."

An ambulance and a police car pulled up on the street just as her grip loosened and her hand fell to the sidewalk.

I moved aside to make room for the emergency medical technicians. One of them asked the crowd if anyone knew her. I raised my hand.

The EMT handed me antiseptic tissues to wipe my hands, then squirted them with a solution. I rubbed my hands vigorously and looked down at my dress, which miraculously didn't have even a drop of blood on it. The EMT pulled out a pen and pad, and the police officer did the same.

"I don't know her well. Her name is Cara Melton. She's a reporter for *The DC Chatter*." I didn't know her address or phone number or next of kin.

A hefty man in the crowd said, "Looked like you two were having an argument."

The atmosphere changed immediately. All eyes were on me, and they were no longer friendly or even indifferent. They gazed at me in horror. "Well, yes. She's been following me. I asked her to stop."

The police officer took new interest in me. He motioned to me and I followed him to the alley. "Why is Cara following you?"

I glanced at my watch, which probably wasn't the right thing to do, but I hated to be late for anything. Eric would be at the café any minute. I explained as quickly as I could.

"Did you report her behavior to the police?"

"No. I thought she would stop. I guess I didn't think she would harm me."

"Did you stab her?"

"No!" I cried out far too loud. I was getting frustrated. "I never touched her. I just spoke with her."

"You seem pretty agitated."

"I am *now*. I can't imagine what happened. I walked away and she started calling me. I ignored her and then I heard a noise. She must have knocked over the sign when she fell.

That was when I ran back to her, and she was bleeding from her neck."

"Did you see anyone running away?"

I tried to remember. "I don't think so. To be honest, I was focused on Cara. I didn't realize she had been injured and was bleeding. I thought she had just tripped or something. It didn't occur to me to look for someone who might have attacked her."

"May I check your purse?"

"For what?"

"A weapon."

That took my breath away. I knew better. I thought he needed a warrant, and yet, under the pressure of the moment and my overwhelming desire to be cleared of any involvement, I said, "Of course," and handed it to him.

My cross-body purse wasn't large. If I had stabbed her and hidden the weapon in my bag, the leather would have bloody fingerprints on it.

He unzipped the compartments and found nothing of interest. With an annoyed look, he handed it back to me. "Flip your hands over."

I placed the strap around my neck and then held out my hands and showed him both sides.

He scowled at them.

"Address and phone number."

It wasn't a question. He wrote them down on a small pad.

Should I mention Eric's name or not? It might be helpful. "If you need a reference for my character, I was on my way to meet Eric Jonquille for breakfast." My phone buzzed and I glanced at it. "That's him now."

The cop shot me a doubtful look and held out his hand for my phone. I gave it to him.

"Eric?" He walked away from me. I presumed he didn't

want me to hear their conversation. While I waited, I turned
to see how Cara was doing. The crowd had dispersed, and the
ambulance was merging into traffic. The siren shrieked and
the ambulance picked up speed. I found myself hoping she
would be all right. Only minutes ago, I had been furious with
her, but now I hoped she would be okay. As long as she
would leave me, my family, and the Maxwells alone.

The cop returned and handed me my phone. "He's waiting for you. Have a nice breakfast."

I wondered what had happened, but I didn't ask. Sometimes it was better to grab an opportunity. I thanked the cop,
said goodbye, and tried not to look like I was in a hurry to get
away.

Eric waited at the café, seated at an outdoor table. I kissed
him and dropped into the other chair. "Thanks for waiting."

"I was getting worried. It's not like you to be late."

"I appreciate whatever you said to that cop."

Our server arrived and said to Eric, "I knew she didn't
stand you up."

Eric smiled at her. "Bagels and lox for me, please. Orange
juice and more coffee?"

The server nodded and looked at me.

"Sounds great. I'll have the same."

"So what happened exactly?" Eric asked.

I ran through the whole saga again, glad to be able to talk
about it. I stopped briefly when the server brought our food
and waited until she left. "It was the strangest thing. Cara was
perfectly fine, if a little nuts, but a few minutes later, she fell
and was bleeding from her neck. I can't imagine what happened to her."

"No one else was with her?"

"Not that I'm aware of. I didn't see anyone. We were
close to an alley, so I suppose someone could have disappeared
quickly."

He set down his coffee and frowned at me. "Florrie, this is very disturbing. Unless a total stranger ran up to her, stabbed her, and ran off, which I admit could happen but is unlikely, it means someone was following either you or Cara with the intent of murdering her."

Despite the warm weather and hot coffee, a chill ran through me. "She kept trying to say something: 'R-faux.'"

"'Are'? Like she was asking a question?"

"I don't know. 'R' and faux' were as far as she got. But she said it several times."

"Evan."

"That doesn't make any sense." I laughed at Eric. "'Revan'? I don't think so. 'Arthur' would be more like it."

"Was your argument about Evan or Arthur?"

"His name didn't even come up." I studied his expression. "Are you saying there could be a connection between the attack on Cara and Evan's death?"

"R-faux," he mused aloud. "What else could she have meant?"

"'Arc,' 'arm,' 'art,' 'arithmetic.'"

"Do any of those hold meaning for you?"

"Not in relation to Cara."

"Arthur." Eric tilted his head coyly, nodded, and bit into his bagel.

"But Cara didn't have anything to do with Arthur. Not that I know of, anyway."

"The key words there would be *not that you know of.*"

"I know better than to exclude a connection, but if we look at the two cases, then it's hard to imagine that someone attacking Cara could have anything to do with Arthur. Or do you know something you haven't told me?"

"It's early days yet. And I have to point out that both Cara and Evan were at the party on Saturday evening."

His phone rang and he glanced at it. I knew he was being polite by not answering. "Go ahead and take it."

"Hey, Bridges." He held the phone to his ear. I could hear Bridges speaking but could only catch the random word. *Witness. Argument. Her.* I had a bad feeling *her* referred to me.

Eric thanked him and ended the call. "They want to talk with you."

I shrugged. "Okay. I don't have a problem with that."

"They have a witness."

"It must be that dry-cleaning guy. He probably saw us arguing." I took out my wallet and paid our check. But when I tried to stand up, Eric grabbed my hand. "Florrie, Cara is dead."

Chapter 20

The words sliced through me. "Noooo! I knew she had lost a lot of blood, but I didn't expect this. She was so young." I sank against the back of the chair.

Eric signaled the waitress. "I think we'd like another coffee if that's okay."

"Sure." She shot me a pitying look.

Was I pale? Probably.

After she brought the coffee, Eric said calmly, "Let's go through this again. Exactly what happened?"

"Eric, I didn't kill her!"

"I know you didn't. But someone did. You saw blood, so something happened to her. Do you recall anyone passing by? Someone who ran or jogged by you after the argument?"

"It wasn't really an argument. It was me begging her to leave me, us, alone. Are they saying I murdered her?"

"I don't know. But it's not a good sign that they want to talk with you."

"I have a totally clear conscience. I don't know what happened to her. I'm horrified and so sad that she died, but I had nothing to do with it." I paid for the extra coffees and left a generous tip since we had tied up the table for so long.

"Thanks for breakfast, Florrie."

"I'm going over to the police station right now. Who should I ask for?"

"Maybe you should take an attorney."

I blinked at him. "Did you not hear me? I have nothing to hide."

"You can be very stubborn. I'll take you there. But I still think you should call a lawyer."

"Thanks, Eric," I muttered through my teeth. Didn't he believe me?

He drove me to the police station. I had the feeling that my interview happened more quickly because Eric was involved. Or maybe they had just been waiting for me.

Sergeant Bridges took me into a small room and offered me water. For the third time I went through the details.

"If you need confirmation that she was following me, both Fish Gordon and Eric Jonquille saw her in the bookstore when I had to ask her to leave. And both of them helped remove her from the party when she pretended to be a photographer."

Bridges made note of that. At least he was listening to me.

"But you didn't press charges."

"I thought she would stop. She practically ran out of the bookstore when she saw Eric and Fish. Seriously, if you were forcibly removed from a party, wouldn't you just give up? Besides, what with Evan's death, I didn't even give Cara any more thought until today when she turned up again."

"We have a witness who says he saw you with her just before she collapsed."

I nodded. "The dry cleaner. When I was speaking with her, she seemed fine. I stalked away. I was in a hurry to get to breakfast with Eric. How do you know the *dry cleaner* didn't kill her? I had my back to her. He could have darted out of his shop, stabbed her, and run back inside to dispose of the knife."

"Is that what you think happened?"

I chose my words carefully and spoke slowly and clearly. "I walked away from her. My back was to Cara. I was not watching her. I didn't even turn to look at her. She screamed and then she called my name. Twice, I think. Only then did I look back." I snapped my fingers. "Why would she have called to me for help if I was the one who hurt her?"

"The witness didn't hear her call for help."

"I had my back to him. I don't know what he was doing. Probably killing her." I stood up abruptly. "Are we through?"

Bridges nodded. "For now."

Eric waited for me outside the interview room. "How'd it go?"

"You'll have to tell me. Just as I thought, the dry cleaner tried to pin it on me."

I covered my face with my hands. "I want to sob for Evan and for Cara." Eric stroked my shoulder and I looked up at him. "But I can't because I'm so angry and frustrated."

"I have a few hours before work. Why don't we go somewhere and talk?"

It was so sweet of him. I ran my hand over his arm. Tempting as his offer was, I had some investigating to do. I wouldn't be able to relax after what had happened. "Thanks, but I'll be okay."

I left the police station in a hurry. Outside, I sucked in deep breaths. I had read about a breathing square that was used by high-level military to help them focus when they were in dangerous situations. Breath in for a count of four, then hold your breath for a count of four. Exhale for a count of four. Count to four again. Repeat as necessary.

After doing it a couple times, I smiled. The summer sun glowed high in a clear blue sky. I had the day off and could do anything I wanted. And the worst was behind me. I had survived the police interview.

My moment of pleasure didn't last long. Evan's and Cara's deaths quickly returned to hang over me. I strolled through beautiful neighborhoods, wondering how someone could have murdered Cara so quickly. Had he run by her and stabbed her? Had someone tapped her on the shoulder and thrust a knife in her throat?

Suddenly, I became very aware of my surroundings and who was walking nearby. I turned quickly to see if anyone was behind me. A man rode a bicycle past me. If he had abruptly stopped next to me, I wouldn't have darted away. Maybe it was easier than I would have thought to kill someone quickly and move on.

Cara had said *R* and *faux*. Were they two words or one? Was she trying to spell someone's name? Give me the first letter of the attacker's name? Robert? Rufus? Riley?

I found myself listening for footsteps as if she were still alive. I turned around a couple of times to see if someone was behind me. A little girl holding her mother's hand stumbled along the sidewalk.

Cara had worried me more than I thought if I was still looking for her. I shook my head, my feelings torn. I was relieved that she wouldn't be tailing me or taking pictures anymore. But I never wanted her to die!

I stopped in a park and took in the pinks and purples of azaleas in full bloom. They even had the rarer apricot-colored ones.

The problem with Cara's murder was that there were no leads. Well, except for that obnoxious dry cleaner. I headed straight to confront him. In a nice way, of course.

They say that criminals like to revisit the scene of the crime. At least they often did in mysteries. Consequently, I felt just a little bit guilty as I approached the spot where Cara had been stabbed.

The only sign of her life and death at this spot was the dark splotch on the sidewalk. It seemed larger now than I remembered, and I realized that someone had poured water on it. People walked by chatting and going on with their lives, unaware that anything untoward had happened here only a few hours ago.

I stepped inside the cool dry-cleaning business. A portly man with a balding pate held out one hand like a cop stopping traffic. "Go away. You are not welcome here."

How annoying. "There's a counter between us and you're twice my size."

"I have seen what you can do. If you come any closer I will call the police."

I was pretty sure he had a slight Indian accent. "Mr.? I'm sorry, I don't know your name."

"Rajat Bakshi."

I reached my right hand toward him. He shook it reluctantly, his body positioned to spring away from me.

"Can you tell me exactly what you saw?"

"You were arguing with that poor girl. And then you ran away, and she collapsed."

"Did any customers come into your business about that time?" I spied a pad on the countertop and whipped it around so I could read it. I snapped a quick photo of his pickups that morning. "Maybe a Jan Milchek?" She had written 9:35 by her name.

"The purple silk dress. It had an olive-oil stain on it. We did a very good job of getting it out. She was quite pleased."

"That's good to know. Did she examine the dress?"

"Yes. Of course. I showed it to her to be sure she was satisfied."

"You sound like a very conscientious dry cleaner."

"I take pride in my work."

"As well you should, I'm sure. When Jan Milchek picked up her dress, did you also look at the place where the stain had been?"

"Yes. It was no longer visible."

"Did she bring you something else to clean?"

"She is a very good customer. She left several of her husband's shirts. But that child! I don't know why they can't make it stop crying. I have children of my own. It's not normal crying. He screams. I do not wish to offend Mrs. Milchek, but it takes great strength for me not to cover my ears. I am glad I am not her neighbor. This isn't a very wide room. It bounces off the walls! When I am in the back, I can hear them coming down the street. I gave him a lollipop. Why are you asking me all these questions?"

I was reluctant to tell him that I felt better knowing these things. Obviously, his eyes had not been on Cara and me the whole time. He'd been conducting business, complete with handing a screaming child a lollipop. He would be a terrible witness if the police pursued me as Cara's killer.

"Florrie Fox!" The voice behind me did not sound happy.

I whirled around and came face-to-face with Sergeant Bridges. "You are a thorn in my side. Two cases and you are knee-deep in both of them. That doesn't happen often." He shifted his gaze to Rajat. "Is she bribing you?"

"On the contrary. Florrie has been very nice. Just asking me questions."

Sergeant Bridges sighed. "I'd like a word with you, Florrie." He gestured toward the door.

"Thanks, Rajat." I shot him what I hoped was my most winning smile.

On the sidewalk, Bridges focused on the splotch of blood. "I'm told that you have been involved in solving homicides before. But neither that nor your relationship with Jonquille qualifies you as a detective. Do not interfere with my investigation. Do you understand me?"

"I'm not interfering. Everyone has a right to defend themselves. If you question your sole witness a bit more, I believe you will find that he was actually conducting business when Cara was murdered. Ask him if he saw the murder weapon. Or if he heard a child screaming."

"I don't need you telling me how to proceed with an investigation. May I remind you that I am a trained police officer, and you draw coloring books."

It was a low blow. But I thought I knew what would cause him to wince. "Your mother would be so disappointed in you."

I walked away certain he must be watching, but I didn't turn around. It wasn't easy, but I tried to focus.

Jan Milchek must have seen *something*. She arrived and left right around the time that Cara was murdered. Chances were good that she lived around here somewhere. People didn't usually go out of their way to use a dry cleaner. She probably frequented these stores, and if her child screamed as Rajat had described, I bet everyone knew her. But these days, store clerks didn't give out addresses. I didn't. People had asked me for the addresses of our customers on occasion and I had declined to reveal them. The world was a wacky place.

I spotted a small café, ordered a latte, and settled at a tiny table outside to search for Milchek on my phone. To my complete surprise, Jan Milchek showed up on Google without much searching. Her Facebook page indicated that she worked at Salon Solei. I phoned the salon to make an appointment with her but was informed that she was taking a leave of absence. However, I could book someone named Mika because she had an opening right now. I thanked the receptionist but declined.

Just as I was about to leave, I heard screaming. Surely Cara's murderer wasn't some neighborhood freak who roamed the streets plunging knives into people's throats!

I leaped from my seat. The woman at a table opposite mine groaned and picked up her muffin in haste. As she left, I asked, "What's going on?"

"Nothing. I have calls to make. I can't do it with that child screaming."

"How do you know that's a child? A woman was murdered in this neighborhood this morning."

"What?" Her eyes narrowed. "Then why are you here?"

"I'm, uh, following up on it."

She shook her head and took off in a hurry, away from the wailing. A woman and a child in a stroller emerged around a corner. It could only be Jan Milchek. The red-faced child in the stroller didn't let up. How could he breathe? He didn't even take breaks to suck in more air.

I hurried toward them. "Excuse me, are you Jan Milchek?"

She looked at me with tired eyes. "I am willing to try anything. What's your magical method of getting a child to stop screaming?"

"Gosh, I'm sorry but I don't have any idea. I wanted to talk with you about what you might have seen this morning when you went to the cleaner's."

She blinked hard.

I wished with all my might that I had a lollipop. "Can he have ice cream?"

She nodded and turned the stroller toward an ice cream store.

"I'll get it. What flavor?"

"Blue bubble gum. I know it's probably bad for him, but he'll scream if it's not blue."

I popped into the store and returned with the requested blue bubble gum ice cream in a cone. The color of Carolina blue, I was certain it had dyes in it, but the second the baby saw it he held out both hands and screamed.

And then, blissful silence.

Jan's entire body sagged with relief. "They tell me he'll outgrow this. My husband and I are hoping he'll be a rock star who screams onstage and makes a lot of money to support his parents."

I smiled at her humor. While her son blissfully licked the blue ice cream, I said, "This morning while you were at the cleaner's, a woman was murdered just outside."

She gasped. "You mean that could have been me?"

"Possibly. I'm wondering if you saw anything or anyone. Noticed someone lurking or running past you?"

"I'm sorry. I barely remember being at the cleaner's."

"You picked up a purple dress."

"That's right! He did a great job. I can't say I remember anything in particular."

A dead end. I sagged. I dug in my purse for a pen and came up with an indigo-blue pencil. I jotted my name and phone number on a scrap of paper. "Would you call me if anything comes to mind? Anything at all?"

"Sure"—she looked at the paper—"Florrie. Are you a cop?"

"No. I was a little farther up the street and they're trying to blame me."

Her eyes grew wide.

"I didn't do it!"

Uneasily she said, "Of course you didn't."

Trying to be casual, especially now that she thought she was talking to a killer, I said, "That's a pretty watch."

She held her arm out and looked at it like she'd never seen it before. "Thanks. Look at the time! We'd better go."

"Um, what time do you have?"

She stared at me like I had lost my mind. Her gaze swung to her watch. "Twenty-two past one."

I glanced at my own watch. Twenty-two past one. Dead-on. "Thank you."

She winced a little, and when she smiled at me, it was more of a grimace. "Thanks for the ice cream." She shoved the stroller along the sidewalk.

Jan Milchek was a dead end. But if Bridges ever tried to bring a case against me, all I had to do was arrange for Milchek to bring her child to the courtroom. I wondered if a person could subpoena a child. No wonder Jan hadn't seen anything. Who could focus with that kind of noise going on all the time?

She was already out of sight when I, and everyone else within a one-block radius, knew that her little boy had finished his ice cream.

I walked toward the office of *The DC Chatter*, wondering if Cara had pursued any other people in her quest to break a big story. My family and the Maxwells had nothing to hide and were consequently annoyed by her preposterous idea and impolite behavior, but we were not dangerous. None of us would have knifed her to stop her. What if she had stumbled upon someone with a real secret? It didn't even have to be related to the story she was working on. Maybe she had tread on the wrong toes.

I stopped to gaze at paintings in a gallery window and a shock ran through me.

Chapter 21

Out of the corner of my left eye, I saw a figure dart into a doorway. It couldn't be. Cara was dead. Had someone else been stalking me all along?

I had to be imagining it. Cara had pursued me for too long and now I was imagining things. Trying my hardest not to look to the left, I turned my back on a potential stalker and continued up the street. The store windows gave me a great reason to continually look to the left. I paused again at a woman's clothing store and pretended to look at the display.

It wasn't my imagination. Once again, I saw a furtive figure rush for cover like a rat.

I tried to walk casually, so he wouldn't realize I had spotted him. I paused one more time and pretended to window-shop. But I knew that to the side of the store was a sign that said THE DC CHATTER. 2ND FLOOR.

Again, I saw a person in dark clothes and a hat shuffle into a shadow.

I darted to the stairs and ran up them. Hopefully, my stalker hadn't seen me and would continue on his way, looking for me farther up the street.

I swung open the door. The newspaper office was far

smaller than I had expected. A tall, pale, tired-looking man glanced up from his work. "Yeah?"

I hadn't prepared anything to say. "I'm so sorry for your loss."

He stopped working and looked up at me. "Somebody die?"

"Cara Melton. I'm sorry, you didn't know?" Now I felt terrible. I thought they would have been informed.

He punched one last thing on his keyboard and a printer began to whir behind him. "I don't know who you're talking about."

"I thought Cara Melton had an internship here."

A voice in the back yelled, "It's that girl. The one with a crush on you." A plump woman with a dark complexion and her hair pulled back off her face into a neat bun walked toward me. "She's dead? What did I tell you, Tony? I knew that girl was gonna stick her nose where it didn't belong. Didn't think it would end this way though. How'd she die?"

"I don't really know yet. I believe she was stabbed."

"Stabbed!" the woman shrieked. "Have mercy! Right here in Georgetown?"

"I'm afraid so."

"She crossed the wrong person. I *knew* she was going to get herself into trouble. That poor, poor child."

"I was wondering if you could tell me what stories she might have been working on?"

"Nothing for us," said Tony. He flicked a look at the woman. "We did *not* hire her, Charlie."

"You told her if she brought you a good story, you would look at it."

Tony waved his hand around the room, palm up. "Do you see her bringing us a story?"

"Well, now she can't because she's dead!" Charlie looked at me. "Are you with the police?"

"No. She was following me. Trying to create a story out of an absurd theory."

"Who are you? And why would she follow you?" asked Tony.

"I'm Florrie Fox. I work for John Maxwell."

Tony took a closer look at me. "Are you related to the Maxwells?"

"No! I manage Color Me Read, the bookstore."

"Oh!" cried Charlie. "I love that place. With the fire in the parlor and hot chocolate in the winter. Y'all have that adult coloring club, don't you? I've thought about joining it."

"Coloring?" Tony snorted.

"Hey, you think you're so smart," said Charlie. "Coloring soothes the soul! It lowers your blood pressure, too. You ought to consider it."

Tony made a face.

"We would love to have you join us, Charlie."

"But what did Cara want with you?" Tony persisted. "What did you do?"

"I didn't do anything. And I can assure you that none of the Maxwells nor my family would ever have hurt her. Do you know of any stories that Cara might have been working on?"

Tony shook his head. "I'm sorry about what happened to your friend, but we had nothing to do with it."

Tony was not paying attention. He took the document from the printer and yawned.

Charlie looked me straight in the eyes. "That girl." She shook her head. "Bless her little heart, she thought she could get an interview with Griffin Corbyn."

Griffin! That figured. An interview with him would get a lot of attention. We wanted Griffin to do a signing at the store. Poor man. By being a recluse, he had made himself a target. Everyone wanted access to him. Cara probably thought she would meet him at Jacquie's wedding party.

"Did she have any luck with that?" I asked.

"Shoot, no! You'd have heard about it. She was following you, huh? Wouldn't surprise me if she tried to follow him, too."

My breath caught in my throat. Had she found him? Could Griffin Corbyn have flipped out and murdered Cara? According to his wife, he wasn't in town. But the Chesapeake Bay wasn't far away. He could easily have driven back. It probably wouldn't take him more than one or two hours each way. He had an alibi. Granted, it couldn't be confirmed by anyone. Unless he stopped for gas, cameras probably wouldn't have caught him. They might have picked up his car, though. But Griffin wrote about people who evaded cameras and capture. If anyone knew how to commit a crime unnoticed, it was Griffin.

"You okay, honey?" asked Charlie.

"Yes. Sorry, I was just thinking. Griffin is out of town right now."

The horror on Charlie's face told me I shouldn't have said that. "You think he came back here to murder her?"

"No." I shook my head and smiled. "Of course not."

"Strange things happen, you know."

"I do know. If you think of anything that might be relevant to Cara's death, would you give me a call?" I wrote my cell phone number on a scrap of paper and handed it to Charlie.

"I will. That poor girl. What did she get herself into?"

I left their office and heard the lock click behind me. When I turned to look, Charlie opened the door. "Nobody's gonna come in here and stab me!" She closed the door and locked it again.

Maybe she had a point. If Cara had learned something so damaging that someone had been driven to silence her, that person might fear the newspaper office already knew the information, as well.

I paused at the sidewalk, looking both ways for the person who had been following me. Everything looked placid and normal. Some people bustled on their way, others carried shopping bags and gazed in store windows. The scent of something delicious wafted through the air. Burgers? Pizza? Maybe both?

"Florrie! Florrie!" Jacquie waved and hurried in my direction. She wore a white suit. I was used to seeing her in casual clothes. It looked like a Chanel with pretty buttons and trim. It could have been a knockoff, but I didn't think so.

"Are you hungry?" she asked. "I'm starved."

"Actually, I was just enjoying the smell right here. Where do you suppose it's coming from?"

She sniffed and grinned. "It has to be Antoine's. My treat."

We ducked into a passageway that led to a quiet walking-only alley. The host recognized Jacquie immediately and led us to an outdoor table shielded from the sun by a big royal-blue umbrella.

Jacquie placed her briefcase on an extra chair, and we ordered lunch. She raved about their scallops, but we both ordered spiced shrimp salads. The server brought iced tea for both of us.

"You look exceptionally lovely," I said.

At that moment the server arrived with the most beautiful salads I had ever seen. They were works of art. I hated to dig into mine. Crisp greens formed the base; the center appeared to be a mixture of pea shoots, onion slices, and tomatoes, all surrounded by alternating rosy shrimp and soft slices of avocado. Dressing had been applied in droplets on the plate, and the whole thing had been garnished with sunshine-yellow and bright orange nasturtiums.

The server placed mini gravy boats by each of our plates. "Extra dressing on the side."

We ate quietly for a few minutes, but then Jacquie leaned toward me and whispered, "I'm sure Evan's death was an accident."

I whispered back, "Who brings brownies to a black-tie affair?"

Jacquie choked and coughed. "Some people might." She stared at her salad. "It's the kind of thing Arthur would have done. He always tried to be the cool one. But he never was into drugs."

"Do you think Evan brought them and basically killed himself?"

She winced. "No."

"Who else attended the party that might have done something like that? Who else would have wanted to be the coolest person at the ball?"

"If I knew that, I'd have told the police. Oh, Florrie! I feel so guilty. I was so happy that day and poor Evan was suffering. If John and I had married in a tiny private ceremony, none of this would have happened. Evan would still be alive today."

"You don't know that. He didn't die because you threw a party or because you got married. Jacquie, have you heard of anyone else eating brownies that night?"

"No."

"Don't you find that odd?"

She thought for a moment. "Now that you mention it, I do. I hadn't thought about it before, but someone would surely have made a joke about it or asked why some people got cupcakes while others had brownies. Of course, most people probably didn't open the favor boxes until they were at home. But you're right. It does seem like someone would have mentioned them. And that would mean . . . Evan was the only one who received them. But the favors were all in the foyer, for people to take as they departed. It would have been the luck of the draw."

"Maybe. I saw a few people noshing on the cupcakes before they left."

"Maybe we should have served another round of food. An after-after-party buffet or something."

"The party was perfect just the way you planned it. Don't second-guess yourself. Everyone had a wonderful time."

"Except for Evan."

I gazed at her. She looked fabulous. Like she was ready for a photo shoot. The professor thought she knew some things that she hadn't yet volunteered, but in light of Evan's death, they could be important. I dared to ask.

Chapter 22

"Jacquie, what happened the night before the party, when you left the house?"

She signaled the server. "Two napoleons, please, with hot tea for both of us." To me she said, "They have the best napoleons anywhere in Washington. I think I use the salads as an excuse to come here when what I really want is the delicious, creamy napoleon."

I couldn't believe that she was dodging my question. Our desserts arrived immediately. The napoleon looked great, but I was fixated on her not responding to me.

After a bite of napoleon, Jacquie said, "I received a text from Arthur at two in the morning. It said, 'Urgent. Must see you tonight. Need help. Branigan's.' I debated it. Really, I did. The wedding was the next day. I was comfortably in bed. But as I told you before, there are some people for whom we drop everything when they need help. Arthur was one of those people for me."

She paused and ate more of her dessert before continuing, "Oddly, he had received a similar text from me." She shook her head. "I didn't send it. I hadn't been in touch with Arthur in ages. And as I said, I was tucked in bed and wasn't sending texts to anyone. I've done a little research since then. Apparently, there are ways to send texts that look like they come from someone else. Honestly, Florrie, why would anyone ever do that?"

"Kids. They're so savvy about technical things. You know how kids like to play tricks on each other."

"I can't imagine that kids set this up. Someone clearly wanted Arthur and me together for some reason. I met him at the bar, we had drinks and realized that neither of us had sent the other one a text. The next thing I remember is that little dog barking at me and seeing you."

"What? That's crazy."

"No kidding. It was the same for Arthur. He woke up in a park not far from the bookstore. That's why he came looking for me when we were having our hair done. He wanted to be sure I was all right."

"Rohypnol. It makes people black out."

She nodded. "That's what I think. Someone slipped something into our drinks. It was last call when we met at two thirty in the morning. They were closing in half an hour, so we had to leave soon. Perfectly orchestrated. Thank heaven neither of us were attacked physically. But our money, wallets, and phones were gone."

Aghast, I set my fork on the side of my plate. "Someone knew your phone numbers and brought you there to incapacitate and rob you?"

"It's all I can figure out. Arthur and I have very public profiles. And there are so many of those dreadful online sites that tell you everything about a person: addresses, phone numbers, family members. Nothing is truly private anymore."

"But you didn't report it to the police. . . ."

Jacquie winced. "I chose not to."

She wasn't getting away with that answer. "Why? Why wouldn't you want to tell them so it wouldn't happen to other people?"

Jacquie looked pained. "For Arthur's sake." She calmly ate the last bite of her napoleon.

"For Arthur?" That didn't make any sense at all. He should have gone to the police, too. How would it protect Arthur to stay away from the cops? Unless she thought Arthur set her up. Thoughts spun through my head. "You think Arthur stole your money and phone?"

"He claims he didn't. But I have a feeling he was in dire straits. I didn't want any publicity about that. It was wrong of Arthur, of course. But he would only do something like that if he was truly desperate."

I could understand helping a friend. Assisting someone in saving face made sense in some situations. But theft and, even worse, drugging her?

I stared at her, almost speechless. And then, out of the blue, I understood. At least partly. There hadn't been much time between Jacquie's return and the party. And then Arthur's assistant, Evan, had died. He had died at the Maxwells' house under suspicious circumstances the very next night.

Neither Jacquie nor the professor would have killed him. They were good people, and they barely knew Evan. Even if the professor had known Jacquie had been drugged, he wouldn't have retaliated. He might have had Arthur removed from the festivities, though.

Jacquie reached across the table and placed her hand over mine. "I wish I could remember. But I just don't know what happened that night. I can't explain it. I haven't told Maxwell, of course. He will have some choice things to say about it. You understand. I didn't want to start our new marriage that way. It has taken us years to get to the point where we can be together again. I was not about to bring Arthur into the equa-

tion. I chose to put it behind me. I can't prove anything anyway because I don't remember anything."

I told her about Cara and then remembered the little green
pig. "Did Mr. DuBois show you the green pig we found?"

Jacquie laughed. "He must have forgotten. How odd that
a pig would be green."

"Sort of a poisonous-apple green. It glows! Mr. DuBois
said he thinks it's jadeite."

Jacquie became serious. "No kidding? DuBois knows his
gems. He's such a curious fellow. He tells me that butlers were
trained to know all sorts of things like sewing and fabrics because something might need mending, and china, crystal, and
silver care for proper entertaining, but his knowledge is far
broader than that. When he first came to the Maxwells, they
had a cook. But she retired, and since it was only Maxwell and
DuBois at that point, he took up cooking."

"He's very good at it."

"It's something of a hobby for him, I think. Plus, he likes
to eat and abhors prepackaged frozen foods. Did you know
that he regularly invites the housekeepers from the neighborhood for tea?"

"I knew he was linked into the neighborhood grapevine."

She laughed. "He's the leader of the pack when it comes
to neighborhood gossip."

Jacquie graciously picked up the tab for our lunch and we
parted ways. I returned to the bookstore to retrieve the pig
from the safe. Feeling relieved once I handed the expensive
piggy over to Mr. DuBois, I crossed the driveway to my
home.

Peaches yawned and stretched when I entered the carriage
house. She deigned to rub around my ankles. I bent over and
picked her up. She purred and rubbed the back of her head
against my jaw.

I was still trying to wrap my head around the things I had

learned. What a day it had been. I changed into an oversize T-shirt and skorts, then settled on my sofa with my sketch pad.

I flipped through the pages, flashing back on Evan's horrible death. But that wasn't where the strange things began. They started with Cara tailing me. I drew her face as she had looked this morning. Sort of innocent, actually. She was determined to make her mark by breaking a huge story, but she must have crossed the wrong person in the process.

Then Jacquie went to meet Arthur in the middle of the night. I sketched them side by side, surprised to see that they looked good together. Someone had knocked them out and stolen their belongings. As I thought about what had been taken, I drew little images. Dollar bills, credit cards, identification, phones. What a scam!

As I studied my drawings, I wondered if some people out in the world were now passing themselves off as Jacquie and Arthur. People doctored photos easily in movies and books. I had to think it wasn't that difficult. Buzz Powers probably knew how to do it.

Then it dawned on me that it might not be so difficult to figure out if Arthur had set up that scenario to steal money from Jacquie. I sketched his face again. He didn't look like a thief. He had a rugged look. A handsome, long, lean face with deep lines in his forehead and bracket winkles on both sides of his face when he smiled. His eyes slowed me down. Try as I might, I couldn't find cruelty in them. Bad boy, yes. Definitely a scamp, but not a vicious man.

Had he perpetrated this theft by Rohypnol on someone else who sought revenge and mistakenly killed Evan instead of Arthur? The professor had said Arthur collected information on people. Whom had he crossed? Margarite Herbert-Grant, the vicious reviewer? His agent, Sloan Rogers?

On the other hand, if Arthur had summoned Jacquie, if he had doctored her drink and stolen from her, then it was extremely likely that some of her possessions would still be in his house. They might even be out in the open, such as on top of a dresser. The money would probably be gone, but he hadn't had time to sell her driver's license.

I wondered how I could get into his house.

I took Peaches to work with me the next day. When I unlocked the door, I took a deep breath, enjoying the scent of books. I switched off the alarm and turned the classical music on. It was so soothing that I was tempted to lock the door behind me and spend the day alone browsing through books. "You wouldn't mind that, would you, Peaches?"

She glanced at me on her way to her favorite display window. She leaped into it with the grace of a wildcat. She didn't knock over a single book.

I retreated to the kitchen and started coffee. Then I walked up to the second and third floors, turning on lights as needed. The professor wasn't in his office. He and Jacquie had intended to be in Hawaii now. Maybe he was taking the week off.

Back on the main floor, I flipped the sign on the door to OPEN and placed the early-morning international newspapers in their proper places in the parlor. I fluffed some pillows and snagged a candy bar wrapper that someone had discarded on the sofa. Honestly, did people leave things like that on their furniture at home? Probably. Maybe it was a kid who had to hide it from his disapproving mom.

A corner of a book stuck up from behind a cushion. Or maybe it wasn't a book. It didn't look thick. I pulled it out. The top said PASSPORT.

There was something people didn't lose in bookstores every day. I flipped it open. Buzz Powers's serious face stared back at me from the photo. I checked the name. *Buzz Powers.*

The bell on the front door tinkled. I hurried to the front desk. A gentleman asked if we had a copy of *Goodnight Moon,* because his grandson was coming for a visit. I showed him to the children's room and made a bet with myself that he would appear at the checkout desk with a whole stack of books.

Veronica finally arrived. "I'm so, so sorry to be late." She glanced around furtively and whispered, "Buzz isn't here, is he?"

"No, but his passport is." I held it up to show her.

"I thought he would never leave yesterday. Maybe we've made the parlor too comfy."

"Maybe he *lost* his passport so you would have to call him, and he would have an excuse to return."

She stashed her bag away. "I know! Although I may have finally discouraged him. You know that cop friend of Eric's? The one called Fish?"

Uh-oh. "What did you do?"

"It wasn't anything terrible. I asked him to act like we were a couple. And I think it might have worked. Buzz left shortly after that."

"I'll call Buzz." I flipped through the pages to see the exotic places he had been. It wasn't any of my business, but I didn't see the harm in it. "Veronica, there's only one stamp in his passport."

"Maybe it's new."

I checked the date of issue. "Nope. Seven years old, but the only stamp is from Bermuda."

"Let me see that." Veronica flipped through the empty pages much as I had. "Do they issue special passports to people on dangerous missions?"

"You mean under false names?"

"Yeah. They would have to do that if they were working undercover. Right?"

"That would make sense," I said. "But I fear it confirms that your daring FBI agent was in human resources and not out in the field." I eyed Veronica. "Why would he be carrying his passport around town?"

She shrugged. "Because he needed it as an extra form of identification?"

"Like if he lost his wallet with his driver's license and needed a replacement."

She nodded. "Probably something like that."

Lowering my voice so our customer wouldn't hear, I filled her in on Cara's death and what had happened to Jacquie. "Do you think someone drugged Buzz and stole his wallet?"

Veronica was still reeling when the phone rang. I picked it up, "Color Me Read bookstore, Florrie speaking. How may I help you?"

A voice whispered, "Don't come home."

The call disconnected.

Chapter 23

"That sounded like Mr. DuBois!" I called him back.

He picked up the phone. "Maxwell residence."

"Mr. DuBois, what is going on?"

"I am sorry, but Florrie is not here at the moment."

"Clearly you can't talk. Who's there? Should I call the police?"

In a whisper he said, "The police are here looking for you. They have a warrant! Run, Florrie, run!"

"The police are looking for me?"

The line disconnected again.

Veronica yelped. "They'll be at the bookstore next. You'd better go. I can handle everything. Go to Mom and Dad's house to hide out."

"I don't have a reason to hide."

"I'm calling Eric." Veronica pulled out her phone and made a call.

I had a slightly different idea. I knew I couldn't afford Maxwell's attorney, but I had met a retired lawyer who lived on our street. Gene Germain was a little cranky, but he seemed to know his stuff. I looked up his number and called him.

When I explained the situation, he said he would pop over to the mansion to find out what was going on.

I knew I wasn't guilty of anything and yet a tremor rumbled through me. Was this tied to Rajat and his mistaken belief that I had assaulted and murdered Cara?

For the next forty-five minutes, I forced myself to concentrate on unboxing orders and shelving books. Every time the bell on the door rang, my heart skipped a beat out of fear that the police had arrived.

I felt queasy even when Eric entered the store. "Are you okay?" he asked before dropping a sweet kiss on my cheek.

"What's going on? I feel like I'm a suspect, but I haven't done anything."

"It's the autopsy. The person who killed Cara jabbed her with a really weird little spear. The end of it broke off, which is why it wasn't visible. I suspect that's also why the killer was able to stab her so fast and then be gone."

"I thought it was a knife. It broke off? Eww."

"Since the dry cleaner said he saw you, the police want to make sure you don't possess that kind of little spear or the broken end of it. They'll be over here soon to check out the professor's office. Don't be nervous."

The bell on the door tinkled. I relaxed a little when I saw that it was only Gene Germain. Portly with graying hair and a long straight nose that reminded me of an arrow, he was a little bit intimidating. Rumor had it that he made the rounds of widows in the neighborhood in hopes of scoring homemade dinners. He was exactly the kind of fellow I wanted on my side.

"I see you beat me here, Eric. Ah, the benefits of youth." He smiled at me. "I don't think you have anything to worry about, Florrie. Unless you're in possession of strange small spears."

"I can honestly say that I'm not." Then I told them both the details about Rajat and his claim that I had stabbed Cara when he was actually engaged with a customer and her shrieking child.

"Excellent work, Florrie!" exclaimed Gene. "You're quite the sleuth. They had a warrant to search your home."

"Not again! I don't have anything to hide, but they make such a mess. I'm glad I brought Peaches to work so no one let her out."

"The good news is that they didn't find anything of interest. I'll tell you what. For a retainer of five dollars, you may call me at any time. I don't expect there will be any developments in your direction. Just keep your nose clean."

I darted to retrieve my wallet and promptly handed him a five-dollar bill.

"Thank you." Gene spoke in a most serious tone. "Should anyone give you trouble, you may refer them to me, and I'll take care of it."

"Thanks, Gene."

"Now, who would have wanted to murder this Cara?"

At that moment, a worried Jacquie marched into the store, followed by her assistant, Roxie, and Sergeant Bridges, who looked tired.

Jacquie paused next to us. "Sergeant Bridges has a warrant to search the premises."

Bridges scowled. "I'm only interested in Professor Maxwell's office. I understand he has a collection of artifacts."

I smiled as sweetly as I could. "I'll show you the way."

I could hear the others whispering as he followed me up the stairs.

When I opened the door to the professor's office, Sergeant Bridges whistled. "This is like a little museum." He glanced around and then walked closer to each wall, methodically peering at each item on display. He shook his head. "Has he got any that aren't out? Maybe they're in boxes or some kind of storage?"

"Not that I'm aware of. He takes a lot of pride in these. Many of them were gifts from people he met during his travels."

Bridges pulled open drawer after drawer, rifling through them. I had a hunch Jacquie had convinced the professor to stay home. He would have been outraged by the intrusion.

"You went through the artifacts awfully fast."

"They don't look anything like the weapon—" He looked up and stared at me. "You really don't know, do you?"

"I thought it was a knife. I could tell she was bleeding from her neck, but I couldn't see anything. I heard it broke. That must have been so painful!"

"I thought she was following you."

"She was."

"But you're worried about how painful her death was?"

"I wouldn't wish that on anyone. I didn't like her stalking me or promoting ridiculous ideas, but I certainly didn't want her to die."

His eyes narrowed as he studied me. "Someone did." He finished browsing through the desk drawers and asked what was in the room next door.

"That's my little office."

He walked into it and looked around. "No knives on the walls."

"I'm not an international adventurer like the professor." He smiled at the large promotional poster of *Bats at the Beach*. I didn't say a word when he opened the drawers of my desk or the filing cabinet.

"Florrie! Florrie, are you up here?"

I recognized Professor Goldblum's voice and stepped out of my tiny office. "Right here. Is something wrong?"

He panted from running up the stairs. "They have found glass spearheads on Rottnest Island in Western Australia." He inhaled deeply and beamed at me.

I had no idea what he was talking about and worried that he might be having a stroke.

But Sergeant Bridges bolted out the door past me. "Rottnest Island? Is that some place Professor Maxwell has been?"

I shrugged. "Not that I know."

Bridges glared at Professor Goldblum. "What do you know about glass spears?"

Goldblum, in his adorably clueless way, launched into a history of the glass spears on Rottnest Island. "Some were glass and other spearheads were made of broken china. They were used for fishing and hunting. The ones newly found are deemed to be about one hundred years old."

When the professor drew a breath, Bridges demanded, "I mean, how do you know we're looking for a glass spear?"

Goldblum blinked. "Jacquie told me."

Bridges breathed, "Jonquille," and ran down the stairs.

"What did I do wrong? He's so upset."

"Professor, what exactly did Jacquie tell you?"

"Only that the police were looking for a glass spear."

I nodded, thanked Goldblum, and hurried downstairs. Bridges and Eric were on their way out the door.

Jacquie and Roxie watched them leave.

"What happened?" asked Roxie.

"He was very upset that Jacquie knew they were looking for a glass spear."

"That's so crazy. Wouldn't a glass spear break?" asked Roxie.

"Apparently it did."

"He was so obvious." Jacquie sighed. "If he wanted to keep that a secret, then he should have been more discreet. He was fascinated by my Murano-glass hummingbirds. Their beaks are long and tapered to a fine point. I could tell from the way he was examining them that they must have found glass somewhere. He felt the points of the beaks several times. What was I supposed to think?"

"I still don't get it," said Roxie. "Glass is so fragile."

Jacquie raised an eyebrow. "Haven't you ever broken a glass and gotten a sliver of it in your hand when you were cleaning up?"

Roxie gasped. "I see what you mean. Those chunks have to be handled just so or they'll slice into you."

Jacquie stared at me and uncomfortably chewed her lower lip. "The birds were gifts from Arthur."

Chapter 24

"Arthur has a thing for venetian and Murano glass." Jacquie tensed and her breath came a little too fast. "Maybe we should pay him a visit."

I held up my palms in protest. "Are you saying that Arthur might have killed Cara?"

"Noooo." It came out slowly, reluctantly, like a child who had to fudge an answer. "But he might know where one would get a glass weapon. Besides, he must be devastated about Evan's death. I've been so self-absorbed that I didn't think about the fact that Evan was Arthur's daily connection to reality. Come with me, Florrie. I'll distract him while you look around."

"Look around?" I squawked. "You just said he didn't kill Cara."

Her eyes narrowed. "I'd like to talk with him. See how he's doing. Please come with me. I don't want Maxwell thinking I went there alone."

"I can't leave Veronica in the store by herself."

"I'll fill in for you," offered Roxie.

She worked for Jacquie, but it might not be a bad idea to

hire Roxie as an extra hand when Jacquie didn't need her. "Sure. Is that okay with you, Veronica?"

"Go." Veronica swished her hand through the air. "The two of us will have fun."

As Jacquie and I set off, she asked, "Have you called Arthur about the signing this Friday?"

"Not yet." I felt the flush of embarrassment flooding my face with heat. She was right. We had been so distracted by everything that was going on that we were forgetting about the day-to-day things we needed to do. "Don't let me forget to ask him when we're at his house." I tried making a mental note about it.

"To tell the truth, I'm glad I never married Arthur. It would have been miserable for both of us. Well, for me anyway. He is an interesting person and I'll be eternally grateful that I knew him, but he would have made a lousy husband."

Arthur's house blended with the other three-story houses on the street. A corner house partially hidden by massive evergreens, it had been painted white and the exterior was classically Federal-style.

Jacquie knocked on the front door.

We waited but no one answered. She knocked again. "Arthur? Arthur!"

Her brow wrinkled. "I hope he's okay. He might have drunk himself into a stupor over Evan's death. I hadn't even considered that possibility. Poor Arthur." She signaled to me to follow her, opened a gate, and slipped around the side of the house to the backyard.

Jacquie pushed aside evergreen branches and squeezed between two trees. "Oof! It has grown quite a bit in the decade or so since I was last here."

"Do you think this is legal?" I asked, brushing pine needles off my clothes.

"Well, of course it is! We're friends checking on his welfare."

She had a point.

Arthur's backyard rivaled that of the mansion. It was much smaller, but towering pines shielded it from view by neighbors or passersby. They would have no idea that a luxurious swimming pool shimmered blue in the sunlight. Patio chairs with plush white cushions almost beckoned one to sit down and lounge. Ivy grew out of an oversize birdcage.

Jacquie had her back to me as she peered in floor-to-ceiling windows. "I don't see him." She called his name again, then looked around. "He always kept a key outside so he could get in if he lost his house key."

Jacquie eyed a large terra-cotta pot in the grass that contained a hibiscus plant with platter-size sun-yellow and maroon flowers. She grunted when she tried to tilt it. "Florrie, could you give this a shot?"

"What exactly am I supposed to do?"

"Just lift one side. I'll look underneath for the key."

I grabbed the top edge and lifted. It went nowhere. "Are you kidding?"

"Mmm." She looked around. "Aha!" She fetched a fireplace poker and aimed it at the bottom of the pot. "You only have to raise it enough for me to wedge this underneath. Then it will act as a lever."

This time I placed my hands below the rim and pushed upward on one side. The pot moved ever so slightly, but it was enough for Jacquie to slide the poker under the bottom edge.

"Perfect, Florrie!" Jacquie lifted the poker and the pot tilted far enough to see what was underneath.

Dirt. That was all I could see.

"Hold this, will you?"

I took control of the poker while Jacquie knelt and scratched at the dirt with a stick. "How annoying. It could be inches down if he hasn't used it recently. Wait, wait! I feel like I hit something." She tossed the stick and clawed at it with her fingers. "Got it!"

She pulled out a filthy can and brushed it off. "'Nuts,'" she read. "It used to be in a little box." She turned the top. A snake leaped out and hit her in the nose.

Chapter 25

Jacquie and I screamed simultaneously. I dropped the poker and the pot flipped into place on top of it.

Jacquie jumped to her feet, her chest heaving.

A timid female voice on the other side of the dense pines asked with a tremor, "Are you all right? Who's over there?"

Jacquie took a deep breath and bent to pick up a rubber snake. "We're fine, thank you."

A head of white curls poked through the trees. The woman shook the curls out of her face and studied Jacquie for a long moment. "Oh my stars! Are you that author?"

Jacquie brushed off her hands. "Yes, I am. Jacquie Liebhaber."

The rest of the white-curled lady pushed through the trees. "I forgot there was a fence here. Hah! The trees have overgrown it all with the gate open." She brushed off her clothes. "I can't believe it's you! I knew you were a friend of Arthur's. He talks about you all the time. Oh! I wish they hadn't taken my phone away. I would so love to have a photo of the two of us."

I pulled out my phone. "I can email one to you."

She clasped her hands together as if it were the greatest joy she had experienced.

The two of them stood side by side smiling happily.

I snapped several shots in case one of them closed her eyes like I always managed to do. "What is your email address?"

With a twinkle in her eye, she spelled, "K-A-Y-L-E-E-8-7 at M-Y-N-E-T."

I sent off the best of the pictures. "All done!"

"What are you doing here at Arthur's house?"

"I'm sorry, Mrs.—" Jacquie stopped midsentence.

"Jezebel."

"Not Jezebel Fish?" I asked.

She giggled. "The one and only. Have we met before?"

"I don't think so, but I met your grandson Fish Gordon."

"My favorite," she said slyly. "I love all of them, of course, but he's special. The only one in my family who doesn't treat me like I'm incapacitated."

From the other side of the trees, we could hear a voice, probably inside the house, calling, "Mrs. Fish? Mrs. Fish, where are you?"

"Want to have some fun?" she asked. A long cord with a pendant hung around her neck. She pulled it over her head, and then, slinging it in her hand like a lasso, she let it go over the trees. It landed with a splash on the other side. She pulled her shoulders back. "Bull's-eye!"

Jacquie asked, "What was that?"

"It's one of those infernal monitors. They want to know my every move. I'm no longer allowed to leave the house. There are guards hovering over me all the time. They shove children's games in my face all day long. They even watch me sleep. Sometimes I hold my breath just to scare them!"

I flashed a look at Jacquie. I wasn't sure what to think. Jezebel seemed to be fully in control.

"Guards?" asked Jacquie.

"They call them my *friends*. Always puttering around me. There's a different one most every day. I've never met them before. I may be getting up in years, but you can't fool me by calling them my friends. My children live in Phoenix and Duluth. They want to put me in an old folks' facility, but I plan to stay right here in my own home until the good Lord calls me. So far, he hasn't even sent me a text."

Next door a hysterical voice said, "She sent me a picture of her posing with some lady and . . ." A scream reverberated. "Her medical alert is in the pool!"

Jezebel bent double with silent laughter. "May I borrow your phone?"

I handed it to her.

She had no trouble whatsoever making a call. "Hello, sweetheart."

Someone yammered at her. She held the phone away from her ear. "Are you through?" She listened for a moment. "These are my demands. The guards leave. Every single one of them. I am perfectly capable of feeding myself. Dorothy may continue to come weekly to clean. Now call off the guard or I'm not going home." And she hung up. "So you never mentioned what you're doing here."

A phone played a metallic tune on the other side of the fence. "What? Where is she?" A pause. "As long as I get paid for today."

Jezebel smiled and winked. "Sometimes you have to play hardball."

"You probably read that Evan passed," said Jacquie gently.

"Broke my heart. I always enjoyed his company. Such a nice young man. Too bad he never did find the right girl."

"We thought Arthur must be terribly upset and we wanted to check on him. He's not answering the door. He used to keep a key under that pot, but when I dug it up, a snake jumped out of this can."

Jezebel howled with laughter. "That Arthur! He is a man after my own heart. Darlin', he moved the key after that girl finally left. She must have loved him something awful because she kept coming back. He'd wake up and find her in the bedroom, which was horribly frightening. One time he was sitting at his desk writing when he saw her slinking around the back to get the key. When he went outside to confront her, she hid in these evergreens. Another night, he brought home a new lady friend—he is quite the ladies' man, you know—and the previous girl ran her right out of the house in her drawers. They were nice ones, looked to be silk, but it's hard to tell anymore unless you touch it. Polyester can fool the eye."

Jezebel walked over to a sundial. "The key moved around over the years. Arthur trusted people too much and told too many of them where it was. But right now, it should be here." She smiled as she pulled a shiny key from the birdcage.

Jacquie thanked her and unlocked the back door. The three of us entered. Every step we took seemed to echo through the house.

"Arthur?" called Jacquie.

We heard a light thud. Not a minute later, six cats ran into the room like a herd.

The three of us stopped to pet them.

Smiling, Jacquie said, "Arthur always has been a sucker for cats."

The entire back of the house was glass. Enormous sheets of floor-to-ceiling glass looked out on the swimming pool and evergreens.

To the left, carefully curated modern furniture rested on a faux-fur rug before a granite fireplace. On the right, eight silver-and-gray dining chairs surrounded a glass dining table.

Black chandeliers hung above it from the ceiling, the arms reflecting light. I peered at them. Were they black crystal? They were eye-catching and surprisingly attractive.

I had only seen pictures of places like this in architectural magazines. And had certainly never expected to find such a modern interior behind the traditional façade.

Jezebel and I followed Jacquie to the foyer. Given the formal exterior of the house, I had expected the kind of traditional décor popular in Georgetown. But the foyer was a giant square room with a soaring ceiling and a huge abstract painting on each side wall. A three-foot-tall glass sculpture gleamed in every color of the rainbow. Striations of yellow, blue, green, and red stretched upward in a wide ribbon, reminding me of pulled sugar. An open staircase zigzagged up three stories.

"Hello?" called a woman's voice. She appeared on the staircase, her heels clacking as she trotted back and forth down the stairs. "I thought I heard someone."

She reached the foyer and stopped in surprise. "Hello. My goodness, did I leave the door open?"

She wasn't the only one who was shocked.

"Mia!" Jacquie exclaimed.

Mia Woodham, the artist who had drawn sketches of guests at the party, smiled at us. "How nice to see you again. Hello, Jezebel. I've missed you! If you're looking for Arthur, I'm afraid he's not home."

The air was thick with unasked questions. She was probably wondering how we got in the house, and we were itching to know what she was doing there.

"Will he be back soon?" asked Jacquie.

"I doubt it. You know Arthur."

"I *do* know him," said Jacquie oh so smoothly. "I didn't realize that you were friends with Arthur."

"Can I get you ladies a cool drink? You must be parched."

Jacquie jumped on it, and the two of them chatted as they walked away.

Jezebel frowned at me. She seized my elbow as I was about to join them. "That's Mia," she hissed. "She's aged a lot, but it's her. What's she doing back?"

"I don't know."

We trailed them into a sleek, modern kitchen. Endless high-gloss wood cabinets without handles or knobs surrounded us. Mia opened the matching fridge and took out a carafe of iced tea.

Cats milled around us as if they were hoping to hear the sound of a can being opened.

"Mia," said Jacquie softly. "You're *that* Mia?"

Mia smiled brightly and chuckled. "I guess I am. I hadn't seen Arthur in years, but then he showed up at your party, and things just clicked again between us."

"This is a remarkable house," I said. "He must have made a lot more money than I thought."

"Some of his books sold very well." Mia leaned against a kitchen counter, totally at ease. "They were translated into a dozen languages and sold all over the world. And Arthur came from a superwealthy family, too. When he inherited this house, he tore out everything and hired a decorator. That was a nightmare. We lived here through the construction. I thought it would never end. He used to joke that he was house rich and cash poor. He sank all his money into this place, and then when his other books didn't do so well, he found himself pinching pennies. I noticed that one of the paintings is gone. He probably sold it because he needed cash." Mia smiled at me. "You've never been here?"

Mia led us into a library. Except for one window, every inch of three walls was filled from floor to ceiling with books and venetian glass in the shapes of animals and abstract designs. The fourth wall was glass, with a desk looking out over the pool and greenery in the backyard.

"That's where he writes." Mia sipped her tea.

I sidled over to the desk and examined the top of it. A laptop computer rested on it, along with notes. Piles and piles of scraps of paper covered the desktop. On each he had scribbled a few words or merely a letter. In the trash bin beside the desk were more, mostly the letter *J* in beautiful calligraphy. But some of them went further and spelled out Jacquie's name. I wondered how Mia felt about that.

"Jacquie," I said, "you have to see the view from here."

She walked over to me and looked out the window.

How on earth could I get her to look at the trash? I faked tripping over it.

"Are you all right?" asked Jezebel.

I fudged while Jacquie slowly placed papers back in the trash bin. "Um, yes. I was just thinking of Evan, who worked here. Arthur must be lost without him."

"I didn't know Evan," said Mia. "Arthur is a wreck about Evan's death. He was like a zombie when he got the news. But I'm doing my best to help Arthur and make sure nothing falls between the cracks."

Jacquie stood up straight. "Arthur must be broken by Evan's death."

Mia nodded. "It has shaken him to the core. I thought he would never budge from this place, but he's decided to sell the house. If you know anyone who is in the market for a house in Georgetown, please tell them. It's one of a kind."

"Sell?" Jacquie blurted. "Where will he go?"

"He's talking about Portland. He says Washington isn't the town he knew anymore. He wants to get away and start fresh."

Jacquie's eyes met mine. Smooth as silk she said, "We've

taken up enough of your time. Thank you so much for the tea. It's warm today!" She walked toward Mia and the two of them left the room.

Jezebel stuck her tongue out.

I stifled a laugh and took her empty glass to the kitchen with mine.

Thanking Mia, the three of us left through the front door.

"Did you ever tell her how we got inside?" I asked.

Jacquie smiled. "I think she forgot about it. I still have the key. I'm just so surprised that Arthur took up with her again."

We walked toward Jezebel's home.

"So much for that," said Jacquie. "I guess I should be happy for Arthur. Do you think she's moving in?"

Jezebel shrugged. "Probably. She was with him for nearly twenty years. My windows don't look out on Arthur's house much. Now if you had asked me about one of the homes across the street, then that might have been different. Although the guards were always trying to force me to play children's games so I couldn't watch the neighborhood like I used to. Did I tell you they wouldn't let me have a cat or a dog? I think that's inhumane."

Jacquie gasped. "Who wouldn't let you?"

"My children! They said I would trip over them, and it was too much for my prison guards to have to take care of them."

"Oh," Jacquie said weakly, staring at Jezebel.

"I used to walk my little schnauzer every day. We explored all over the neighborhood. I knew everyone. Is there anything you'd like to know about them? I knew who was out late, and who got up early. Who was having an affair, and whose spouse knew or didn't know about it. Oh, I have dirt on all the neighbors!"

"I wouldn't go around saying that," I advised. "You're likely to be knocked off!"

Chapter 26

Jacquie eyed Jezebel. "How long have you lived here? How well did you know Mia?"

"It's too bad you weren't involved with Arthur when he moved in here, Jacquie. I'd have liked having you as a neighbor. Certainly better than Mia. She was so young. I remember being quite upset about it."

"Surely she was old enough . . . ," said Jacquie.

"I imagine she was, legally speaking, maybe nineteen or twenty? He must have been twenty years her senior. She wasn't out of the house a day before Lena started showing up. And then, well, I can't even recall all their names. It was a steady stream with quite a turnover. Pity, he would have made someone a nice husband."

"Actually, he would have been a terrible husband." Jacquie smiled. "That was why I left him!"

"He had a lot of venetian glass," I said. "You were right about that, Jacquie. Are the black chandeliers Italian blown glass, too?"

"I would bet on it," said Jacquie.

"Too bad Arthur wasn't home. We don't know a thing more about Cara's murder," I griped.

Jezebel placed a cool hand on my arm. "That was so sad. Don't worry, Florrie, I heard on the news that they have a witness who saw the whole thing and they already have a person of interest, which means it won't be long before they arrest him."

She could not *possibly* have said anything more worrisome to me.

She didn't seem to notice. "Poor Evan!" said Jezebel. "Such a nice young man. I only wish he had fulfilled his dream of being published before he died. Arthur said he'd tried to get his agent to take an interest, but that Evan's writing wasn't 'ready for prime time' yet."

"Will you be okay by yourself?" asked Jacquie.

"Okay? I'll be fantastic! This is the first time in ages that I can do what I want without some stranger bossing me around. I'm going to eat what I'm not supposed to and watch a good murder movie on Netflix."

We watched Jezebel unlock her front door and waited until she was safely inside.

"Are you upset?" I asked Jacquie as we walked back to the store.

"No. But I expect Maxwell and I will be equally problematic for you when we get to her age."

I laughed, pleased to be thought of as family. "I meant about Mia."

"Not a bit. I'll admit that I was surprised. But you know, it's not unlike Maxwell and me getting married again." She pulled out of her pocket one of the slips of paper on which her name had so beautifully been written. "Arthur loved me. But those days are long gone. Maybe seeing Maxwell and me so happy together let him know that he had to move on. If he and Mia spent twenty years together, they must have had a special bond. I'm so pleased that they found it again. And at my wedding! What could be better than that?"

"No wonder you write romances. You're a romantic through and through. I wanted to talk to you about Roxie. I need to hire a couple of people to help us out at the store. Not necessarily full-time. I thought Roxie might be a good choice if you don't need her full-time. She knows the bookstore, and everyone loves her. She's diligent and trustworthy—"

"You don't have to sell me on her. I know how great she is. That's not a bad idea. It would do her good to be around people more. She's very outgoing. I'm sure that sitting around taking care of details for me must be somewhat lonely for her. Maybe we can figure out a schedule that would work for all of us."

I tried not to do a little jig on the sidewalk. We would probably need one more person, but Roxie was a great start.

When we returned to Color Me Read, I proposed the part-time job to Roxie.

She turned to Jacquie. "Don't you need me?"

"Absolutely. But this would give you an opportunity to be out and about and meet people. Besides, you know perfectly well that when I get into writing a book, I go for hours without stopping, except to refill my tea."

Roxie beamed. "I would love the job. Both of them!"

An hour later, we had worked out a tentative schedule and Roxie was officially on the payroll. We agreed to be flexible while we worked out the kinks.

It was almost eleven when Peaches and I got home that night. I fed her a late dinner of mixed tuna and salmon. She snarfed it but was looking about as tired as I felt. I noshed on a piece of leftover wedding cake that would be going stale soon if I didn't eat it and went straight up to bed.

I was running early the next morning, but that gave me more than enough time to buy a ham biscuit and coffee and enjoy the summer air for a bit before work. I left Peaches at home and strolled toward a local diner for takeout. On my way, I spotted Arthur half a block away. I smiled and waved at him. He looked straight at me but didn't wave back. He turned and went into a building. Well! That was a major snub. I consoled myself by imagining that he didn't remember me. Why would he?

I was standing in line to buy my breakfast when someone whispered, "Hi, Florrie."

I looked to my right and found Celeste Sorello looking at me. She seemed even thinner than before. Her complexion was sallow and her eyes were red as though she'd been crying. "Hi!" I lowered my voice to a whisper. "Can I get you something?"

I could barely hear her response: "Just a plain coffee."

I felt like I was channeling my mother when I ordered two breakfast specials, one plain coffee, and a latte. I handed the coffee and one of the breakfast specials to Celeste.

"What's this?"

"Breakfast. You have to eat." My mother had said those exact words a million times.

She followed me outside into the sunshine. We found a bench in a small park and sat down.

Celeste took one bite of her ham biscuit and launched into a coughing fit.

I patted her on the back and could feel every vertebra on her spine.

"I'm so sorry," she sputtered. "I hate making scenes. It's embarrassing."

"It's fine. Everyone chokes sometimes."

She looked at me with big watery eyes. I thought she might start crying. "What's wrong, Celeste?"

"You're being so nice to me."

"I can't imagine anyone not being nice to you."

She smiled shyly and sipped her coffee. "I'm enjoying the coloring sessions. Such kind people. And that Goldblum, he's a hoot. He always makes me laugh."

"I'm glad about that." I had no trouble eating my ham biscuit and eagerly took another bite. The cinnamon scent of fried apples wafted up to me.

Celeste ate a bite of her apples. "This is good. I wonder why I never tried their food before. I always order a plain coffee."

We ate quietly while she devoured every single thing in her breakfast box. I began to wonder if she didn't eat anything at home. When she finished, she sipped her coffee. Intentionally avoiding my gaze, she studied the grass and blurted, "My husband is having an affair."

Chapter 27

I swallowed hard. "Grady?" It was a stupid question since she only had one husband, but his name slipped out anyway.

She nodded but didn't raise her eyes.

"How do you know?"

"He claims he's going to meetings and conferences, but he doesn't. I've called and asked for him. He's not there. He hasn't checked into the hotel. And sometimes when he's home, he sneaks out at night. I pretend I'm sleeping but I wait for him to return. He's usually gone for two or three hours, sometimes a little longer. I've thought about following him. . . ." She bit her upper lip. "Oh, Florrie! I haven't been able to tell anyone. . . ."

I wasn't sure why she chose me. Maybe because I didn't know her that well? I wasn't in her inner circle of friends, who would share the news within an hour of learning it? Or did they all know? Were they Grady's friends who wouldn't rat on him?

"The night"—she choked back a sob—"the night Evan died, Grady went out and didn't come back until just before dawn."

A shiver ran through me. "Did Grady know Evan before the party?"

She nodded, finally turning her head toward me. "It's such a relief to tell someone else. I just didn't know what to do. I . . . I feel like I'm betraying him. He's my *husband*."

"Were Grady and Evan friends?"

"I don't think so. Not in the regular way. From what I gather, when Arthur ran short of money, he would drive an Uber. Something about getting ideas for books. Meeting the common man, that sort of thing. Apparently, Evan did the same thing. I guess he thought if it worked for Arthur, it might work for him, too. It seemed like every time Grady needed an Uber, it was Evan who picked him up."

"Did he call for an Uber a lot?"

"Several times a month. If he was going out of town and didn't want to leave the car at the airport—" She stopped short. "Of course, who knows where he really goes. He might have been snuggled up with the other woman in some hotel right here in town. Or at her house!"

One person knew where he went—Evan. But he wasn't around to tell anyone. Not anymore. "Do Grady's friends know about his affair?"

"Friends? We hardly have any. I feel terribly ungrateful for complaining. Grady is hardly ever home even though he claims to be semi-retired. We live a comfortable life because of him. I've never had to pinch pennies or scrape to get by or wonder how I was going to buy food or clothes for the kids when they were young. He's been a good provider. Maybe that's why I feel so guilty about ratting on him. He's a decent person, Florrie."

I blinked and tried hard not to say what I was thinking, namely that he was a rat of a husband. I pondered how to say it without berating her. I didn't think she could take that.

"You're telling me facts, Celeste. There's no reason to feel guilty. A good man does not cheat on his wife."

She cringed. "Maybe he's doing something else that he can't tell me about?"

Like murdering people? I was ashamed of myself for even thinking it. But who knew? He seemed like a nice enough man, but one had to think that a person who disappeared on false pretenses was up to no good. "Where else could he be going, Celeste?"

"Another job? Maybe he's doing something for the government that he can't tell me about. That's not uncommon in Washington."

I could tell she had reasoned through his absences. "Then why do you think he's having an affair?"

"The credit card statements. He hides them but I know where they are. Hotels, restaurants, even the occasional jewelry store. He was in Hong Kong recently and spent quite a nice sum at a jewelry store. I guess he might be saving his purchase as a holiday gift for me, but I don't think so."

"Sounds like an affair to me."

"But the night Evan was killed . . ."

I placed my hand on her arm so she would look at me. "Why do you think he murdered Evan?"

"Because Evan knows Grady's secret and . . . Grady eats that brand of pot brownie."

I almost wanted to laugh. She was so innocent and angelic that I couldn't imagine her buying or partaking of laced brownies.

"He claims he has achy joints."

Grady was a character. More information for me to pass along to Eric.

"The son of friends of my parents just became a private investigator. Would you like his number?"

For the first time it appeared to me that she had a back-bone. "Yes. I most definitely would. If I knew where he was going and whom he was meeting, then I might know what to do."

I texted my mom for Norman's number.

She texted back immediately. *Did you break up with Eric?*

No! Someone needs a PI.

That time she sent the number. I pulled a sunset-purple coloring pencil out of my purse and jotted it on an extra napkin.

I handed it to Celeste and checked my watch, because there was something else I wanted to ask her while I had the opportunity, but I couldn't be late opening the store. I still had plenty of time. "Celeste, what happened the day Caroline disappeared?"

With a sharp intake of breath, she closed her eyes. "I will never recover from that day. Every morning when I open my eyes, my first thought is of Caroline. I can barely look John and Jacquie in the eyes. It was my daughter's birthday. Every year since then, when we celebrate her birthday, I can't focus. I go through the motions. Of course, she's an adult now with children of her own, so I rarely see her on that day anymore. I used to bake a cake, sing 'Happy Birthday,' and clap when she blew out the candles, but all I could think of was John and Jacquie. Because while we were eating cake, they knew it was the day they lost their daughter. I will never forgive myself."

I studied her eyes, her kind face, and tiny frame. The day Caroline disappeared had changed her life and left a wound that had never healed.

She took a deep breath. "It was a nice day, sunny and bright. Nine little girls came to her party. We gathered outside in our backyard. They played games and ate hot dogs, which were my daughter's favorite. We had put up pink streamers. A couple of the moms stayed to help, and I paid a neighborhood teenager, too, so the girls had plenty of supervision. Plus the man whom we hired to bring two ponies."

She took a deep breath. "Little Missy Bowlers had an accident. I left my husband in charge and took her inside to clean her up and dress her in a pair of my daughter's panties. And when I returned, there were only eight girls. We searched everywhere. Sheds, garages, other people's yards." Her lips quivered. "I still look for Caroline and check faces everywhere I go. I realize that they wouldn't look like they did back then, but that doesn't stop me. I examine every face for a hint of those girls. They were just gone."

"What about your husband? The other moms?"

"Everyone was engaged with one of the girls. Frankly, I think the moms were talking to each other and my husband was probably ogling the teenage neighbor. It's incredible to me that not one of them saw anything."

I laid my hand on her arm. "I'm sorry, Celeste."

"I wish I were as clever as you. Maybe I could have found them. If I had only turned over more stones. Confronted people, made some noise. But I didn't have it in me. Just like I know I should follow my husband. If I were braver, I would demand answers from him. But I stand by watching like a fearful doe."

Fearful? That was worrisome. "What are you afraid of?"

She turned her large eyes toward me. "That the truth will be worse than not knowing."

I probably wouldn't learn what her husband had been doing. But the thought crossed my mind that if Evan turned up every time her husband needed an Uber, perhaps they were engaged in something unlawful together. What was that old saying? Two can keep a secret if one of them is dead. I tried not to be too obvious when I glanced at my watch, but when I saw the time, I jumped to my feet. "It's been lovely having breakfast with you, but I have to go. It's time to open the bookstore. I hope we can talk again sometime."

She nodded and smiled in that calm, sad way of hers. "I'll clean these up. You run along."

"Thanks, Celeste." I almost ran—okay, it was a half run at best—but it was fast for me. I glanced back before crossing the street. Celeste had gathered our take-out boxes and was placing them neatly in a public trash bin.

As soon as the light changed, I hustled across the street. Bob lumbered up to the bookstore just as I arrived. I could see Veronica striding toward us in absurdly high heels.

"Have a good day off?" I unlocked the door and dashed inside to turn off the alarm.

"I wanted to talk with you about that." Bob stopped at the customer side of the checkout desk and Veronica joined him.

"I'm working a lot of hours," said Bob.

"I know you are. I hired Roxie part-time yesterday, and I'm still looking for one more employee."

His face brightened. "No kidding? That's great! It's like you read my mind."

"We all need to cut back a little bit. I can't keep asking Goldblum to fill in. He's a good egg to help out, but I know it's an imposition."

"I'll let you know if I think of anyone."

"You can be here tomorrow for the signing, right?"

"Are you kidding? I can't wait. Wish Griffin were coming, though."

"Me, too. But he continues to be elusive."

The day progressed in the usual manner until a woman about my mother's age walked in and stared at me. Three people stood in line to check out, so I said, "Good afternoon. I'll be with you in a moment." She didn't smile or say a word.

I focused on the people buying books. When the third one was walking out the door, I asked the waiting woman, "How can I help you?"

"Are you Florrie Fox?"

"I am."

Her chest heaved and she stiffened, her jaw twitching.

"Are you all right? Maybe you should sit down."

I came around to the front of the checkout desk, but she backed away from me. "Why did you do it? Why did you murder my daughter?"

Chapter 28

I wasn't sure who was more horrified. Me, to be accused of murder, or the woman, who thought she was in the presence of her daughter's killer.

I inhaled noisily. "You must be Cara's mother. Could I get you a cup of coffee, Mrs. Melton?"

Her mouth fell open. "Aren't you the smooth one. Is that how you fooled my little girl? By making her think you were a friend?"

What if a customer came into the store and heard her? I tried to coax her into the parlor. "Please come in and sit down."

"I wouldn't go anywhere with you," she huffed, her eyes brimming with tears.

I was having trouble holding back my own tears. "I didn't murder Cara. I didn't even touch her until she fell, and that was only to help her. She . . . she was holding on to my arm while we waited for the ambulance to arrive."

The tears crested her lower lids and drizzled down her face. "Don't lie to me. Sergeant Bridges told me what you did."

"But I didn't. I was already way down the street when it happened. I didn't see who killed Cara. Honest. She called out to me. I wouldn't have even looked back if she hadn't called my name asking for help."

Mrs. Melton dabbed her eyes with a tissue. "Then why does he think you killed her?"

I could tell her the whole story about the dry cleaner, or I could simplify it. "Because I was there. But I didn't want her to die." I tried to put a positive spin on Cara's behavior. After all, this was her grieving *mother*! "Cara was spunky. She was trying her level best to get a big story for a newspaper. I'm so sorry her life was cut short. She would have been a tenacious journalist."

"I don't believe you. If you didn't kill her, then who did?"

"I wish I knew! Mrs. Melton, do you know of any stories Cara was working on that might have upset someone?"

She looked like she might start sobbing. "Besides the one on you and the Maxwells? Oh! She was looking for that author. The one who is a recluse."

"Griffin Corbyn?"

"That's the one! She was determined to locate him."

Maybe she had found him. "I hope they catch her killer. She had a lot of life to live ahead of her."

Mrs. Melton swallowed hard. She pointed her forefinger at me and shook it. "You better find her killer if it's not you. Otherwise, I hope you go to prison for the rest of your life."

She barged out the door.

Bob ambled up to me. "Who was that? Are you okay?"

"I'm fine." To tell the truth, I was shaking like a leaf. My entire body quivered. What if Griffin had murdered her? Had he killed Evan, too? I gazed at Bob. Was Griffin walking among us, looking like an ordinary guy in a T-shirt and jeans? Not that I thought Bob was Griffin by any means, but wouldn't that be the easiest way to hide? To blend in and look like an average Joe? Gabriella had been friendly. Maybe I could weasel information out of her. I would have to know the make, model, and color of his car, along with the license plate number, to get the police to search highway cameras. How in the world could I discreetly get that information? There had to be a way.

Veronica joined Bob, and the two of them watched me like they thought I might explode.

"We have to do something, Florrie." Veronica wrapped her arms around me for a hug. "Color Me Read would be a disaster if you weren't here to run it."

"Very funny," I groused. "I need a reason to pay Gabriella a visit."

Bob grinned and disappeared for a moment. He returned with a copy of Buzz Powers's book. "We were talking about Buzz at the party, and she told me she hadn't read his book yet."

I thanked him and tied our signature ribbon around it. "Technically I'm off at six today. I'll be back as soon as I can."

Veronica said, "Bring pizza if you're coming back this way."

"Will do."

On my way over to Gabriella's house, I took a detour by Arthur's place. Mia hadn't been kidding. A FOR SALE sign stood in the yard. I couldn't really blame Arthur. I would feel the same way after being duped into going to Branigan's, where he was drugged and robbed. While I wasn't at all certain that Arthur's real intent might not be to escape someone to whom he owed money, I couldn't overlook the commonality of drugging by Rohypnol in a drink and then drugging by the high-potency brownies. For the life of me, and in this case my life and freedom might be at stake, I couldn't tie them together in any meaningful way, except that they both involved Arthur. Maybe I could drop by Arthur's house later for a chat with him.

I made my way to Gabriella's pretty place, let myself through the gate, and knocked on the door. I could hear her moving inside. She answered the door breathlessly and shoved her hair back off her face. "Florrie! How nice to see you. Come on in."

I handed her Buzz's book and walked inside. "Bob said you wanted a copy."

"He's such a nice guy. I'm surprised that he remembered. Could I offer you some lemonade?"

"That would be great!"

Her expression suggested that she had offered in the hope I would decline.

She disappeared into the kitchen. "Are we still on for to-morrow?" she called.

"Yes. I'm looking forward to it." I quickly scanned the room. It looked almost as perfect as it had the last time I was there. A throw had fallen to the floor, though. I picked it up, revealing a pair of men's shoes. They were light tan slip-on loafers made of lovely soft leather. Griffin! He was home! I looked around. Had he dashed upstairs when I knocked on the door?

"Is Griffin coming?" I asked, hurrying over to the big boots by the door. I compared the sizes. The loafer looked small compared to the boot. I checked the size of the loafer. Twelve. Was that why Griffin avoided publicity? Because he wasn't a big strapping guy? That would be silly, but stranger things had happened. I put the boot back and scooted across the room to replace the shoe and cover them with the throw.

"I love your house!" I said, heading into the kitchen. It was every bit as sweet and romantic as the living room. A window over the farmhouse sink let in light and offered a view of the backyard. Shabby-style white cabinets mixed with open shelving, which showed off her collection of teapots and teacups. Four chairs painted the green of milk glass surrounded a rustic tawny wood table. A chandelier hung from the rafters that crossed the ceiling.

"This is beautiful. What a treat to cook in here."

Gabriella smiled. "I love this house. I have to show you my little porch. I call it my studio." She opened a door and led the way into a good-size room decorated in white, pink, and milk-glass green. A sofa covered in colorful chintz sat under a window. On the other side, a long desk ran the length of one wall in front of a window. A computer and a printer rested on the top, surrounded by papers and notes. Two easels flanked it. One held a partially finished painting of flowers in a bucket. The other was being used as a storyboard.

"This is my work in progress." She had attached images of people and castles from magazines. Index cards were pinned in straight rows.

"Do you have a title yet?"

"I'm still working on it. Do you like *One More Kiss* or *The Last Kiss?*"

I was considering when I turned around to a small stone fireplace. A long-haired cat looked up at me. "Is that Chewie?"

"He loves it in here. This used to be a porch, but I had it enclosed. It's my little hideaway."

"It's so cozy. I think I like *The Last Kiss*. It contains a note of melancholy in it."

Gabriella sucked in air. "Exactly! That's what I think."

"Does Griffin have a writing space of his own, too?"

"Of course! Each of us needs a quiet space of our own. Besides, all our little notes would get mixed up if we worked in the same area. What a nightmare that would be!"

Chewie jumped up on the desk to be stroked. Gabriella indulged him by scratching his cheeks. She was on her way back toward the kitchen when he rubbed against something that clinked. I looked over at him.

Four venetian-glass sticks were clustered in a bowl. They were bold indigo blue, sea-glass green, gold, and apricot. I backpedaled and pulled one out. It didn't appear to have an obvious purpose. On the end of each was sort of a clear-glass flame with a tip sharp enough to slice my finger open when I touched it. I grabbed a tissue and wrapped it around my finger. "Do these have a use or are they just pretty?"

Gabriella returned. "They're calligraphy pens. A gift from Arthur. Calligraphy is another interest that we share."

Arthur again. I examined the tip of one. I had already proven that it could easily pierce skin. A chill flooded through me. "Does he have a set?"

"Probably. That's how I shop, don't you? One for this person, one for that person, and one for me."

They were the kind of thing he probably kept in his work-room. Had he thrown them out because they were evidence? Or were they hidden from sight? "Did you know that he's selling his house?"

"No! He loves that place. No way. I don't believe it."

"I saw the FOR SALE sign on my way over here."

"I'm stunned. I have to give him a call."

Trying to buy time, I sipped my lemonade slowly and eyed the pens. "Where do you put the ink?"

"You have to dip them. See the point on the clear end? Arthur is crazy for venetian and Murano glass. It's the only thing he really collects. That and enemies."

Now she had my attention. "Why do you say that?"

"I love Arthur. Not in a weird way. He taught me a lot about this crazy business of writing and publishing. But he wasn't close to many people. Those few, like Jacquie and me, and his mom, could do no wrong. He accepted us warts and all. But he was wary of other people. They thought he was delightful because he asked so many questions about them. It seemed as though he was showing real interest in them, you know? Initially, I thought it was because he was a writer. Part of the natural curiousness about people one must have to cre-ate characters. But as I grew to know him better, I realized that he was digging for their dirt. People told him remarkable things about themselves. And if they didn't, he did his own research. He knew about the dark, dusty corners of their lives. The things they didn't want brought out into daylight. I think it helped him develop characters, but sometimes I wondered if it wasn't to have an upper hand. Arthur is a class-A manipulator of people. He gets what he wants from them, and it isn't by being kind. You see, when he knows someone's secrets, he holds all the cards."

"Did he know your secrets?"

Gabriella laughed. "I'm not a genius. But I learn fast."

"Are you saying that he blackmailed people?"

"Not in the conventional way. I don't think he ever demanded money. He had enormous wealth, even when he ran through most of the investments. He could always sell some expensive paintings that he owned. He could have taken a mortgage on his property. It's worth millions. But he told me he would never put himself in the position of having to sell his house. 'Gabriella, darlin',' she said, mimicking him. 'I have been extraordinarily lucky in my life. Every time I need money, it arrives.' Plus, it wasn't beneath him to take on odd jobs for money. He told everyone it was research for a book, but I knew the truth about that."

"What kind of jobs did he take on?"

"He was an excellent bartender. And he loved driving for Uber. He liked to say, 'Everyone has a story.'"

"Did anyone ever threaten him?"

She giggled. "That was a regular occurrence." She lowered her voice to mimic a man's. "'Bedlingham, if word gets back to my wife, I'll ruin you.' They were all idle threats from people who were sorry they'd blabbed so much."

I saw the time on a clock and felt terribly guilty for having been gone from the store so long.

"Did he have children? Do you know who would inherit the house?"

"He didn't have any children. He had a lot of girlfriends, but he never married or fathered children." Gabriella shot me a glance. "That I know of."

I followed her to a closet. She bent over, looking for something.

Griffin's coats hung there. One was a camel-colored winter coat. It looked small for a guy who wore those huge boots. Next to it hung an extra-large black raincoat. I could see the size on the label.

Gabriella held out a garment. "Hold that for me, will you?"

The scent of lavender drifted to me from a bulky sweater with traditional leather patches on the elbows. "Is this Griffin's?"

"Sure is."

I wondered how he felt about the lavender smell. There was no reason in the world that men couldn't enjoy nice scents. But it was a size small. About right for me. If the boots and this sweater belonged to Griffin, then he had an unusual build. A thin body with giant feet.

"Here they are! I knew I ordered bookmarks for my next book." Gabriella took the sweater and handed me a stack of bookmarks.

"Thanks! Our customers will love them." I returned to the kitchen and set down my lemonade glass. Gabriella was right behind me.

"When you worked for Arthur, was he into drugs?"

"Funny thing about that. Arthur read a lot and was always current on trends and what was cool. He told me he smoked one joint and one cigarette and that was enough for him to know what they were all about. He had a reputation as this incredibly cool guy. He wasn't like other stuffy teachers, he had seen and done it all. His students saw him as sort of a generational icon. But in truth, drugs didn't interest him."

She rinsed the glasses. "He flaunted the latest thing, the best thing, the most expensive thing."

"Have you spoken to Griffin?"

"No. He must be in the zone, concentrating on his book."

"That's too bad. I do wish he could come tomorrow. Where is he again?"

"The Chesapeake Bay."

"That's what? A two-hour drive?"

"Something like that."

I crossed the room, hoping for a glimpse of something, anything really, that might tie Griffin to Cara. I tried to appeal to her. "Gabriella, I'm in trouble. Did you hear about Cara Melton's murder?"

"It was terrible! Right here in our neighborhood, too. And in broad daylight!"

"The police are trying to pin her murder on me."

"What?" She backed away from me.

"I didn't do it! Here's the thing. Cara desperately wanted to break a big story. That's why she was following me and taking photos of my parents. She was also trying to unveil Griffin."

Gabriella slowly lowered herself onto the couch. Her face had gone pale.

"That's why *I'm* eager to talk to Griffin. To find out what he might know about her or someone who might have been out to get her." There, I thought I managed that without claiming Griffin could have killed her. But from the look of shock on Gabriella's face, I suspected she read neatly between the lines.

She placed her open palms on the couch on either side of her legs and stared, wide-eyed, at me.

I stopped talking, hoping she would finally put me in touch with Griffin.

"This explains so much. I thought I heard someone in the back about a week ago. I bet she was following me, too."

"Or Griffin."

"Or Griffin," Gabriella repeated weakly. "This is so disturbing. I had no idea. So you think she was tailing someone else. Or had dirt on them and that's who murdered her?"

"That would make sense. I'm afraid she went too far pursuing someone. Maybe she found out someone's deep, dark secret and he killed her to keep it hidden."

Gabriella's eyes finally met mine. "Someone dangerous." Her voice was breathy, almost like a whisper. "Florrie, you have to be careful!"

"Why? I don't know anyone's secret."

"But in investigating, you might encounter that person. Or maybe you already know the secret, but you don't realize it."

Chapter 29

That was a horrifying thought. What could I possibly know that no one else knew? As she talked, it occurred to me that Jacquie and Arthur's bizarre night before the wedding could fall into that category. But I didn't know who had arranged that. It could have been set up by Arthur himself.

I tried to bring her back to Griffin. "Please, Gabriella, if I could just talk to Griffin. Maybe *he* knows something."

"I'm pretty sure he doesn't. He would have mentioned it to me."

"Can we try? Could you just call him?"

She looked at her watch. "I'll try to reach him tonight. I'll let you know what I find out." She stood up, a signal that she was dismissing me.

I wished that I could grab her phone to get his number. I wished she had the number lying around on a scrap of paper somewhere so I could memorize it. But wishes weren't going to make anything happen. I thanked her for my lemonade and left the house. I stood outside on the sidewalk, deciding where to go. Back to the store or over to Arthur's house? I stashed the bookmarks in my purse.

I turned left, and when I walked by Gabriella's house, I

could definitely make out two people inside. I couldn't tell who they were, but I had to believe they were Gabriella and Griffin.

Every fiber of my being itched to run back to the door, hope it wasn't locked, and barge in on them. But I couldn't bring myself to do it. Gabriella had probably locked the door. If that was the case, Griffin could disappear upstairs again. And then what? I would chase him through the house? Look in the closets to find him?

Arthur had met Griffin. Maybe he could give me some advice or smooth the way for Griffin to be willing to meet me. That might be the safer course of action.

I crossed the street and gave Gabriella's house one last look before heading for Arthur's home.

As I neared Jezebel's house, a shiny white Cadillac Escalade pulled up in front of Arthur's house. Two men stepped out. One looked familiar. I hurried forward, trying not to trip over my own feet.

"Florrie?" said the taller man, whom I recognized as Professor Maxwell's brother-in-law, the one married to the professor's odious sister, Liddy.

"Walter! What are you doing here?"

"I came to see this house." He introduced me to his Realtor, who knocked on the front door.

"They're supposed to be out, but I have learned the hard way never to assume anything," said the Realtor.

"You're moving? Where's Liddy?"

"I would love to respond to that with *who cares*." Walter grimaced. "Liddy and I are splitting up. I'm shopping for a house for myself."

"I'm sorry to hear that."

"Don't be. I'm not a young man anymore. I believe I am entitled to some years of joy and peace. Heaven knows I have earned them."

"Yes, I believe you deserve that. What will Liddy do?"

The Realtor swung the door open and beckoned to Walter. I could see the magnificent glass sculpture glowing as the sun hit it.

"Would you give us a moment, please?" asked Walter.

"Certainly." The Realtor stepped into the house.

Walter took a deep breath. "This isn't easy for me. I can only imagine the terrible stories Liddy will invent. I don't know if I will ever see Maxwell and Jacquie again. Would you please let them, and Mr. DuBois, whom I hold in such high esteem, know that Liddy has found someone else?"

"She told you?"

"Liddy admit wrongdoing?" He smiled sadly. "The night of the wedding, Liddy left our room. I pretended to sleep, but when she didn't return, I ventured into the house, thinking perhaps she couldn't sleep and was having a drink with Jacquie. But I ran into Jacquie. Liddy wasn't with her."

"Where was Rosie?"

"Snoring in our room. I imagine the party wore her out. Jacquie poured each of us a glass of exquisite sherry and took me upstairs to the attic, which she plans to renovate as her office. She showed me the floor plans. It will be wonderful. Not unlike a Parisian garret in some ways. Each of us went off to bed, but Liddy didn't show up until just before dawn."

"You don't suppose . . ." I didn't want to say it aloud.

"That she killed Evan?" He squeezed his eyes closed in pain for a moment. "Jacquie told me about the brownies. They're the brand Liddy buys."

"Are you saying that Liddy partied with Evan and accidentally killed him?"

He whispered, "I don't know. It's possible. She's been getting texts from someone. I don't know who. But I do know something is going on. I've moved out of the house. I . . . I'm ashamed to say it, but I couldn't sleep in the same house with her. I was afraid of what she might do to me." He felt in his pocket for a business card and wrote on it before he handed it to me. "That's my new private number. Please don't give it to Liddy." He looked me in the eyes. "Thank you for listening to my sad story."

"I think I speak for Maxwell, Jacquie, and Mr. DuBois when I say that you are always welcome at the mansion and the carriage house."

He leaned over and kissed me on the cheek. "Thank you, Florrie."

Walter turned and walked into the house. The door closed behind him.

His news came as a shock, but I knew he would be much happier without having to deal with Liddy anymore. I just hoped she wouldn't be moving into the mansion. I cringed at the mere thought.

On the way back to the bookstore, I stopped for a pizza. Half meat lovers for Bob and half roasted veggies for Veronica. When I delivered it, I ate a slice while I brought the two of them up to speed. I worked the floor the rest of my shift, while Veronica concentrated on her social media magic, reminding people that we would be hosting an author signing on Friday.

I trudged home at seven thirty, on the lookout for anyone following me. I didn't see anyone. Still, I locked the door behind me as soon as I was in my cottage. Peaches stretched as if I had awakened her and ambled toward me purring.

I made myself a roast beef sandwich from thawed wedding leftovers and a heavenly horseradish mayonnaise. I gave Peaches a choice between shrimp in aspic or chicken and liver for kitties. She chose the chicken and liver, though I was pretty sure she didn't actually know what was inside the unopened can she rubbed her cheek on.

After dinner I settled on the sofa with a cup of steaming

tea and my sketch pad. I had so many thoughts that I hardly knew where to begin.

But I started on my phone, checking men's shoe sizes. Hmm. The average shoe size for men was between nine and twelve. So those size twelve loafers of Griffin's were actually on the large side. What was going on with those huge boots? I sketched the boots and the loafers. That didn't help at all. I moved on to Jezebel's sweet face with surprisingly few wrinkles for a woman her age.

But perhaps the most significant thing wasn't a person, but an object. I drew the glass calligraphy pens as I recalled them. They weren't long. About six inches, I guessed. That seemed too short, so I grabbed a measuring tape and checked the length of my pens. I was shocked to find most were only five and a half inches long, although I had a collection of colored pencils that measured seven inches.

For purposes of murder, though, that was probably enough, as long as the tip was sufficiently sharp to break skin and hit the jugular. I'd been cut by broken glass before. It might not be enough to kill someone by a punch in the shoulder, but the neck contained the jugular, which would bleed out fast. The tips of the pens were tiny and angled so the pen would be suitable for the sweeping thin-to-broad lines of calligraphy.

I looked up glass calligraphy pens and found the exact ones that I had seen at Gabriella's house. They came in a set of five. But Gabriella only had four. If I was right about the calligraphy pens, that narrowed down the suspects in Cara's death to Arthur, Gabriella, and Griffin. I discounted Gabriella because I liked her. That wasn't a good reason, and I knew it, but I just couldn't imagine her trying to kill anyone.

I wished I knew how to get into Arthur's house to snoop. Jacquie still had a key, but Arthur, Mia, or both were likely to be there. How stupid could I be? All I had to do was pose as a buyer. I didn't think I would be credible in that role, though.

I called Jacquie and explained the situation. She readily agreed to call a Realtor friend. I felt guilty about taking up a Realtor's time on false pretenses, but Jacquie quickly said, "Good grief, Florrie, this is murder we're talking about!"

We ended the call, but she texted me ten minutes later to say we could meet at the house at eight thirty the next morning.

I returned to my sketches, drawing Walter. He had lost weight, I realized. Was he afraid to eat food at home? He'd said he couldn't sleep out of fear of what Liddy might do. He had come to the store when his son was murdered, and I had felt terrible for him. He seemed like a nice man.

Peaches and I were up early the next morning. I dressed in a sky-blue top that picked up on the blues in a peach, pink, and blue flower-patterned skirt. The flowing design always made me think of watercolors. I apologized to Peaches for leaving her home and promised to let her spend some time out in the garden soon.

At exactly eight fifteen, I knocked on the back door of the mansion.

Jacquie bubbled with enthusiasm for our project. "I would have suggested that we meet somewhere for breakfast, but DuBois goes to so much trouble for us. It's almost an insult to him if I go out for breakfast. He's kind of sensitive that way."

"I've noticed that. Has he showed you the jadeite pig?"

"It's so sweet. I'm putting it in a book. On its face it's sort of silly, I guess, but I'm imagining a man in love bringing it back from a business trip to Asia as a gift for his true love so she will always have good fortune."

Jacquie was such a romantic. I described what we were looking for and asked her to divert her friend's attention.

The Realtor turned out to be nearly as talkative and out-going as Jacquie. As soon as they moved toward the kitchen, I scrambled upstairs as fast and quietly as I could. I sped through modern bedrooms with clean lines and virtually no bric-a-brac. The master bedroom offered more in the way of décor, but as I gazed into the wastebasket, it dawned on me that if I had attacked someone with a venetian-glass calligraphy pen, I would have thrown it away. In fact, I would probably have bothered to drive out of town and pop it into a dumpster somewhere. My brilliant idea to search the house was nothing but a big, fat bomb.

I could hear the Realtor's and Jacquie's voices as they walked up the stairs. When I saw them on the landing, I said, "I hope you don't mind me skipping ahead. I've seen most of the downstairs before. The master bedroom is beautiful."

That started them on a new topic, and I raced up the open staircase to the third floor with cats following me.

The room on the third floor should probably have been broken into several rooms. The absence of walls was both daunting and freeing. The back of the house and the ceiling were all glass. It was an artist's dream. Natural light flooded the entire area. Two cozy chairs overlooked the garden and tree-tops. A few roofs were visible beyond them. I looked around for an easel. There was none, but a table and fancy desk chair offered space to work. The room took my breath away. Forcing myself to concentrate on the task at hand, I searched for cabinets or drawers where one might stash art supplies.

I found the drawers cleverly built into a wall. If I hadn't been looking for storage, I would never have noticed them. And there, among bottles of ink and stacks of beautiful paper for calligraphy, lay a collection of special pens. Among them, four venetian calligraphy pens in indigo blue, sea-glass green, gold, and apricot.

Chapter 30

I could hardly wait to call Eric. But Jacquie and the Realtor had just walked into the glass room and were gushing over the light and the view.

While they raved, it dawned on me that I hadn't seen a storyboard like Gabriella had. Mia had said Arthur worked downstairs. Maybe the third floor with all the gorgeous windows became too hot or too cold for hours of writing.

I walked down the two flights of stairs, thinking they would be treacherous if one was intoxicated, as rumor had it that Arthur often was. In the room that I thought of as a library because of the walls of books, I gazed around for any sign of writing. Arthur's laptop lay on the desk as it had before. The trash had been emptied and the scraps of paper with *J* on them were gone. I told myself I was getting carried away. Not every writer used a storyboard. And maybe Arthur was taking a break. Maybe he wrote in fits and then stopped entirely for a week before he started again. There were loads of explanations.

Still, the missing calligraphy pen was evidence.

Jacquie and the Realtor returned to the first floor. I could hear Jacquie thanking her. I joined them to add my thanks and say goodbye. Jacquie and I stepped outside.

"Well?"

"One of the pens is missing. I'm going to let Eric know. It's not definitive. I'm sure glass pens break all the time. What I don't know is what Cara might have discovered about Arthur that led him to kill her."

We paused on the sidewalk and heard a rapping noise. Like a woodpecker hitting glass.

The two of us looked around.

"There!" Jacquie pointed at the second floor of Jezebel's house and waved.

Sure enough, Jezebel rapped on the window and waved at us vigorously. I waved back.

"I know Arthur. He could be verbally vicious, but I never saw him be violent. If all the evidence leads to Arthur, then I'll be astonished."

We walked as she talked.

"Arthur took his anger out on his characters, not on real people. Does that make sense to you? He put his anger on the page."

"Is his house always that tidy?"

She laughed. "He's a neat freak. He would rather have one, usually expensive, item that he loves than one hundred tchotchkes. Like that venetian glass sculpture in the foyer. The one with all the colors? It's one of his most prized possessions. He's the same way with clothes. I have a closet full of things I can't even fit into anymore, yet I keep them in the hope that I'll whittle off twenty pounds. Not Arthur. He purchases expensive clothes, but not many. It's very difficult to buy him gifts. All he likes are books. And they are precious to him. Did you see the library? They are organized in precise order, and heaven help you if one gets misplaced on a different shelf."

We had reached Color Me Read. "What about the night you don't remember?"

"I no longer think Arthur had anything to do with that. My credit card company has informed me that it was used by someone before I was able to report it. The person who took it bought a pair of inexpensive sneakers, socks, an expensive video game, and a take-out dinner from a fast-food place. That doesn't sound like Arthur at all."

"Seems like a lot of trouble to go to for those purchases."

She shrugged. "On the bright side, I'm looking forward to tonight. See you later!"

I unlocked the bookstore and turned off the alarm. I still had fifteen minutes before we opened. I put on the coffee and was sorry I hadn't stopped for baked goods. While the coffee brewed, I grabbed a sapphire-blue pencil and a sheet of paper to try to make sense of things.

Arthur's lean figure went at the top with an *R*. No matter what Jacquie wanted to think of her former beau, he was involved in whatever was going on. And Cara had said *R* in her dying moments. Not to mention *faux*. Had she not been able to make a *th* sound? Then I drew the victims, Evan and Cara. I did not want to draw Gabriella. But she and Griffin had major connections to Evan and Cara.

I studied the paper and shuddered at the thought of seeing Arthur at the signing. The bell tinkled over the door, letting me know that someone had entered. I was relieved to see Veronica. Even better, she was carrying a box of doughnuts!

"I know these aren't the healthiest, but I was starved and running late this morning, so I picked them up on my way."

I poured each of us a mug of coffee and filled her in while we munched on pillowy doughnuts covered with chocolate icing.

"Let's look at this from a different angle," said Veronica. "Who left their rooms the night Evan died?"

"Jacquie, Walter, and his wife, Liddy. But Walter claims he ran into Jacquie, and they talked about renovating the attic as her writing room. So that leaves—"

"The wicked witch?"

"That's the one! And Walter says that she eats the same brand of brownies with high-potency pot in them."

"Ohh, now we've got something. And who has the glass pens you think could have been used to murder Cara?"

"Arthur, Gabriella, and Griffin."

"And clearly Arthur could have walked over from his house to make sure Evan died. *And* Arthur was with Jacquie the night before the wedding when she disappeared."

"And Cara said *R-faux* when she was dying."

"There you have it!" Veronica clinked her mug against mine in celebration.

"I'm going to tell Eric. The trouble is there's nothing conclusive, except Jacquie's fingerprints on the brownie box." Customers entered the store, breaking up our conversation.

Just before eleven, my mother arrived with her friend Mrs. Spratt, mother of the unappealing yet persistent Norman.

"Florrie! Thank heaven you're safe." Mom placed her purse on the checkout counter and extracted her wallet. "Now I want you girls to take an Uber to and from the store for the time being. I saw on the news that there's a murderer on the loose in Georgetown. He killed a girl about your age in broad daylight. They have a suspect, I think they call them 'persons of interest' now, but I don't want you two walking around Georgetown until they arrest him." She placed a wad of bills on the counter and patted them with her hand.

I debated telling her that I was the suspect. Maybe not in front of her friend, though. I didn't want to embarrass Mom. I shoved the money in her direction. "Thanks, Mom, but I feel quite confident that we're safe."

Mrs. Spratt clutched her handbag with both of her hands as though she expected someone to seize it from her and run. "Norman told me how kind you were to refer business to him. His father and I appreciate that, but we know you run with a rough crowd, so please don't ever do that again."

The thought of delicate Celeste as part of a *rough crowd* amused me.

My mom shook her head. "We are so sad for the woman whose husband is having an affair. The woman in the photos is a pretty blonde but it's horrible of her to be seducing someone else's husband!"

My mouth dropped open. "He showed you the photos?" Wasn't there some kind of regulation against that? Celeste's problems weren't anyone else's business.

I started to say so, but Mrs. Spratt wasn't finished yet.

"I must tell you that I have mixed feelings about your renewed interest in Norman." She shook her forefinger at me. "Do not involve him in your murderous escapades. I wish I could stop you from loving him. He's the most wonderful son and I won't have anything bad happen to him. But your adoration for him is so deep that you don't listen to me and stay away from him." She dipped into her handbag for a handkerchief and dabbed at her eyes.

My head spun. Why, oh why, would Mrs. Spratt think I was in love with Norman? I tried to smile reassuringly. "Mrs. Spratt, I have no interest in your son." Did that sound cold? I added cheerfully, "I'm still dating Eric!"

Happily, Veronica happened by, and Mom launched into her spiel about the murderer who was loose.

Veronica handed the money back to her. "You have nothing to worry about. Florrie is the person of interest."

I thought Mrs. Spratt might faint.

"That's not even remotely funny, Veronica," scolded Mom

as she and Veronica helped Mrs. Spratt to a chair in the parlor. I brought her a glass of cold water, but my mother intercepted it and downed it in one long drag.

"Tell me that is not true," she hissed. "That Veronica is joking around."

"I happened to be nearby when she was murdered."

Mom gasped. "You mean it could have been you who was murdered?"

"No, it couldn't have. Mom, the woman who was murdered was the one who pretended to be a wedding photographer and took pictures of you and Dad at the wedding."

Mom sat down next to Mrs. Spratt. Her brow furrowed. "I don't understand."

"She wanted DNA from you and Professor Maxwell in a wildly misguided notion that you are actually Caroline Maxwell."

Mom sat up straight. "But that's crazy."

"Exactly."

"And that's why you killed her?" shrieked Mrs. Spratt, pushing herself back against the chair cushion as if she thought I might do her in, too.

"Mrs. Spratt, I did not kill her. Someone else did."

"Then why do they suspect you?"

"Because I was there."

"Why didn't you tell me this?" asked Mom.

"Because I didn't want a scene like this!"

At that exact moment, Jezebel, her eyes wide and her white curls frizzing around her head like a Chia Pet, burst into the parlor out of breath. "Help me, Florrie! Help me!"

"Who is that?" asked Mom.

"Part of the rough crowd I hang with."

I walked over to her and helped her to a chair. "Let me get you some coffee."

She grasped my hand. "She'll find me here!"

"Who?"

"Kaylee!"

She popped out of her chair, totally unaware that Mom and Mrs. Spratt were watching as if a TV drama were unfolding. "Where can I hide?"

"Come back to the kitchen with me." When we passed Veronica, I whispered, "Mom and Mrs. Spratt are all yours."

I settled Jezebel in a chair with a cup of coffee and closed the door to the kitchen. "What happened?"

Jezebel relaxed. "I hate being old. Why do they think they have to treat me like a child? I am still compos mentis." She snorted and giggled. "Kaylee told me I couldn't watch my soaps unless I ate my applesauce. So I went to the fridge, got out the applesauce, and threw the whole jar on the tile floor. Then I asked her, 'Do you still want me to eat it?' While she was cleaning it up, I snuck out." Jezebel smiled dreamily. "It was *wonderful* to see people and store windows and dogs again. So refreshing to see life going on all around me. And the smells! I have to find out where that delicious smell was coming from."

I offered her a doughnut. "Mercy! I forgot doughnuts exist." She bit into it, shaking her head from side to side. "Mmm. Dee-licious!" She finished her doughnut, ate a second one, and downed it with coffee. "Do you think my children are getting revenge? I thought I was a kind mother. But they must hate me to put me through this."

"I bet they worry about you. Would you mind if I called Fish to let him know you're safe and sound?"

"All right. Fish is the only decent one in the whole bunch. But don't you dare tell him where I am."

I nodded my agreement. "I have to get back to work. Are you okay here? Do you need anything?"

"I'm happy as a lark."

When I returned to the checkout desk, Veronica was getting rid of Mom and Mrs. Spratt.

"Is that old lady all right?" asked Mom.

I stared at the two of them. "Why don't you take her to lunch with you? She's a lot of fun."

Mom said, "I bet she never goes out. Veronica, go get her."

"Honestly, Linda, I think your girls get their alarming behavior from you," said Mrs. Spratt. "Who takes a stranger to lunch?"

Mom just laughed. "We do!"

"Now watch out for someone named Kaylee. Jezebel is on the run from her. But it's all right. I'm calling her grandson to let him know she's safe."

Jezebel was delighted to join them for lunch. As they left, I whispered to her, "Don't believe anything Mrs. Spratt says about me."

Jezebel rubbed her hands together. "Oh, I can't wait to hear the dirt!"

I phoned Fish to let him know Jezebel was in good hands. He promised to call off Kaylee.

Time had flown by. Bob brought folding chairs up from the basement while I shoved furniture around in the parlor to make room for the signing. In between helping customers, we put out books by our guest authors.

At ten minutes past two, I answered the store's landline phone.

"Hello. This is Arthur Bedlingham." He spoke slowly in a low voice and coughed.

Chapter 31

"Hi! This is Florrie Fox. We met at Jacquie's party."

"I . . . remember you. About the signing. I'm not up to it today."

"I hope you're not sick."

"Not well at all. So sorry." The phone clicked and went dead.

And just like that, we were down to three authors. I hoped *they* would come! I even hoped Griffin would have a change of heart and join us.

We put out a few of Arthur's books anyway, especially his biggest seller, *The Death of Mrs. Grimkill.*

Mom brought Jezebel back. And Bob left to pick up sandwiches for us to eat and assorted pastries that I had ordered for the signing.

Veronica and I set up one long table where the authors would sign. The podium was in place. Jezebel threw a yellow-and-white tablecloth over another table in the back.

The bell rang at the checkout counter, and I rushed to help the customer who was waiting to pay for three books and a coffeepot. Behind her, the next customer bought two books and three boxes of assorted teas.

I was beginning to wonder what was up since coffeepots and tea didn't usually fly out of the store. As I walked toward the kitchen, I heard Jezebel saying, "If I were you, I would buy some of these darling packs of note cards as favors and order pastries from Antoine's. I just had lunch there and they were fabulous. Isn't that really all you need? I mean these are adults, they're not expecting balloons and ice cream."

I scuttled back to the checkout desk and within minutes, a woman plopped twelve adult coloring books on the counter. She followed that with twelve packs of elegant floral note cards, two oversize rolls of wrapping paper, and twelve romance books by Jacquie and Gabriella. "I'm hosting my book club tomorrow evening. I love your employee with the white hair. She had the best suggestions! I spent all week worrying about what to do, and she solved all my problems in minutes."

That Jezebel! She continued to surprise me.

Jacquie arrived at five thirty, followed by Gabriella and Buzz. We planned to begin with a chat involving all three of them. Veronica offered to be the moderator, which suited me just fine.

To my great surprise, book reviewer Margarite Herbert-Grant strolled in. She wore a silk blouse, trousers, and a bulky black leather jacket that looked expensive but fit her like a sack. She strolled over to me. "Hello, Florrie. I'm pleased to see so many readers. You have a fine turnout."

"Thank you for coming. I believe you've never been here before. There are two more floors of books."

Her eyebrows rose. "That's larger than I expected." She scanned the parlor. "Where's Arthur?"

"I'm afraid he had to cancel. He's home sick tonight."

"Pity. Have you heard anything about the content of his upcoming book?"

"Only the publicity his publisher has put out."

She wandered over to Jacquie. They exchanged a few

words before Jacquie hustled over to me. "What's the deal with Arthur? Is he really sick?"

"He sounded sick on the phone. Are you going to call him?"

"No." She said it firmly, and I thought I detected some anger. "Arthur is my past. I have fond memories but it's time for me to look to my future with Maxwell. I wish Arthur well, truly I do. But he is no longer on my middle-of-the-night rescue list. Those days are over." With that she wiped her hands against each other dramatically.

The professor joined us, and Jacquie melted into the arm he placed around her back. "Are you ready to go onstage?"

"Have I ever told you how wonderful you are?" asked Jacquie, looking up at him.

"In a million little ways."

Veronica called the authors to their seats and began the discussion. I hustled to the doorway that led from the parlor to the checkout desk so I could assist any customers who had questions or might leave early and want to buy a book.

Veronica asked great questions about their research and how they came up with ideas. The audience paid rapt attention.

I hustled behind the checkout counter to help a customer. The line grew and Bob stepped in to help.

By nine thirty the crowd had cleared, and we had sold a boatload of books. I ventured into the parlor to personally thank each of the authors.

Jacquie hugged me and whispered, "I'm glad Arthur didn't come. He would have tried to steal the show."

Gabriella beamed. "This was so much fun. I think I may have gotten some new readers."

Buzz shook my hand. "Thank you for inviting me. I hope we can do this again."

Jezebel had taken it upon herself to wrap up the leftover pastries and wash the coffee and hot-water urns.

"I feel like I should pay you," I said.

She laughed. "That's funny. I feel like I should pay you. This is the most fun I've had in a long, long time. What a wonderful day. Be sure to thank your mother again for taking me to lunch. Mrs. Spratt is a bit of a pill, but your mom was simply delightful!"

"Would you like me to call Fish to walk you home?"

"Don't bother him! I know these streets like the veins on the backs of my old hands."

I couldn't let her walk alone. "All right. Wait for me so we can walk home together." I didn't give her a chance to refuse.

When I was on the third floor, Veronica sidled up to me. "I was worried about seeing Buzz. I guess he figured out that I was avoiding him because he was polite but distant."

"You achieved what you wanted, I guess."

She took a deep breath. "I'm glad that's over."

Shortly before ten, Veronica, Bob, and I had been through every room in the bookstore to make sure all the customers had left. Relieved and exhausted, I locked the door, ready to go home and relax. But first, I had to walk Jezebel home.

Jezebel clutched a signed copy of Gabriella's latest book and carried it like it was a treasure. The two of them walked in front of Buzz and me. Night had fallen on Washington, but the streetlights lighted our way. Someone, probably Kaylee, had left the lights on for Jezebel.

No lights glowed at Arthur's house. I hoped he was okay. As we walked, I watched the dark windows of his house for any sign of life, but there was none.

At her front door, Jezebel bent over and dropped the book she was carrying.

Gabriella and I looked at each other quizzically.

"May I help you?" I leaned over to pick up the book and caught a glimpse of Buzz's shoe. My breath caught in my throat.

Surely that was the same leather loafer I had seen under the throw in Gabriella's house.

I straightened and handed Jezebel her book, trying my best to avoid looking at Buzz. I held out my hand to Jezebel. "The key?"

"It's under the flowerpot with the geranium in it."

"Jezebel!" scolded Buzz. "Never leave your key in an obvious place like that. Every burglar knows to look there."

I lifted the pot and readily found the key, but I lingered for just a moment to double-check what I thought I had seen. The lighting wasn't perfect, but Buzz's shoes looked light tan to me. I pretended to sway and not-so-accidentally touched one of his shoes. Soft as butter. They had to be the same shoes I had seen!

"Oops, sorry about that. It's been a long day." I unlocked the door and handed Jezebel the key. "Maybe Fish can help you find a new place to keep the key. Thanks for pitching in at the store today. You were wonderful!" I hugged her frail frame.

"Can I come again tomorrow?"

Her request took me by surprise. "Absolutely!" I was on the verge of offering to walk her to the store in the morning but decided she might feel differently about it the next day.

The three of us said good night and she closed the door.

"Jezebel!" shouted Buzz. "Lock the door!"

A loud clank sounded in the night.

I thanked Gabriella and Buzz for coming to the signing and crossed the street to go home. I paused and watched them. Were they holding hands?

Keeping my eyes on them, I moved into the shadows and followed them on the opposite side of the street. They turned at the corner. Maybe he was being a gentleman and walking her home. They *were* headed in the direction of her house.

I crossed the street again and caught sight of them. I scurried from tree to tree until they stopped in front of her home. They embraced in a passionate kiss. I *knew* I was right about his shoes!

I couldn't believe it. I had thought her reclusive husband had come home, but it was Buzz who hid in the house while I was there. They were having an affair.

Could Cara have discovered their secret? Maybe she had been tailing Gabriella in the hope she would be led to Griffin and had caught her in flagrante with Buzz.

But then why had Buzz been interested in Veronica? As a decoy? Was Veronica supposed to throw Cara off track? I gasped. Had he been spying on us? Had he used Veronica and gossip at the bookstore to find out if anyone knew about his relationship with Gabriella? He was FBI, after all, even if he had only been in human resources. Or had he simply given up on Veronica and hooked up with Gabriella?

I turned to go home and out of the corner of my eye saw someone dart toward me. I'd forgotten about my own stalker!

Chapter 32

I had no weapons. Nothing, not even a whistle. I held on to my purse by the long over-the-shoulder strap and slung it around at the person's head. It made impact with a satisfying smack, and as I ran away, I heard someone moan. I didn't look back.

My breath came hard, and I knew I couldn't outrun the average fourth grader. Why was I on a residential street where I couldn't dodge into a building? I didn't dare slow down enough to search for a hiding place in the dark. I chugged on, motivated by fear. I almost cheered when a bar came into sight. I dashed across the street, flung open the door, and darted inside. I found a window that looked out on the street and leaned against the bar, panting.

My heart rate slowed. The place was packed with people, and I felt secure there. No one walked along the street looking around for me. I didn't see a single suspicious person.

Now, how to get home? I ordered a ginger ale but didn't leave my post near the window. What was I thinking? I dated a cop, and he was probably working right now. I pulled my phone out of my bag. The screen had shattered. It must have hit the person. Ouch.

Happily, the phone still worked. I called Eric and told him where I was. "If you have time, I could use an escort home. Someone has been following me."

Eric arrived five minutes later. "Are you okay?"

"I'm fine."

He pulled me to him and hugged me fiercely. "Do you know who's following you?"

I shook my head. "But I think my purse gave him a good whack." I showed him my phone.

Eric spoke into his radio. "I'm now officially on my dinner break. What do you say we grab some something to eat?"

Tired as I was, I agreed. We hadn't seen much of each other lately, and I wanted to tell him my theory about the venetian-glass pens.

We walked to a small Italian restaurant where everyone seemed to know him. He introduced me as his girlfriend, which made heat rise in my cheeks.

Eric led me to a small table with a blue-and-white tablecloth.

An older woman with an Italian accent shuffled over to me and whispered, "Don't let this one go. He is *un tesoro!*"

I wasn't sure what that meant, but I was betting that she thought he was a treasure. I smiled at her, and she patted my shoulder.

We didn't order or even see a menu. They brought us salad, lasagne, a bowl of spaghetti with meatballs, and a basket of bread.

"They love you here!" I whispered.

"Restaurants like to have cops drop by. Makes them feel safe. So when did you notice someone tailing you?"

With a great deal of regret, I admitted, "Before the wedding. But I thought it was Cara. In fact, I'm sure it was Cara. Even after we asked her to leave the bookstore and we threw her out of the wedding, she was still on my track. She was tailing me the day she was murdered."

"I think we can confidently say it was someone else this time."

I sagged. "No kidding."

"Do you have any idea who it might be?"

"No. But I have discovered a few things. They don't lead to a killer, but, who knows? People go to extremes to protect their secrets."

"I'm listening." He took a bite of the lasagne.

"Sergeant Bridges needs to know this, but if *I* told him, he would probably haul me in and lock me up."

Furrows formed across Eric's forehead. "I can take a hint. What do you need to tell Bridges?"

"I think the murder weapon was a glass calligraphy pen. I saw them for the first time in my life at Gabriella's house. There were four of them. I found them online. They come in a set of five. The red one was missing. But then Jacquie and I went to Arthur's house to have a look around, and I found the same set, with the red one missing again. Do you know if there's any red on the portion that they found in Cara's neck?"

"Maybe the red ones break easily. And what were you doing snooping around Arthur's house?" Eric frowned at me.

"Don't look so perturbed. The house is for sale, so Jacquie and I went to see it. It has the most amazing glass room on the top floor. That was where I discovered the calligraphy pens. Arthur had a thing for venetian glass."

"Are they expensive?"

"They're not cheap as ordinary pens go but they're affordable."

Eric took a deep breath. "Then no one stole them for resale, I guess. And really, probably hundreds of people have them in the greater DC area."

"Could be. I don't know if they're popular." I ate a forkful of heavenly lasagne.

"I'll pass this information along to Bridges. He's not a bad guy, but this is his first murder investigation and he's feeling a little frustrated."

"I wouldn't mind if he would identify another suspect instead of concentrating on me."

"Got any ideas?" Eric cut into a giant meatball.

"It appears that Gabriella and Buzz are having an affair while her husband is out of town."

Eric's eyebrows shot up. "And you know this how?"

"I saw his shoes at her house. And they smooched at her door, right out in the open where anyone could see. I thought maybe Cara, in her zeal to get an interview with Griffin, found out about their affair." I helped myself to more salad, laden with olives, cherry tomatoes, and bits of ricotta salata.

"Did Buzz or Gabriella have any reason to kill Evan?"

"Not that I know of. I went to Evan's apartment with Gabriella to get his cat. He seemed like a pretty average guy." I surveyed the food. I was getting full, but everything tasted so good. I helped myself to just a little bit more of the pasta. "Do you remember the Sorellos, who sat at our table at the wedding? The wife looks very timid and thin? She thought her husband was running around with someone and it turns out he is."

Eric shook his head. "That's too bad. I liked the Sorellos. But that doesn't implicate him in Evan's death. Or Cara's for that matter."

"I guess not. It would depend on who he's seeing. But Evan drove an Uber and often picked him up."

"I presume you know who it is?"

"My mother reports that she's a pretty blonde."

Eric tilted his head and laughed. "Your mother is involved with the PI?"

"Do you remember Norman Spratt?"

A broad grin crossed Eric's face. "My rival for your love!"

"Hahaha," I uttered dryly. "Apparently, he dropped out of the police academy and now he's a PI. He took photos and showed them to his mother and to mine!"

Eric took a deep breath. "He has a duty of confidentiality to his client. For Pete's sake!"

"I thought that might be the case."

Eric checked his watch. "I would love to linger, but I have to get back to work. Come on, I'll walk you home."

I felt spoiled to be able to walk home with my own body-guard. But I was also relieved and grateful. Eric didn't linger long once I was inside, but I understood. He had work to do.

Besides, I was bushed. Peaches purred, clearly glad that I was home. I opened a can of filet of beef, which I guessed wasn't as fabulous as it sounded, but Peaches thought it quite tasty and licked her bowl clean.

I made sure the door was locked and went up to bed. But try as I might, I couldn't sleep. So many questions were in my mind, and I leaped from one to the other, never able to put them together, like mismatched puzzle pieces. I turned the light back on and retrieved my sketch pad. Sitting up in bed with my comforter over my knees and Peaches watching me, I reviewed my drawings.

They began with the beautiful lanterns at the wedding. That was where it had all started. No! That wasn't right. It all began the night before when Arthur texted Jacquie and met with her. He had to be the link.

Evan worked for him, a clear connection. Whether Evan died because he was murdered or by accident, he had a strong tie to Arthur. Why would anyone want to kill him? He seemed like a quiet sort of fellow, absorbed in his quest to become a published author.

Arthur's link to Cara was more tenuous. She had said *R*,

which could mean the letter *R* or the beginning of a word, in this case Arthur's name. I drew the letters *A r t h u r* in a mock-calligraphy manner. Arthur faux. Arthur pho. Arthur fo. Foe? Was Arthur her foe? That seemed wrong, even if her brain wasn't working at full capacity in her panic. I sounded it out. Photon, photo . . . phone! She protected her phone like crazy. I remembered her clawing at me when I was deleting pictures of my parents. What was on her phone?

I checked the time. It wasn't too late to call Eric. He might even still be working.

He answered the call immediately. "Hi! I thought you'd be asleep by now. Are you worried about your stalker?"

"Thanks for reminding me about him," I said sarcastically. "I can't sleep. I was thinking about Cara saying *R-faux*. Maybe she was trying to tell me something about her phone. Do the police have it? There could be something on it that would lead us to her assailant." I would hope someone had examined it by now, but maybe it had slipped through the cracks.

"I'll check to see. How long will you be up?"

"I don't know. But it doesn't matter. Call me regardless." I thanked him and disconnected the call.

I woke the next morning with my phone under my hip and my sketch pad poking me in the jaw. Memories of the previous night flooded back to me. I called Veronica.

"Mmmf."

"Have you noticed anyone following you?"

"Wha? Florrie, it's six in the morning."

"Now that you're awake, maybe you could answer my question."

"Do you know what I like about working in a bookstore?"

I knew it wasn't the books. "Meeting new people?"

"That I don't have to be there until ten."

The dial tone buzzed in my ear.

When it played my ringtone, I smiled. Hah! Veronica was calling back.

Instead of saying hello, I snarked, "I knew you'd call!"

"Florrie? Is that you?"

I recognized the voice. "Jezebel?"

"They're taking me to a home. I need your help! Now they're taking my phone away." Her voice faded. "Help me!"

Once again, I was listening to a dial tone.

Chapter 33

I jumped out of bed and called her back while I dressed. No one picked up. I brushed my teeth in haste, and without brushing my hair, I pulled it back into a ponytail.

I dashed downstairs, fed Peaches, and pondered. Would it be faster to walk or to drive? Even on a Saturday, traffic might slow me down. And what if I couldn't find a place to park? I decided to walk and set out moving as fast as I could.

The person who could help Jezebel the most would be Fish. Did he know what was going on with her? I found Fish's phone number and called him.

"Hi, Florrie."

"I apologize if I'm waking you up."

"No problem."

"Jezebel called me. She said they're taking her to a home. Do you know anything about that?"

"Who's taking her?"

"She didn't say. The last thing I heard was her saying, 'Help me!' I'm on my way there now." I could hear that he was moving around.

"Let me phone my mom and see what I can find out. I'll call you back."

I was making relatively good time, and when I saw the traffic, I thought I'd made a good choice. As usual, I tried running, but I didn't think I was making better time. I was just wearing myself out. I rounded the corner. Jezebel's house was in sight.

Several cars were parked along the street, but I knew from personal experience that it was hard to find parking spaces in Georgetown. Those cars could belong to people who were on the next street over or eating breakfast in some restaurant. In any case, I didn't see an ambulance or anyone trying to force Jezebel into a vehicle.

I stopped to assess the situation from the street. I didn't hear any shouting or wailing. Maybe I had missed them, and they were already gone? No one peeked out the windows.

Taking a deep breath, I walked up to the front door and knocked.

A burly woman opened it.

I tried to sound cheerful. "Hi! I'm looking for Jezebel Fish."

She placed her hands on her hips. "She's not here."

She started to close the door, but I jammed my foot in the opening. "Just a minute, please. Where has she gone?"

"Who *are* you?" she demanded.

"A friend of Jezebel's."

She laughed but it sounded more like a cough. "I doubt that."

"And you are?"

"Kaylee Brewster, her caregiver."

Kaylee wasn't someone I wanted to tangle with. Built like a truck, she wore what I suspected was a perma-scowl. I imagined her as a drill sergeant shouting orders.

"Were you in the military?"

"You betcha. I was a drill sergeant."

Okay then.

"Listen," she said confidentially. "I have never lost a client. Some of 'em died, but you can't count that. I am not about to lose one now. She was supposed to go to the old folks' home this morning, but that little sneak got away from me. I shoulda given her a dose of sleeping pills in her coffee this morning. They're not gonna pin this on me."

"That's too bad. I'm sorry to hear that. How about I look around back?"

She shrugged. "Suit yourself." She closed the door in my face.

Well, at least it wouldn't be trespassing if I snuck around the house to look for her. I scanned the street first. How far could she have gotten?

I headed around the side of the house, into the beautiful backyard. Vibrant purple rhododendrons, bold red and baby-pink azaleas, and white clematis had carefully been planted just beyond a pool surrounded by a concrete deck. Most of the outdoor furniture remained covered, with the exception of one chair and a tiny side table. "Jezebel?" I whispered. "It's Florrie!"

All I heard were bird calls and distant traffic.

I knew *one* of Jezebel's escape routes. I eyed the dense evergreens that formed a privacy barrier between her property and Arthur's. Using both hands, I pried the branches apart and peered through. I didn't see anyone. "Jezebel!" I hissed, wedging myself into Arthur's backyard.

I didn't think he would mind my intrusion if he knew Jezebel was missing. He probably liked her. "Jezebel!"

I brushed pine needles off my clothing. My phone rang. It was Fish.

"Everything is under control. Mom doesn't know what's wrong with Grandma. She thinks Grandma has developed dementia. She's making up stories and acting out, which isn't like her at all."

That didn't sound right. "What do you mean by making up stories?"

"She thinks she works at a bookstore."

I burst out laughing. "She did yesterday! There's nothing wrong with her."

"Are you sure? My mom is flying in to move her to a nursing home."

"Unless she went bonkers in the last sixteen hours or so, she's fine. Lucid and lovely. She had a wonderful time with us yesterday."

A movement caused me to look up. Arthur stared at me from a window. Anyone would have noticed his Hawaiian-style shirt in screaming yellow and red.

I smiled and waved at him.

"I'm glad she's all right," said Fish. "I'd better let Mom know so she can postpone the move."

"Thanks for checking on the situation. She must be home, then." I disconnected the call and looked at the window again. The curtains had been drawn.

Oof! That was a sign, for sure. Maybe he was still sick and didn't want company. I could take a hint.

Instead of going around Arthur's house, I pushed my way through the evergreens and brushed the little bits of greenery off me.

Kaylee stood next to Jezebel's pool with her hands on her hips.

"Hi! Could I please see Jezebel?"

She blinked at me. "Are you daft? I just told you she ran away, and I can't find her."

"But I just spoke with her grandson and . . ." Uh-oh. I'd better keep my mouth shut about Jezebel's grandson and what someone had told his mother.

She approached me, wagging her forefinger. "Now you listen here. I am not losing this job because of a crazy old woman.

I *will* find her. And you"—she chucked me under the chin like a child—"will keep your fat mouth shut and git out of here."

No problem. Mustering what little dignity I could, I turned on my heel and left.

I tended to believe Kaylee about Jezebel having run off. It would do a lot of damage to the caregiving service if they lost a client. But then, where was Jezebel?

I smacked myself on the forehead. She thought she had a job at Color Me Read. I knew exactly where she was. I hurried along the sidewalk, stopping only for two lattes and two breakfast specials of scrambled eggs, bacon, and pancakes with maple syrup and fresh strawberries.

As I approached the bookstore, I realized with enormous relief that I had been correct. Jezebel sat on the bench outside Color Me Read with Celeste Sorello.

"Hi!" I called as I walked up to them.

"I'm sorry that I'm so early, but I didn't have anywhere else to go," said Jezebel.

"She's been telling me about her troubles." Celeste reached out and patted Jezebel's hand. "And I thought *I* had problems!"

"Why don't we go inside and have some breakfast?"

I unlocked the door and turned the alarm off. "I only bought two, but we can share."

In minutes we were seated in the parlor, enjoying warm lattes, savory eggs, and fluffy pancakes.

"Jezebel, how would you like a job here at the store? It doesn't have to be full-time. We could use some part-timers to help us out."

"Do you have openings?" asked Celeste. "Can I apply?"

I felt like I had been handed a gift. "Done! You're hired."

Celeste smiled. "That was the easiest job interview ever."

This was turning out to be a great day.

"I would like that, too," said Jezebel. "I just need to figure out how to get everyone off my back and let me enjoy my life."

"I'll make an appointment for you with my lawyer," said Celeste. "She's quite good. A Ms. Strickland."

"I know her," I said. "She's the professor's attorney. I think that's a great idea."

"Florrie, I want to thank you for referring me to your friend Norman. Did you know he's crazy in love with you?"

"Oh no. Is that what he told you? Honestly! I went out with him once. Only once!"

"You and Eric make such a cute couple. I felt terrible for him. But"—she handed me a manila envelope—"he knows his stuff. Go ahead, look inside."

I set down my latte, opened the flap, and pulled out photographs of Celeste's husband, Grady, and a blond woman entering a local hotel. I gasped. This was the woman my mom had said was pretty.

"Do you know her?" asked Celeste.

"I'm so sorry that he's having an affair, Celeste. I do know her."

Chapter 34

"She's Liddy Woodley, Professor Maxwell's sister."

"She was at the party! I thought she looked familiar. Oh my gosh. They were both there. Right under my nose!" Celeste sat still as a statue. "My husband likes to show off. I wore a simple blue gown the night of the party and meant to take a small bag that he brought me from Hong Kong. It's beaded and very pretty, but he insisted that I carry an Hermès Birkin. It was way too big and totally inappropriate for that kind of event, but it cost a small fortune. I bet you anything he was showing off for her. I've been such a fool!"

"No, you haven't, Celeste. No one ever wants to think that the person they trust most in the world would hurt them. He let you down." Jezebel smiled at her.

"Thank you, Jezebel. I needed to hear that." Celeste checked her watch. "Should I call my lawyer and see if she can fit you in? We have an hour before the store opens and she's not located far from here."

"Let's do it!"

I told them not to worry if they weren't back exactly at ten. "And, Jezebel, I feel like we ought to let Fish know where you are. Just so no one will worry. Is that all right with you?"

Her mouth twitched uncomfortably. "I will phone him right now. May I borrow your phone?"

After she called Fish, the two of them left, on their way to a brief appointment with the lawyer. While they were gone, I took care of the paperwork necessary to put them on our payroll.

My phone rang. I expected it to be an irate Fish. Or maybe even his mother, but it was Eric.

"Thanks for dinner last night," I said. "We have to go back to that place. Everyone was so nice, and the food was delicious."

"You're on! Florrie, I checked the inventory of what they found on Cara when she died. There's no phone. She did *not* have a phone on her."

"But she did! I'm not saying that I don't believe you. She took a picture of me with her phone. I remember her holding it up and aiming it at me."

"What are you saying? That someone murdered her for her phone?"

"Yes. She took pictures of everything. Maybe she had something on her phone that someone was willing to kill for. Cara might not have even realized that she had a photo that important."

"She could have dropped the phone."

"You're right. But the cops checked that area right away. Surely they would have noticed it. And I went back later on—"

"You did? What for?" Eric asked.

"To talk with the dry cleaner. It was *not* there. Do you have her number? Is there any way you can track it? Or has too much time passed?"

"Looks like they tried but the battery was dead."

"Bummer. Another reason to remember to charge my phone."

"In case you go missing?"

"Yes."

"But then we couldn't go back to the Italian restaurant," he joked.

"Very funny." I said goodbye as Veronica strode in.

Much to my surprise, everyone arrived to work on time. I spent the next hour walking Roxie, Celeste, and Jezebel through the store, explaining how we did everything and showing them where various genres were shelved.

I hovered behind Jezebel as she rang up her first sale. She caught on quickly, and I went back to work deciding which books to order to replenish our stock of children's titles.

Jezebel said, "I saw Arthur this morning."

"Is he feeling better?"

"He must be. He had been swimming."

"Really? When I saw him, he drew the curtains, which I took to mean he was not interested in seeing me. Oh well! What did Fish have to say?" I hoped she wouldn't feel like I was pressuring her. But it would be awful if people were looking for her.

"He was fine. My daughter isn't happy about it, but I told him they have to call off the guards."

I checked to be sure everyone knew their schedules. Bob would work until closing with Roxie to teach her how to close up. Everyone else could leave at six. Except for me. I was taking the rest of the day off.

On the way home, I stopped at the grocery store, where I could not resist the lush strawberries, which were in season. I was placing a box in my shopping cart when I spied Sergeant Bridges. My instinct was to hide, then it dawned on me that it could be Bridges who was following me!

He darted out of my line of sight. I charged down the aisle and turned, looking for him.

He pretended to be examining something in the meat display. He saw me coming toward him and immediately looked away.

But I had had enough of him. I didn't stop until I was directly behind him, boxing him in with my cart. "Are you following me?" I demanded.

He and a chubby woman about my height turned to look at me.

"Uh, no."

I stared at his cheek. If he was my stalker, he might have a bruise from being hit by my purse, or even a scratch from the buckle that held it closed. I didn't see anything.

"You followed me into this store."

"Honey, who is this?" asked the woman.

Honey? She was old enough to be . . . his mother. A flush of hot shame rose in my cheeks.

"Mom, this is Florrie Fox. Florrie, meet my mother, Eleanora Bridges."

"Hi, Mrs. Bridges. I'm so sorry. I thought your son might be my stalker."

In a no-nonsense tone, Mrs. Bridges asked her son, "Are you following this young woman?"

"Mom, please. Stay out of this."

"I'm so sorry, honey. I'll see that he leaves you alone." She whacked her son in a motherly way on his upper arm.

"Mom—"

"He thinks I murdered someone."

She drew her head back and scrutinized me. "Did you?"

"Of course not!"

"There, you see? She told you she didn't do it. Didn't they teach you anything in the police academy? Anyone would realize that this sweet thing isn't a murderer!"

"Mom, please." He whispered, "She's a suspect in an investigation."

"Well, you just better find yourself another suspect because she didn't do it."

I smiled at him. "Does it look like the left side of his face is bruised?" I asked her.

His mother reached up, clasped her hands on his jaw, and turned his face for a better look.

"Mom!"

"I don't think so, honey. Did you slug that guy who was following you?"

"Hit him with my purse."

"Ohhh, good for you! You stand up for yourself."

"Wait," said Sergeant Bridges. "You mean someone else was following you?"

"So you *have* been following me."

"Just answer the question."

"Yes. I managed to lose him and called Eric."

He narrowed his eyes and studied me.

His mother said, "You be careful now, honey. And you call him if you need help."

Yeah, like I would do that.

"It was nice meeting you, Mrs. Bridges. If I recall correctly, you like to read. I run Color Me Read bookstore. You should come by sometime."

"Do y'all have a mystery reading group?"

"We do. They meet on the first Tuesday of each month at six o'clock and take turns bringing dinner for everyone."

"I like that! I'll see you there."

I smiled again at Bridges, feeling snotty for doing so, but I couldn't help it. The guy had turned on me.

I picked up some cheese and the strawberries, paid for them, and walked home. Still worried about who was following me, I pretended to stop several times, hoping to catch someone, but I didn't see a soul. Knowing that Sergeant Bridges had been following me was irritating, yet comforting, too. I knew he didn't mean me any harm. He just hoped I would lead him to answers about Evan's and Cara's deaths. I'd like to know those answers myself.

I paused again at Poole's Auctions and looked slyly to the side. I didn't see anyone darting behind me. But when I gazed back into the fabulous show window, a glass sculpture drew my attention. It contained every color of the rainbow. Striations of all the colors stretched upward in a wide ribbon, just as in the foyer at Arthur's house.

I pushed open the door and went inside. I didn't see the man I had met with regarding the jadeite pig, but a woman asked if she could be of assistance.

"I'm interested in the glass sculpture in the window."

"That will be in next Saturday's auction."

"Can you tell me who the seller is?"

"I'm afraid not."

"Please? This could be important." Oh, boy. I was going to have to lie again, and it would have to be a humdinger. No. I was not going to lie. I would be straightforward.

"Is the name Bedlingham?"

"No." She smiled at me, which was probably meant to be friendly but seemed condescending.

Oh, shoot! What was Mia's last name? Mia . . . Mia . . . Woodham! "Is the seller Woodham?"

The woman's face showed her dismay. "How did you know?"

"I can't imagine there are too many sculptures like this one. At least not locally. Thank you so much." I scuttled out of there as fast as I could, thinking that Jacquie had been right about Arthur all along. He was probably hard up for money. I hated to think he was selling his beloved possessions, but if he sold the house, he might not have a spot for that big sculpture anyway. And glass like that had to be hard to transport.

I was deep in thought when my skin crawled and I realized someone was behind me again. Out of the corner of my eye I caught sight of a figure, and when I stopped to pretend to look in a show window, I heard a scream and scuffling.

Bridges had tackled a man who wrestled to get away. I ran toward them, pulling out my phone to call for help.

But Bridges managed to roll the man over on his stomach and placed handcuffs on him.

"Who is it?"

"I don't know yet," said Bridges. "I thought I'd better follow you home. Okay, you. On your feet," he ordered.

The man on the ground struggled to rise. Without his hands, and with his rather prominent belly, he couldn't get to his feet. But he was starting to look familiar.

Bridges took him by one shoulder, and I grabbed the other. Together we hoisted him to a standing position.

"Norman!" I cried.

"You know this guy?" asked Bridges.

"Yes. You can take off the handcuffs. How long have you been following me?"

"I'm not admitting to anything. You're a suspect in a murder. You need security."

I looked at Bridges. "I can't believe this. Norman, you had me scared half to death."

"I'm pretty good at my job. Mrs. Sorello said so. Now will you go out with me?"

Bridges started to snicker.

"No. I do not date men who stalk me."

"I'm not stalking you. I'm protecting you." Norman gestured at Bridges. "Tell her there's a difference."

Bridges bit his lower lip to keep from laughing.

"If you ever follow me again, Norman Spratt, so help me, I will tell your mother that you jumped a man with a knife and almost got killed in the process."

"Aww, you're teasing me. You wouldn't do that."

"Just try me."

Bridges nodded. "I think she means it, pal. You better get going."

I crossed my arms over my chest and narrowed my eyes, trying to look tough. Beside me, Bridges snorted. "Wait until I tell Eric."

I turned to him. "And exactly why were you following me?"

"Whoa. I'm as scared of my mom as your buddy Norman is of his mom. I believe I'll just walk away now."

So I was still a prime suspect in Cara's death. I trudged on.

Glad to be home, I greeted Peaches and snuggled with her before making the batter for my strawberry cupcakes. I could use something sweet to cheer me up. While they baked, I retrieved my sketch pad.

The pictures I had drawn told stories, but they didn't connect. We knew that Grady and Liddy had left their rooms the night Evan died. Chances were good that they were together. I drew their faces side by side.

Jacquie had been up and about as well, but Liddy's husband had gone in search of Liddy and could provide an alibi for Jacquie.

The mansion's alarm system had been turned off because of all the guests. I wondered who knew that. The sad fact was that if someone intended to kill Evan, they could have handed him the brownies during the party, which narrowed the number of suspects down to over five hundred people.

What had the professor said? It revolved around Jacquie and her writing friends.

I paged back to Margarite. She wasn't young, but anyone

who'd pole danced might still be surprisingly limber. Maybe *she* could have stabbed Cara. But if she was going to kill anyone, it would surely have been Arthur.

I flipped over to see my drawing of him. He was good-looking for his age. And a bit of a charmer. Definitely a ladies' man. But the way he had looked at me today and then drawn the curtains shut made me wonder if there was another side to him. Hadn't Jacquie said that she left him because she couldn't deal with his jealousy and the way he treated her when she became a successful author, and he didn't? Everything seemed to come back to Arthur.

I flipped the page to Gabriella. Had she knocked Cara off because she had photos of Griffin on her phone? Or had Griffin killed her while supposedly writing out in the woods near the Chesapeake Bay?

And what about Buzz? I examined my drawing of him. The human resources employee who wrote a cloak-and-dagger-style thriller. And now he was involved in an affair with Gabriella?

That just made me sad. I liked Gabriella. Why was she cheating on her husband?

I got up to take the cupcakes out of the oven, then went back to the sofa and my sketch pad. The heavenly aroma wafted to me.

Arthur, Gabriella, and Griffin were my top suspects. They had the most at stake. And all three of them had easy access to the glass calligraphy pens.

Griffin may or may *not* have known Evan. I wondered if Bridges had managed to interview Griffin. Would Bridges tell me if I asked?

I had brushed off Arthur's closing the curtains this morning. If he was sick, he might not have been up to having company, or the sun could have been bothering him, or he wanted to sleep in. There were a million good reasons that he might not have felt like seeing anyone. On the other hand, maybe he was hiding something.

I sketched him as I had seen him this morning, with the big white mustache, the contrasting eyebrows, and cold eyes.

Someone knocked on my door. I peeked out and opened the door. "Jacquie!"

She motioned to me to come outside. "I want to show you something."

I locked my door and took the key. There was no point in taking chances. I did not want to come back to find someone in my home.

She led me to the mansion and into the living room, where Professor Maxwell and Mr. DuBois greeted me.

"What do you think?" asked Jacquie.

I looked around and spotted a new oil portrait of Jacquie and the professor on their wedding day. "It's stunning!" I moved closer. Colorful azaleas in the background didn't overwhelm the happy couple. "This is incredible. It's just beautiful. And a perfect likeness of both of you."

"Mia painted it for us," said Jacquie. "When I hired her to do sketches of the guests, she offered to paint us, too. I'm so pleased with the results."

"She's quite talented," agreed Mr. DuBois.

"I just love it," gushed Jacquie. "We have friends whose portraits look so stiff, but this looks natural. She really captured us."

"DuBois," said the professor, "have you made any progress identifying the owner of the jadeite pig yet?"

Mr. DuBois looked at me. "Have you learned anything more?"

I did *not* want to be the one to break the news to them. But they had me cornered, in a manner of speaking. "I believe it belongs to Liddy."

"My sister?" asked the professor. "Why would you think that?"

I took the easy road. "It was found in the room where she was staying. And she does like pigs."

"That explains why she wants to return," said Jacquie. "She plans to look for it."

I was lost. "She's coming back here?"

"Poor thing is all broken up because her husband is leaving her," said Jacquie. "She's going to stay with us for a while because they're putting their house up for sale."

Chapter 35

Why that lying, scheming sneak! I snapped my mouth shut. I stared at Mr. DuBois. Hadn't he told them that someone had locked him in a closet? That someone being the nasty Liddy, who was now returning to stay in the mansion with them?

"You have to tell them," I hissed.

All eyes were on DuBois. "When does she plan to arrive?" he asked.

Oh, a deft avoidance! I scowled at him.

"On Wednesday," said Jacquie. "She'll be bringing quite a bit with her. You may need to hire some help for unloading it all."

"Very well." He tilted his head, as if he wanted me to exit the room with him.

I followed him out.

"I can't tell them now," he said.

"You can't live with her in this house."

"Worse things have happened to me. I'm sure I can handle it."

"Will I have to come home from work every few hours to make sure you're not confined to a closet? They *have* to know."

"Know what?" asked the professor behind me.

I swung around at the exact moment that the doorbell rang.

Mr. DuBois shot me a satisfied smirk and opened the door.

Rosie squealed with glee and trotted into the mansion wagging her tail.

Liddy didn't even acknowledge Mr. DuBois. She flew into the foyer, dropping her bags and a coat on the floor. "It's so good to be home!"

"Liddy, dear!" Jacquie gave her an air kiss over each shoulder. "We weren't expecting you yet."

"I know, but I just can't be around *him* anymore." Tears began to flow, but only Jacquie was sympathetic.

"Come with me. I'll make you a lemon drop. You love those!"

The professor appeared unmoved by his sister's drama. "DuBois! What do we have to know?"

Mr. DuBois said cheerily, "If you'll pardon me, I believe the ladies would care for a lemon drop." He left the foyer so fast I felt the breeze he caused.

"Florrie?" Professor Maxwell strode into the library. I followed and he closed the doors behind us. "Perhaps you can enlighten me?"

"The day we found the jadeite pig, someone had entered the house and pushed Mr. DuBois into a closet from behind. He did not see the person. She took a chair and wedged it under the door handles, effectively locking him in."

"You think it was Liddy."

"I don't know for sure."

"What *do* you know for sure?"

"That her husband, Walter, is considering buying Arthur's house."

Professor Maxwell nodded.

"And that Celeste Sorello hired a private investigator to find out if her husband, Grady, was having an affair. She showed me the photographs he took. I'm sorry, Professor Maxwell. Grady is having an affair with Liddy. And I don't think it's a complete coincidence that Grady was recently in Hong Kong, which is likely where the jadeite pig was purchased. According to the gentleman at Poole's Auctions, it's a symbol of prosperity and good luck and would be a cherished gift." There, for better or worse, it was all out in the open now.

"Is Walter seeing someone?"

"If he is, I am not aware of it."

Professor Maxwell got to his feet and opened the library door. "Liddy! Would you come here, please?"

Holding a lemon drop like the diva she was, she entered the library, followed by Rosie.

The professor gestured toward a chair and took a seat behind the desk. "Did you bring a jadeite pig to the wedding?"

"Do you have it?" she asked eagerly.

"Why would you bring a jadeite pig to a party?"

He was setting her up. Given the way she had treated Mr. DuBois, I didn't mind seeing her squirm a little.

"I didn't bring it with me. I was given it as a gift while I stayed here."

"By whom?"

She took her time answering. I suspected she was working through the implications of her response.

"Walter."

"Your husband, the one who is leaving you, gave you an expensive gift only days ago?"

"Yes." Her tone was snotty.

"Then why didn't you call us and tell us you had lost it?"

I tried very hard not to smile.

"Just stop it. You're so mean to me. Obviously, you know the answer to that."

"Indulge me."

"You are so judgmental! You have your nerve, Mr. Married Four Times. At least I stuck it out with my husband."

The professor appeared pained. "Perhaps I am. But you didn't have to lock DuBois in a closet."

"I can't imagine why you keep him on. Surely you could find someone younger and more useful. He's the most judgmental of all." She mocked him. "Why Miss Liddy, what *would* your mother say about that?" Her tone changed to one of anger. "Besides, the closet wasn't locked—" She stopped dead and turned to gaze at me. "It was you! I should have known you were the one squawking DuBois's name when he was in the closet. Honestly, you have brought me nothing but trouble since the day you moved into the carriage house."

I was tempted to lash out. I wasn't the one who had killed her son. Nor was I the one who was having an affair or had lost the jadeite pig. But sometimes, it was better to keep quiet. She would never admit that none of it was my fault, but I thought she must know that. Besides, I *had* ratted on her, but that was for DuBois's safety.

She huffed and then said in a tiny voice, "I couldn't tell any of you I was having an affair with Grady. He gave it to me the night after the party. I had to hide it from my husband and then I went and lost the thing. It meant so much to me, but none of you could know the truth. What if it got back to Walter?"

The professor picked up the desk phone. "I'd like to reserve a room, please. Starting tonight, for the next month. Liddy Maxwell Woodley. She'll be bringing a pig with her. . . . Yes, it appears to be housebroken. Thank you." He dialed another number and asked for a car to be sent to the mansion. Then he looked up at me. "Thank you for being honest."

"You're welcome," said Liddy.

"You'd better drink your lemon drop very fast," said the professor.

I hustled out of there to avoid being around for the next drama. It would be one more thing for Liddy to blame on me.

Rosie trotted to the door with me. I scratched behind her ears. Her tail wagged and she smiled. She really was cute. "You behave. No running out in the streets. Okay?" She snorted at me and I took that as agreement.

Back at the carriage house, I iced the cupcakes and couldn't help trying one immediately. It soothed my nerves, right up until someone knocked on my door. I peeked out. Uh-oh. Jacquie.

I opened the door, expecting her to let me have it. She burst into the house and wrapped me in a hug. "I love you!"

"What?"

She released me. "Thank heaven Liddy isn't going to stay with us. She would have tried to drive a wedge between Maxwell and me. I know her. She's a menace. Not to mention that she would have expected poor old DuBois to wait on her hand and foot. I cannot believe that he didn't tell us about being trapped in the closet. We are so grateful, Florrie."

Sometimes the truth, even when bad, was a good thing. I offered her a cupcake.

She bit into it. "Mmm. So good."

Handing her a napkin, I said, "I'm going to take some over to the bookstore."

"They'll love them!"

I placed two cupcakes on a plate. "Maybe the professor and Mr. DuBois could use one, too."

When Jacquie left, I packed six cupcakes and told Peaches I would be back soon. She opened one eye briefly and then closed it again.

I didn't notice anyone tailing me and was heralded like a

hero when I arrived at the bookstore. Bob, Veronica, Roxie, and Celeste crowded around and helped themselves.

"Where's Jezebel?" I asked.

"She hasn't come back from lunch," said Bob.

Veronica swallowed a bite of cupcake. "We were going to give her ten more minutes and then call you."

"Did she say where she was going?"

Roxie shook her head. "She seemed fine, though."

"I've been calling her, but she isn't answering her phone." Veronica looked as worried as I felt.

"I'll go to her house. Keep calling her and let me know if you reach her." I shot out the door, down the stairs, and dodged people strolling leisurely along the sidewalk. Huffing, I finally made it to her block. It seemed quiet.

I walked up to her door and knocked. I tried a second time, but she didn't respond. Crossing my fingers, I hoped she hadn't taken Buzz's good advice to move the hiding place for her house key. I almost shrieked with joy when I found it still under the pot where it had been before.

I unlocked the door and shouted, "Jezebel? Jezebel! It's me, Florrie!"

No answer. The house was dark for the time of day, with curtains drawn and no lights on. I took a quick walk through the first floor and found her purse on the dining room table. I didn't know if that was a good sign or a bad one. Surely it meant she was home.

As a precaution, I phoned Fish and let him know what was going on. "Her handbag is here but I'm not seeing any sign of her."

"I'm just a couple of blocks away. I'll be right there."

I listened for moaning or crying but heard nothing. I raced up the stairs. "Jezebel? Jezebel, where are you?"

I checked each of the bedrooms, under the beds, in the closets, and behind shower curtains. There were four bedrooms in all, but Jezebel wasn't there. I was beginning to wonder if Kaylee had snatched her and whisked her off to a nursing home. But wouldn't Fish know about that?

Back downstairs, I found a locked door. I assumed it went to the basement and was about to walk away when I remembered that she *had* to be home because her purse was there.

I studied the locked door for a moment. Why did it lock from the other side? Then it dawned on me that it would keep grandbabies from opening the door and falling down. I pulled out my credit card and wedged it through the crack between the door and the jamb. Wiggling the card toward me did the trick. I heard the latch snap and pulled the door open. I flicked on the light switch, but no lights came on. Peering into the darkness, I made out a small figure crumpled at the bottom of the stairs.

Holding on to the banister, I hurried down the steps. "Jezebel! Can you hear me?"

I leaned over her. "Jezebel?" Her hand was cold. I called 911 and asked for an ambulance. Kneeling beside her, I touched her wrist for a pulse but felt nothing. I tried again on her neck and thought it had a faint pulse. "Jezebel, I've called an ambulance. They'll be here soon and so will Fish! Hang in there."

I glanced around. It was a finished basement, but I didn't see any blankets. I raced up the two flights of stairs to a bedroom and yanked a blanket off the bed. I grabbed the pillow, too, and ran back down the stairs to her.

Tucking the blanket around her, guilt overcame me. This was all my fault. Her family had been right. She needed someone with her all day long. If I hadn't hired her at the bookstore, she probably wouldn't have fallen down the stairs, and she definitely wouldn't have lain there for so long. "Oh, Jezebel," I moaned. "I'm so sorry."

I heard Fish upstairs calling our names.

"Down here! In the basement!"

Sirens sounded. "Jezebel, they're on the way and Fish is here!"

He clattered down the stairs. "Grandma! What happened?" He felt her throat for a pulse. "She's alive."

"I thought I felt a pulse, too."

"What happened to her?"

"I don't know. I thought she fell down the stairs, but the door was locked, so she must have been pushed. I haven't moved her, but I did cover her with the blanket."

"She must have been carrying that pillow."

"That was me, too. I brought it down, but I was afraid to move her head. What if her neck is broken?"

He nodded knowingly.

"Why would anyone push her? Do you think it could have been Kaylee? You know, to make a point that she needed care?" I asked.

"Kaylee wasn't the friendliest person I ever met, but I can't imagine she would harm anyone."

Still, someone had pushed Jezebel.

The sirens had stopped. I left him with his grandmother and raced upstairs to show the EMTs the way. I waited for them upstairs. There was no point in my watching them. I couldn't help and would only be in the way.

They carried her upstairs on a stretcher. Fish followed behind them.

I looked at her. "Jezebel? Can you hear me?"

Her eyes were closed, and she didn't move or moan.

Fish thanked me, more out of habit than sincerity, I thought, since there was nothing to thank me for, and he left in a hurry.

I felt so guilty. I shouldn't have interfered. I meant well! I wanted to help her. I walked down the stairs, collected the pillow and the blanket that had been left behind, and carried them up to the bedroom. I returned to the main floor and looked around. There wasn't anything I could do for her.

Mentally kicking myself, I left the house, locked the door, and slid the key under the pot.

I phoned Fish as I walked home. "How's Jezebel?"

"It's touch and go. She's alive but they're not hopeful. They're running a barrage of tests."

"Is there anything I can do?"

"Don't send anything. She'll be in the emergency room for hours yet."

"Keep me posted, okay? And if you need anything at all, please call me."

Back at home, even my beautiful pink-iced cupcakes didn't cheer me up. I put them in the freezer and gazed glumly at my sketch pad.

I drew Jezebel's smiling, enthusiastic face. What had I done? I would never forgive myself.

Paging back, I gazed at my sketch of Arthur this morning when he had pulled the curtains. Ever critical of my work, I thought I got his eyes wrong today. He tended to hold his head forward or at a tilt, which gave him a mischievous look. His upper lids were heavy, too, which often happened with age. But today I had drawn cold eyes. Eyes that had no depth or compassion.

Unhappy with my drawing, I flipped back to see how I had drawn him before. Those were the right eyes! How had I gotten them so wrong today? Was I seeing a different side of him? Or was it me? Was I just off?

I jumped when my phone rang.

It was Fish calling. "Did you mean it when you offered to help?"

"Absolutely! You have no idea how terrible I feel about Jezebel's accident. I never should have interfered."

"It's not your fault."

It was and I knew it.

"Jezebel wears reading glasses. She hasn't come around yet, but she'll want them if she wakes up."

If she wakes up. The words tore through me. "I would be happy to bring them over. Anything else?"

"If I think of anything, I'll let you know." He disconnected the call.

Feeling sad, I trudged back over to Jezebel's house, retrieved the key, and let myself in. I found her reading glasses in her purse, then went upstairs and looked for a small bag that I could load with clothes.

I found a little duffel bag in a closet. The first thing I checked was her nightstand. Most people kept things there that they used nightly. I found some lotions and creams she might want, and a phone charger.

Curiously, I also discovered a calendar, which Jezebel used as a brief journal. There were entries on each day, along with a number that looked to be the temperature.

In the previous days, she had made notations such as *Foiled Kaylee! Kaylee back, ugh. New job at bookstore!* And one that concerned me from yesterday. *Arthur didn't recognize me.*

Chapter 36

How could that be? Jezebel and Arthur had been neighbors for decades. I wondered about the nature of Arthur's illness. He had remembered to call the bookstore to cancel his appearance, but he had sounded odd. Sort of groggy. Had he fallen and hit his head? Suffered a stroke?

I added a brush, toothbrush, and toothpaste that I found in Jezebel's bathroom. From her closet I selected a top and comfortable-looking trousers, then added a matching sweater. Did she have her shoes on when the EMTs brought her up from the basement? Probably. Just in case she had been barefoot, I wrapped a pair of sneakers in a towel and added them to the duffel bag, along with some undies and socks.

Back downstairs, I glanced through her purse to see if anything was in it that she might need. In the end, I decided to take it along. Everything except her wallet, which I stashed in her nightstand. Fish could bring home anything she didn't want by her side.

I zipped the duffel bag and left the house, taking care to lock it securely. Once again, I bent to slip the key under the plant pot.

But when I walked away, I heard rustling in the bushes

next door. I didn't see anyone, but a branch moved suspiciously. Slinging the duffel bag over my shoulder, I crossed the small lawn to Arthur's house, thinking one of Arthur's cats might have escaped.

The rustling had moved around to the left side of the house. I peered behind the bushes, expecting to see a cat or dog, but it was a person. "Hello?"

Gabriella popped up, twigs in her hair. "Thank heaven it's only you." She motioned to me to crouch. "Something's wrong with Arthur. Look at this." She pointed upward.

I wedged through the bushes to join her. "What am I looking for?"

"Just look inside."

I peered through the window into Arthur's library. Books lay all over the floor like an earthquake had shaken them off the shelves.

"What a mess. I'd hate to be the one who had to clean that up. What do you suppose happened?"

"Hurricane Mia."

"Well, they *are* moving. That's an ineffective way to pack, though."

"She's not packing. She's looking for something."

I hated to imagine that was the case, but it did make more sense. "What is she looking for? Everyone knows Arthur is broke." We sat behind the bushes, side by side, our backs to the brick wall of Arthur's house.

"I have no idea. I'm so glad you're here," said Gabriella. "All we have to do is wait for Mia to leave."

"Arthur may not let us in."

"I have a key. What are you doing here?"

"I was checking on Jezebel."

"I'd almost forgotten about Jezebel," said Gabriella. "I haven't seen her in ages. She's such a hoot!"

I was about to tell her that someone had pushed Jezebel down the stairs when it dawned on me that Gabriella could be armed with a glass calligraphy pen. "Did Cara bother Griffin a lot?"

Gabriella sighed. "I never realized it was Cara until you mentioned it. I'm sorry that she's dead, but I'm convinced that it's because she hounded the wrong person. She must have thought she was paparazzi or something."

"That's my conclusion." I went out on a limb. "I think she was killed with a glass calligraphy pen."

"That can't be. It would have broken off in her neck."

"It did."

"Eww. What a horrible way to die." Gabriella held her hand against the right side of her throat and moaned. "Is that why you were so interested in my calligraphy pens?"

"I'd never seen any quite like that before. They really are like little arrows."

"What a terrible death. She must have been so afraid."

I glanced at her. Would Cara's killer have said that? I didn't think so. Certainly not with that degree of sincerity. "What happened to the red one?"

"Red one?"

"The red calligraphy pen."

"Oh my gosh! You think I killed her? It broke, Florrie. Actually, that's how I know they break easily. I dropped it on the floor, and it smashed into pieces like a candy cane. All except the nub on the end, which remained surprisingly intact."

"Arthur's red calligraphy pen is missing, too."

"Well, that doesn't mean anything. In the first place, there must be hundreds of people in Washington who have them. And in the second place, maybe the red ones break easier for some reason. Or maybe people use them more frequently because they like the color, so they get dropped more."

Gabriella was so reasonable that I found it hard not to like her. I thought I had pushed my limit, though, and didn't ask if Griffin might have stabbed Cara.

"Is Griffin back from his writing retreat?"

"Not yet. I don't think he'll be back for a while."

That was convenient for Buzz!

At that moment, we heard an engine. A sleek black low-slung Jaguar purred by us.

"Mia is driving, and Arthur is with her. Come on!"

We burst through the branches and brushed plant bits off our clothes and hair. "You can't break into his house."

"I'm not breaking in. I have a key."

"How did you get that?"

Gabriella shot me a quizzical look. "He gave it to me. I worked for him, remember?"

She unlocked the front door and drew a sharp breath. "The rainbow ribbon is gone!"

Cats appeared on the open staircase far above us and raced down, mewing.

"It's going to auction on Saturday."

"No! That can't be. He would never give it up. Something is very wrong here."

I paused for a look at the empty pedestal and the Siamese cat that had just jumped onto it. "How did he keep the cats from knocking it over?"

She pointed upward. "It was secured by fishing line from the ceiling. It's barely visible."

"What are we looking for?"

"I don't know. Medications, maybe? I saw him yesterday, Florrie," she whispered. "He looked *wrong*. And he was distant, like he didn't know who I was. I don't understand why he didn't recognize me."

"That's what Jezebel wrote on her calendar. I saw him on Thursday, and when I sketched him later, I got his eyes wrong.

Just like you said. He looked wrong. Squinty, like someone wearing contacts for the first time."

She sucked in a noisy breath of air. "It's not him! That's why he didn't look right. It's not Arthur! I wrote this exact scenario in one of my books. My character grew a mustache, dyed his hair, and wore contact lenses. This guy has Arthur's lean, tall build, but—"

"But you can't change your eyes."

We looked at each other and said in tandem, "Then where is Arthur?"

"Clearly, we need to search the house." I picked up a cat who'd been circling my ankles. "What if they left because a Realtor is coming to show the house?"

"I didn't think of that! The buyers won't be impressed by that mess in the library. Okay, if a Realtor shows up, I'll say they called and asked us to secure the cats so they wouldn't be in the way. Got it?"

I nodded.

"I'll check down here. You head up to the bedrooms and bathrooms."

I placed the cat on the floor and tried to dash up the stairs, but cats surrounded my every step. I could only imagine that they smelled Peaches on me. Or maybe they had that feline sixth sense and they knew I liked them.

I began in what I guessed was the master bedroom. Clothes had been tossed about, making it almost as big a mess as the library. I looked out the floor-to-ceiling window, thinking this was probably where I had seen Arthur or someone who resembled him.

When I ventured into a gleaming all-white bathroom, I spotted the Hawaiian shirt he'd been wearing. A quick check of drawers and closets didn't reveal anything of particular interest.

As I left the bedroom, intending to visit the next one, I realized that all six cats waited for me on the stairs leading to the third floor. "What are you guys up to?"

They turned and zoomed up the stairs.

I followed them. The sun shone into the beautiful glass room at the top of the house. Arthur had kept the furnishings minimal and simple, which only added to the feeling of being in the sky. The cats mewed and paced at the back wall where I had found the art supplies.

"What is it?" I asked them. "Are there mice back there?"

Their tails flicked like Peaches's did when she was upset. I pressed along the seam of the built-in cabinets and saw the art items again. I pressed the next one, and a hidden door swung open. The cats bounded through to another room.

I was more reticent. An attic window at the front of the house let in light. I cautiously stepped inside.

Chapter 37

A figure lay on a bed, covered with a white blanket.

It was Arthur. His complexion had turned ashen and his eyes were closed.

I dashed to the stairs. "Gabriella! Gabriella! Up here." I ran back to Arthur, wondering if he was dead or alive.

As I approached him, I saw the blanket rise and fall almost imperceptibly, but it was there. He was alive!

"Arthur, can you hear me?"

He didn't open his eyes or show any sign of acknowledgment.

A scream rose behind me. Gabriella rushed to him, not nearly as tentative as I had been. "Is he dead?"

"No. I think he's breathing. Arthur? Tap his cheeks lightly. See if he responds."

She tried to revive him. "Nothing. Just nothing," she sobbed.

I pulled out my telephone, and for the second time that day I called 911 to ask for an ambulance. "And send the police, too, please."

When I hung up the phone, Gabriella was sitting on the bed. She leaned against the headboard with Arthur's head cradled in her arms. "He's been drugged. That's the only explanation."

"Maybe he'll be okay."

"Arthur is the closest thing to a father that I ever had," sobbed Gabriella. "My own father died when I was two. I don't remember anything about him. Sometimes I wondered if Arthur didn't feel like I was his daughter. He was lonely, even when he had a girlfriend. They always wanted something from him, you know? Money or fame. Sometimes they were social climbers. They'd hang on until someone better came along. And they dumped him fast when his books didn't do well. It was different between Arthur and me. He never drank around me. Sometimes I thought maybe he was insecure and needed booze to help him be the persona he tried to project. But I saw the real Arthur. The one that Jacquie knew. The one who caught popcorn in his mouth, was in awe of fireflies, could quote Robert Frost and Fred Flintstone, and rescued alley cats, no matter how matted or sickly they looked."

I gazed out the window, only half listening, because I was afraid the black Jaguar might return before the ambulance arrived.

My heart beat faster with each passing moment. I called Eric but he didn't answer his cell phone. I left a voice-mail message. "Eric, I'm at Arthur's house. He's in poor shape. We're waiting for an ambulance and the cops, but I'm afraid his girlfriend, Mia, will be back before they get here. If you're in the area, could you come by?"

Just as I finished, the exact thing I had feared happened. The black Jaguar glided by the front of the house and turned into the driveway.

Chapter 38

I had to keep Mia, and maybe the man who had been with her earlier, at bay. Gabriella was in no shape to be much help. The ambulance or the police had to arrive soon.

It dawned on me that someone had to corral the cats, too. They still lounged around the man they loved. I couldn't leave them here. They would be underfoot when the EMTs arrived.

I ran down the stairs, frantically searched the kitchen for canned cat food and bowls, and looked around for a room with a door. I found a rather large powder room. I was willing to bet they had never eaten in there! I stood just outside the bathroom and slowly opened one can of cat food, hoping the sound would travel up to them.

I heard them before I saw them. "In here, kitties!" I placed bowls on the floor and watched as they barreled in to eat. I left the light on for them and closed the door.

When I stepped out, I could see Mia and the man walking toward the house from the detached garage. Why did this house have to be all glass? There wasn't even a decent place to hide, except for the powder room where the cats were.

Mia and the Arthur look-alike stopped. They were arguing about something.

I had to get to the kitchen. Arthur must have a chef's knife in there. Not that I would use it, but I needed something to defend myself. I dropped to my knees and crawled across the floor to the kitchen as fast as I could. A lovely wood knife rack sat on the counter. Their voices were louder here. I raised myself just enough to grab a knife, then returned to my knees and peered around the corner.

He was the spitting image of Arthur. Tall and lean, with the same eye-catching bushy white mustache. Anyone who didn't know Arthur well would assume he was Arthur Bedlingham. I wondered if he could hold up through an interview. Had he read all of Arthur's books? Studied his mannerisms? They might be able to fool a lot of people. But he and Mia had overlooked one person who knew Arthur well—Jezebel.

"I'm not afraid of you," he said to Mia. "After all, I'm the one who looks like Arthur. I don't need you anymore."

What? Had I heard him correctly?

"You are such an idiot. You just signed a power of attorney giving me complete control over Arthur's estate. Without me, you have nothing."

"I don't have anything anyway. You said there was money in his books. I haven't seen a dime yet. I think the old geezer played you. He lied to you!" The man sneered and then laughed at her.

"That's not true. It's in there somewhere. Besides, there will be plenty of money once this house sells." She paused and gazed at him.

He backed toward the pool. "Hey, *I* am not the one who killed that guy, Evan, or stabbed the nosy reporter."

"You think you're such a good actor. You wouldn't have fooled Evan for half an hour, much less a couple of days. You couldn't even fool that old neighbor who probably has lousy eyesight."

His head tilted just a hair as if he might be realizing she wasn't quite the person he thought. "All you needed was the girl's phone. You didn't have to kill her."

Chills ran through me. Cara had uttered *R-faux*. She hadn't had the strength to say *artist* and *phone*. Cara saw her killer, knew she had taken Cara's phone, and recognized her as the artist at the party.

"You're so stupid. She *saw* me handing him the pot brownies and took a picture. You think she wouldn't eventually have realized exactly what it was that she saw?"

"I did not sign up for killing them two. Only Arthur. And he's looking pretty crummy. We'd better get him down the road so we can throw him out in the desert when his time comes."

"'Them two'? Arthur would never say that. And as I recall, you had no problem putting Rohypnol in Jacquie's and his drinks so we could get his keys and identification." She smiled. "He just laid there on the lawn like a baby while we collected all his financial information. I rather enjoyed seeing him so helpless. He deserves it." Her tone was harsh. "How dare he. I loved him. Loved him! But he used me. For twenty years I was loyal to him. I did everything for him. He could not have asked for a better wife. But he wouldn't marry me." Her tone grew louder. "For twenty years he wouldn't marry me. I never had any children. I never found anyone else to love me. All I got out of it was the shame of being Mrs. Grimkill! He took my life and my love and twisted them into a sad, pathetic character and then he killed her!"

"Now, Mia, you know *I* don't treat you like that."

Her tongue snaked out of her mouth, and she gazed around while she licked her lips.

I didn't dare move. I was pretty sure I stopped breathing.

When she didn't head for the house, I let out a breath of relief. She must not have noticed me peeking around the corner.

"Why, Wayne, didn't you just say that you didn't need me anymore? Maybe both of you will fit into the trunk of Arthur's car." She pushed him into the swimming pool.

She turned, and for a minute, I thought she was looking right at me. I ducked behind the counter. When I looked again, she had grabbed the decorative birdcage, and as the man came to the edge of the pool and sputtered, she used it to push his head down.

He ducked and swam out from under it. He came up for air yelling, "Poor me. If you die first, I'll be Arthur and it won't matter what I signed."

That did it. Her entire body tensed with anger.

He made it worse by laughing at her.

She unlocked the door and stomped toward the kitchen.

There was no place to hide. If I darted out of the kitchen to hide elsewhere, she would see me. Where was the ambulance? What happened to the police?

She stopped dead at the sight of me. Her gaze slid down my arm. She knew I was hiding something behind my back. "Florrie. What are you doing here?"

I swallowed hard. "I was checking on Jezebel because she didn't come to work today."

A corner of her mouth turned up in a smirk. "She lives next door."

I nodded and played along, trying desperately to buy time. "She's not well. She's in the hospital now but it's not looking good."

She shook her head. "You're going to ruin everything. Why did you have to come here?"

"Why did you have to involve Jacquie?" I asked.

"I loathe her. She is my archenemy. You can't imagine what it was like having Arthur hold her up as the perfect woman. He even told me she was his one true love. Can you imagine? The man I adored, for whom I did everything, had one true love and it wasn't me. I had to hear about perfect Jacquie the entire time I was with Arthur. How could I not despise her? And then she turned up asking me to draw pictures of her guests. How crazy is that? The very woman whom I hated came to me! It was like a gift. She needed *me*. She started the whole thing, really. I had met Wayne and could hardly believe the resemblance to Arthur. He's a bit of a dolt though. Doesn't begin to have Arthur's intelligence or wit."

"But why the Rohypnol? You didn't need to do that."

"Oh, but I did. Arthur had removed the key he kept outside. I needed access to his house to get his records, bank account numbers, investment accounts—"

"But he's broke. Everyone knows that. And that has nothing to do with Jacquie. Were you trying to scare her? To be cruel to her?"

"I'll admit there might have been a little satisfaction in it, but she was crucial. Jacquie was the only person he would have gone to meet. His precious Jacquie needing him was the only way to slip Rohypnol in his drink and knock him out long enough for me to get his keys and search the house. He has cash here somewhere, you know. I still haven't found it. If I hadn't drugged her, too, she would have taken care of him and brought him home. Clearly that wouldn't have worked at all. The bonus was this." She passed by me and flipped open a kitchen cabinet door. Inside, someone had taped up a sheet of paper.

Evan McDowell
QT Syndrome
Taking propranolol.
Physician: Dr. Piowtrowski

"You knew!" I was furious. "You killed an innocent man who never hurt you."

"Mmm. Casualty of war." She shrugged, not one bit regretful. "He had to go. Wayne couldn't pass himself off as Arthur to anyone who knew Arthur well. But, you know, it was far easier than I thought to transfer what little he had in banks and investments. Passwords are a handy thing. You don't even have to show up in person."

Her gaze shifted to something behind me. Filled with dread, I turned. Wayne stood in back of me, dripping wet. I was trapped unless I could jump up on the kitchen counter, which I knew was highly unlikely.

Mia wasted no time trying to grab the knife from me. We wrestled for it, but when Wayne seized another knife from the rack, I let go and ran out of the kitchen.

The two of them circled like boxers. I fled for the front door and opened it. Where was the ambulance already?

One of them screamed.

Suddenly it was quiet. Too quiet. I inched back toward the kitchen. Were they planning to attack me?

Mia raced through the house and out to the backyard.

Wayne lay on the floor, the knife handle jutting from his chest. His hands curled around the handle and blood oozed over his wet shirt.

"No!" I placed my hands over his bloody ones. "Don't pull it out. Leave it where it is. Let a doctor remove it. Otherwise, you might bleed out."

"How do you know that? Are you a nurse?"

"I read a lot of mysteries."

Thankfully, the ambulance siren finally sounded outside. Not a moment too soon, either. I wasn't sure whether Wayne or Arthur was in more immediate need of medical attention.

I washed Wayne's blood off my hands and hurried to the front door. I expected the ambulance, but Sergeant Bridges stood there.

"What's the problem now, Florrie?"

I resented his attitude. But this wasn't the time to quibble. I led him toward the kitchen. "Mia Woodham just ran out the back way after stabbing her accomplice, Wayne. And Arthur is on the third floor in terrible shape. Gabriella is with him."

Bridges leaned over Wayne. "Can you tell me your name, sir?"

"Wayne Ridley."

"Who did this to you? Was it her?" Bridges pointed toward me.

"No," Wayne whispered. "Don't leave me alone. She'll be back to finish me off."

"What's her name?"

"Mia. Mia Woodham."

If the situation hadn't been so dire, I might have been tempted to stick my tongue out at Bridges. But that would have been childish.

I could hear the EMTs at the door and rushed to them. "This way, and we have another person on the third floor."

While two of them tended to Wayne, I led the third one upstairs. When she was busy with Arthur, I looked out the window wall. There was no sign of Mia. But I saw Bridges walking around cautiously out in the yard.

Forty minutes later, I stood on the lawn with my arm around Gabriella and watched the EMTs load Arthur into an ambulance.

An additional squad car arrived and Bridges escorted a

handcuffed Mia to the vehicle. She slid into the back seat and stared straight ahead, avoiding eye contact with anyone.

As the car drove away, Gabriella insisted on going to the hospital. "Arthur shouldn't be there alone. He needs an advocate. And he doesn't have anyone else."

I still had Jezebel's bag, so I offered to drive Gabriella.

We returned to the house, where Bridges waited for the crime-scene crew.

"Where was Mia?" I asked.

"Hiding in the back seat of the Jaguar." He walked over to the powder-room door. "What's in here?"

"Cats," Gabriella and I said in tandem.

He opened the door. Six cats yowled and rushed at us. He quickly closed it. "I'll call the pound."

"You will not!" declared Gabriella. "I have a key to the house, and I will come over every day to feed and take care of them. Don't you *dare* touch those cats."

She had more moxie than I thought.

Chapter 39

Bridges appeared to give it some thought. "Okay. Have it your way."

When Gabriella and I arrived at the hospital, we found Fish in the emergency room. Rather than telling the story twice, I invited him to step outside with me while I called Eric. I knew I should be telling all this to Sergeant Bridges, but I thought it might be better received if it came from a fellow cop.

I told Eric everything that had happened. How Jezebel went home for lunch and was pushed down the stairs. That she had mentioned on her calendar that Arthur didn't recognize her, and Gabriella had had a similar experience. That Gabriella and I had seen a man who looked like Arthur in the car with Mia.

When I finished, Eric said, "I'll bring Bridges over to the hospital so he can hear the details for himself."

"Eric, Mia is the one who killed Evan."

"How do you know that?"

"She admitted as much. Her scheme wouldn't have worked if Evan was in the house every day working for Arthur. He died because he was in her way."

★ ★ ★

As if Eric knew that exhaustion had overcome me, he appeared at the emergency room with Sergeant Bridges in tow and giant mocha lattes for Fish, Gabriella, and me.

"You're the best." I drank like I hadn't seen fluids in days. Thankfully, Gabriella backed me up. For once, I hadn't been alone, so Bridges couldn't place blame on me. He listened to the whole story, making notes as we talked. Then he left to check on the crime-scene situation.

Eric stayed with me while we waited to hear about Jezebel's and Arthur's conditions.

Buzz arrived to be with Gabriella, which shocked me to the core. If anyone recognized them, Gabriella's marriage to Griffin would be over.

Two hours later, a doctor emerged to tell us that Gabriella had been correct. Arthur had been heavily dosed with sedatives. Interestingly, Jezebel's blood work showed the same sedative in her system. She had broken her arm, but the CT scan of her head was clear. They would probably be released tomorrow.

I gazed at Fish. I knew what this meant for Jezebel, and it broke my heart. She would be terribly unhappy that she couldn't live in her own home anymore.

On the bright side, both of them would recover.

On Sunday morning, I walked out to the swimming pool at the mansion with my mug of tea. The sun shone brightly. When a light breeze passed, the rays glittered on the pool like diamonds. It was hard to believe that only a week ago I had dragged poor Evan out of the water. Part of me had hoped that his death had been accidental. Somehow it was even worse to know that he had done nothing wrong or evil or troubling. He had just been in Mia's way. They didn't have proof of that yet, as far as I knew, but maybe Wayne would testify against her. With any luck, they would find Cara's phone in Mia's possession, too, proving that she had killed Cara.

"We heard what happened." I recognized the professor's voice and looked around.

He and Jacquie walked out to the pool. Jacquie burst into tears and grabbed me in a bear hug. "We're just so glad that you're all right! I feel terrible." She looked me in the eyes. "I knew something was wrong when Mia delivered the painting to us. She had a huge bruise on the side of her face and a terrible scratch. She tried to hide it with makeup, but you know how that goes. It looks fine when you're in the right light, but when you go outside, it runs or fades. I bet Arthur tried to get away from her."

"The left side or the right side?" I asked.

Jacquie thought about it. "The left."

For a moment I was breathless. "I did that! Someone was following me, and I swung my purse at him and ran. It must have been Mia! I had just walked Jezebel home."

Jacquie scowled. "Why didn't you tell us about that?"

"I'm fine. Nothing happened to me. It's poor Jezebel that worries me. She didn't want to be in a facility and now I'm certain that's what is in her immediate future."

The professor wrapped an arm around my shoulders and squeezed. "What do you say Bob and Veronica run the store this afternoon and you come with us to Arthur's house?"

"Bob has been complaining about working too many days," I protested. "What are you planning to do at Arthur's?"

"Gabriella told us what a mess it is. We thought we'd go over and straighten up his library for him before he comes home. Would you be able to help if Roxie worked for you today?"

"I guess. Wouldn't you want Roxie at Arthur's house?"

"You know more about books. I have a sneaking suspicion some of them might be valuable."

"Okay. As long as it's all right with Roxie."

Although Arthur's house was usually immaculate, I dressed in a jean skort and short-sleeved T-shirt for handling dusty books. I apologized to Peaches for leaving her home alone, but with a tummy full of tuna, she lounged in a sunbeam and didn't appear worried about it.

Gabriella, Jacquie, Professor Maxwell, and I walked up to the front door of Arthur's house. Gabriella grasped the handle and the door swung open before she slid her key into the slot. She drew a sharp breath. "The door wasn't locked!"

The aroma of coffee drifted to me.

"I'll go in first," said the professor. "Be prepared to call for help. Just in case."

I watched from the doorway as he crept through the house. When he left my line of sight, I followed behind him. The sound of his laughter gave me the strength to edge closer for a look.

Jezebel bustled about the kitchen. "Hi, Florrie! We baked some peach muffins for all of us to share."

The light caught on the tops and sparkled. Sugar, I guessed. "They're beautiful. But you have a broken arm."

"Aw, I've had worse. Besides, Fish helped me."

Gabriella made a beeline for the peach muffins and Jacquie planted a kiss on her brave husband's cheek.

"Did you have a big fight with your children last night?" I asked, taking the mug of hot coffee she held out to me.

"I was firm. I told them I went to a supersharp lawyer and that anyone who contests my will gets disinherited. On top of that, she wrote a trust for me that disinherits *all* of them the moment they send me to a home for old folks." Jezebel cackled with glee.

"Is that true? Can you do that?" asked Jacquie.

"That's what the documents say, and it wouldn't hurt for

them to think that's what will happen." Jezebel slapped her thigh she was laughing so hard. "Kids!"

Her kids had to be the age of my parents. Not exactly youngsters themselves.

"Besides," said Fish, "I'm moving in. I can't imagine a better roommate." He winked at us.

"That sounds like a wonderful arrangement." Jacquie smiled at Jezebel, and we made our way into Arthur's office-cum-library.

"What do you suppose is the best way to do this?" asked Gabriella.

"Wait a minute." I looked at Fish. "What about CSI? Won't they need to go through the house?"

"They finished last night."

"In that case, how about if Fish climbs the library ladder?" I offered. "You can pick up the books and hand them to me. I'll make a quick assessment before I give each book to Fish to place back on the shelves."

They handed me books much faster than I anticipated. Happily, Fish was quick at putting them away.

Jacquie handed me a book, saying, "This feels old."

I took a closer look. "*The Hound of the Baskervilles!*" Holding the book carefully lest I damage it, I opened it slowly to see if it might be a first edition. "Bingo!" I cried, closing it ever so gently.

Jacquie reached for it and ran her hand over the red cover and gold lettering. Then she looked up something on her phone.

"What's wrong?" I asked.

"I'm confused. If Arthur was hard up for money, he could have sold this. It will fetch between two thousand and seven thousand dollars. Nothing to sneeze at, yet he didn't sell it."

"Maybe it was special to him," said the professor. "But I've picked up two copies of *Bleak House.*"

"I found one, too," declared Gabriella.

We placed them on a table. So far, we had found three copies.

"The covers are different," Jacquie observed. "They're all different editions."

"Why would he buy so many copies of *Bleak House?*" asked the professor.

"Oh, that one's easy." Jezebel laughed. "I'm always buying things because I forgot I already have one. I have five pepper mills! Do any of you need a pepper mill?"

We chuckled and got back to the task at hand. Our work was interrupted frequently as we found personal favorites among Arthur's collection.

When we paused for a break, I opened a copy of *Bleak House* with care, in case it was older than I thought. Something seemed off. I flipped through thirty or so pages and found a cavity carved out of the remaining pages. Arthur had laid a note on the top.

I was about to read it but decided that the others would enjoy Arthur's little trick. I called them over.

"Look what I found."

Jacquie picked up the note.

> *My dearest Evan,*
> *If you have found this, then I am gone, and you will have to carry the torch for me. You have it in you to be a great writer. Read and absorb King's book On Writing: A Memoir of the Craft, then close it and write. Just write. Turn off your inner editor. Don't doubt your vocabulary. Follow his advice and write for yourself. Enjoy the ride, my friend. Here's a little pocket money to tide you over. See you on the other side.*
>
> *Arthur*

"'Pocket money'?" echoed Jezebel. "Oh no. Evan will never know about this. It would have meant so much to him!"

Jacquie touched the paper in the middle of the pages. "It's glassine."

"What's that?" Jezebel reached over and touched it.

"It's acid-free paper that's resistant to moisture. Artists use it." Jacquie gently pried it open.

"Stock certificates!" exclaimed Jezebel. "My stars! Are they worth anything?"

The professor handled them carefully. "I'll have to check with my broker but some of these could be very valuable."

Bleak House was supposed to be one of the longest books ever written. Maybe that was the reason Arthur owned three copies. He needed a book deep enough to hide things. The title would have been a joke that only Arthur understood.

I opened the second one and found the same thing. A hole in the pages, covered with glassine. The room turned quiet as everyone looked on. I lifted the glassine to find cash. Lots of it in all kinds of denominations.

Gabriella quickly opened the third copy of *Bleak House* and removed the glassine.

"Oh my!" Jacquie pulled out exquisite jewelry. Rubies, pearls, sapphires, and the biggest emerald ring I had ever seen. "They're old. Probably his mother's and his grandmother's."

We closed them all up and placed them well apart on the top shelves.

"I guess we know what Mia was looking for." Gabriella had her hands on her waist and looked fierce. "How could she? Poor Evan. He never hurt anyone."

Gabriella left to pick up Arthur at the hospital while the rest of us finished tidying his house. We ordered pizza, which arrived minutes before Arthur and Gabriella walked in.

"I hope I smell pepperoni," said Arthur. "Gabriella told

me all you did for me. I can't thank you enough. Especially you, Florrie." He walked over and gave me a hug.

We sat down outside at the table by the pool. I brought out iced tea that Jezebel had made and napkins.

Arthur smiled at us and helped himself to pizza. "I'm hungry as a bear after hibernation. Actually, it was kind of like I was hibernating. Very little food and lots of sleep."

"You're lucky they didn't kill you," Gabriella said.

"They would have. I could hear them talking. He wanted to get rid of me, but Mia insisted that they needed me for facial recognition and fingerprints. She couldn't even get into my phone without holding it up to my face. I don't know why, but facial recognition never worked for Wayne."

Arthur ate a bite of pizza. "They were planning to drive to Mexico, and as soon as they had the money from selling the house, they would have left me in the desert, with the driver's license of Wayne Ridley."

"That's the man who looks like you?" asked the professor.

"It is. He's not a dead ringer, but close enough."

"But what about your fingerprints?" asked Jezebel.

"I have to remember in my next book that if the sun dries you out and your bones are picked clean, there are no fingerprints."

Everyone stopped eating, but just for a moment.

I was itching to know more, but Jacquie deftly changed the subject.

We didn't stay long. The effects of the drugs clearly still lingered, and Arthur needed to rest. Gabriella planned to stay over to keep an eye on him.

Chapter 40

One week later, Jacquie and Professor Maxwell left for their delayed honeymoon in Hawaii. Bob finally had Sundays off. After work, Jezebel and I headed for Gabriella's house.

As we entered, the sweet scent of peonies mingled with lavender and garlic. The cowboy boots were gone. Griffin must have collected his belongings.

We followed Gabriella into her charming kitchen, where she poured white wine and offered us bruschetta with pesto. "I made them with basil from my own garden."

"They're heavenly," said Jezebel. "Where are the cats?"

"They're playing upstairs. They might come down later."

We ate outside on a patio that overflowed with summer blooms. The days were longer and the nights mild. Fairy lights sparkled along the brick walls that afforded her privacy from her neighbors.

Gabriella leaned toward us and whispered, "I'm seeing Buzz."

I feigned surprise. "That's terrific, Gabriella!"

Jezebel gazed at her. "How does Griffin feel about that?"

"He doesn't mind. We're getting a divorce."

"Gabriella," said Jezebel, "I'm so sorry. But Buzz certainly does seem exciting and he's not bad looking, either."

"Actually, he's not that exciting, which I find appealing. He's very calm and just about perfect as far as I'm concerned. The two of us have been spending our days together, writing and talking about books."

I was happy for her. When I excused myself for a moment, I passed her desk where a huge stack of pages sat. I couldn't help myself and drifted over to look at it. After all, I wasn't going to read anything but the cover page. There was no harm in that, was there?

The pages were already laid out like a book. Little yellow stickies with notes neatly hung out on one side. The top page showed the copyright and publishing information. It was copyrighted in the name of Griffin Corbyn. I lifted a couple of pages. Sure enough, the title page said, "*The Lions of Rome* by Griffin Corbyn." I paged to one of the stickies. In a feminine handwriting, someone had changed a word. Was Gabriella still editing Griffin's manuscripts?

It wasn't any of my business. I should never have looked at it. What she did with and for the men in her life wasn't my problem. Then it dawned on me. Gabriella *was* Griffin Corbyn! That explained it all. The seclusion and reluctance to make public appearances. The different sizes of clothes.

I heard Gabriella gasp. She bent over with laughter. "I guess you've figured it out. Can you keep my secret?"

"You're Griffin?"

"Yes. I couldn't interest any publishers in my thrillers, so I invented the pen name Griffin Corbyn. I never anticipated that his reclusiveness would only increase the interest in him and his books."

"Wait a minute. Didn't Arthur and Margarite say they had met Griffin?"

Gabriella laughed. "You can't even imagine how shocked

I was when people started claiming they had met him. There are people who have *quoted* things he allegedly said to them! I created a fictional author who took on a life of his own. It's unbelievable!" Gabriella shook her head in amazement.

"Then why do you have men's clothing and shoes in so many different sizes?"

Gabriella blinked at me and then began to chuckle. "I had to decorate with some men's belongings so it would like he lived here. A coat, a sweater, some shoes. Those huge boots that I got for one dollar because they're so big! I went to yard sales and bought a few things that I thought would appeal to Griffin. It never occurred to me that anyone would compare the sizes!"

"You did a good job of misleading me."

"But, Florrie, I make a lot more money as Griffin than I do as Gabriella, so you have to keep it quiet, please. I'm so relieved to have a friend who knows the truth. Whew! I couldn't go anywhere with Buzz because people would have thought I was having an affair, when I'm not married at all!"

I joined in her laughter. "You're getting an imaginary divorce so you can be seen in public with Buzz."

"That's about the size of it. I came in to get something for Jezebel. I'll be right out."

I returned to the patio, remembering that Jacquie had claimed Gabriella couldn't keep a secret. Apparently, she could!

I chatted with Jezebel about how her life had changed now that Fish had moved in with her. In a few minutes, Gabriella returned with a manuscript and held the title page out to us.

" '*The Galactic Wind,*' " I read aloud. " 'By Evan McDowell!' "

Gabriella nodded. "He left all his manuscripts to me. They're actually pretty good. Two publishers have indicated an interest."

"But he's not here to see it happen," I said sadly.

"No. But he lives on in his writing," Jezebel pointed out. "That's quite an honor."

"I have one more thing. A gift for Jezebel."

Gabriella left again and returned with a box. She placed it on Jezebel's lap.

Something inside shifted and we could hear little cries.

Jezebel opened it and two tiny kittens with huge eyes peered at her. One had beautiful orange markings and the other was mostly white.

"They're rescue kitties," said Gabriella. "Which one would you like?"

Jezebel lifted one and then the other, murmuring to them and nuzzling their delicate fur. They mewed for her attention, stretching out their tiny paws.

"If it's okay, I would like to keep both of them." Jezebel smiled as she watched them. "Thank you, Gabriella. And thank you, too, Florrie. You girls have helped me find love and purpose in my life again. Look out, world. Jezebel is back!"

RECIPES

Strawberry Cupcakes

Makes 12 cupcakes

Note: The pound of strawberries will be enough for the cupcakes and the frosting, with a little left over. Use the extra strawberry puree in a smoothie, over ice cream, pancakes, or oatmeal!

3 tablespoons butter
1 pound strawberries
1½ cups flour
1 teaspoon baking powder
5 tablespoons butter
1 cup granulated sugar
2 large eggs, room temperature
2 teaspoons vanilla
½ cup two-percent milk

Preheat oven to 350°F. Place cupcake papers into wells of a cupcake pan.

Melt the 3 tablespoons of butter and set aside to cool.

Wash and hull the strawberries, setting them on a paper towel to soak up the water. Pat with another paper towel. Add all strawberries to a blender. Blend on high or puree until smooth. Set aside. Do not refrigerate.

Pour the flour and the baking powder in a bowl and mix well with a fork.

Cream the 5 tablespoons butter with the sugar until thick

and smooth. Add the eggs one at a time and beat. Add the vanilla and beat to combine. Alternate adding the milk and the flour mixture. Add the melted butter and mix briefly. Pour in ½ cup strawberry puree and mix until just combined.

Fill cupcake papers to the tops. Bake 16 to 18 minutes or until a cake tester comes out clean. Do not overbake!

Strawberry Frosting

The secret to this recipe is having all the ingredients at room temperature, especially the butter and the pureed strawberries.

10 tablespoons unsalted butter, softened
¼ teaspoon fine-grain pink salt
⅓ cup pureed fresh strawberries
3-3½ cups powdered sugar

  Beat the butter with the salt until soft. Add the strawberry puree and beat. Add the powdered sugar ½ cup at a time. Beat for 4 minutes.
  If it's too soft to hold a shape, refrigerate for a while.

Peach Breakfast Puffs

Makes 12 muffins

Butter for greasing muffin tin
1½ cups flour
½ cup sugar
1½ teaspoons baking powder
¼ teaspoon nutmeg
⅛ teaspoon salt
1 egg
½ cup milk (I use two percent)
⅓ cup butter, melted
1½ fresh peaches
½ teaspoon cinnamon
¼ cup sugar
¼ cup butter, melted

Melt ⅓ cup butter and set aside to cool.

Preheat oven to 350°F. Grease muffin wells in the muffin pan.

In one bowl, combine the flour, ½ cup sugar, baking powder, nutmeg, and salt. Mix well with a fork and make a well in the middle.

In another bowl, whisk the egg with a fork, pour in the milk and combine, then whisk in the ⅓ cup melted butter.

Peel the peaches with a vegetable peeler and slice into eighths.

Add the egg mixture to the flour mixture and stir until just combined. It should be lumpy. Do not overmix!

Spoon into muffin pan, dividing evenly, filling each well about half full. Place a peach slice on top of each muffin, pushing it into the batter just a bit.

Bake at 350°F for 20 to 25 minutes.

Meanwhile, stir the cinnamon with the ¼ cup sugar in a shallow bowl large enough to dip the muffins. Melt the ¼ cup butter and pour it into a shallow bowl large enough to dip the muffins.

Remove the baked muffins from oven. While still hot, remove each muffin from the pan, dip into the melted butter, then dip into the sugar.

Serve warm.

Easy Roasted Asparagus

This is my favorite go-to recipe for asparagus. Go ahead and make the whole bunch because it's delicious cold, too, and you can toss leftovers into salads and stir-fries.

aluminum foil
1 bunch of fresh asparagus
about 2 tablespoons olive oil
salt
garlic powder (optional)

Line a baking sheet with aluminum foil and preheat the oven to 400°F.

Wash the asparagus. Grip each stalk around the middle with one hand and toward the bottom with the other. It will snap in exactly the right place to avoid tough parts. Line the stalks up in a single layer across the baking sheet.

Drizzle with olive oil. Sprinkle lightly with salt. Sprinkle with garlic powder if using. Roll the asparagus stalks back and forth with your hand to coat them.

Bake about 15 to 20 minutes depending on how soft you want them and how thick they are.

Roll the leftovers up in the same piece of aluminum foil and refrigerate for the next day.

Blueberry Coffee Cake with Crumble

Use a 9 x 13 baking pan. Note: butter must be softened.

For the Crumble
½ cup flour
⅓ cup dark brown sugar
1 teaspoon cinnamon
4 tablespoons unsalted butter, softened
¼ teaspoon salt

Place all the ingredients in a bowl. Using your fingers, squish them all together, rubbing them between your fingers as you go, until they are all mixed and crumbly. Set aside.

For the Cake
2 cups flour
2 teaspoons baking powder
½ teaspoon salt
¾ cup sugar
6 tablespoons butter, softened, plus extra for baking pan
2 eggs
¾ cup milk
1½ teaspoons vanilla
2 cups fresh blueberries (two 6-ounce clamshell packages)

Grease the baking pan and preheat the oven to 350°F.
Combine the flour, baking powder, and salt in a bowl and stir well with a whisk or a fork to combine.
Cream the sugar with the butter. Add the eggs and beat,

one at a time. Alternate adding the milk and the flour mixture. Add the vanilla and beat briefly.

Stir or fold in the blueberries gently. Pour into the pre-pared pan. Sprinkle the top with the crumble mixture. Bake 40 minutes or until a cake tester comes out clean.

Lemon Drop Martini

Recipe courtesy of Susan Smith Erba

1 cup sugar plus additional sugar for rim of glass
6 cups water (1 plus 5)
5 lemons
vodka
triple sec

Make a simple syrup: heat at medium low 1 cup sugar and 1 cup water until sugar is dissolved. Put in refrigerator to cool off.

Squeeze about 5 lemons—enough for 1 cup of juice. Pour fresh-squeezed juice in a pitcher. Add simple syrup mixture. Add 5 more cups of water.

Refrigerate for a couple of hours. This will be good for lots of lemon drops or for glasses of lemonade!

Pour sugar into a shallow dish. Moisten the rim of a martini glass with juice from a lemon. Turn glass upside down and twist it around in the sugar until rim is coated.

Add 1½ to 2 ounces vodka and 1 tablespoon triple sec to each martini glass, then fill the rest of the glass with lemonade.

Don't miss any of the colorful Pen & Ink mysteries from
Krista Davis, including . . .

MURDER OUTSIDE THE LINES

With Halloween just around the corner, the fall colors in
Georgetown are brilliant. As manager of the Color Me Read
bookstore, coloring-book creator Florrie Fox has arranged
for psychic author Hilda Rattenhorst to read from *Spook-
tacular Ghost Stories*. But the celebrity medium arrives for the
event in hysterics, insisting she just saw a bare foot sticking
out of a rolled-up carpet in a nearby alley. Is someone trying
to sweep murder under the rug? Florrie calls in her
policeman beau, Sergeant Eric Jonquille, but the carpet
corpse has disappeared without a trace.

Then in the middle of her reading, Hilda chillingly declares
that she feels the killer's presence in the store. Is this a publicity stunt or a genuine psychic episode? It seems there's no
happy medium. When a local bibliophile is soon discovered
missing, a strange mystery begins to unroll. Now it's up to
Florrie and Jonquille to expose a killer's true colors. . . .

Available from Kensington Publishing Corp.
wherever books are sold.

Chapter 1

The crate was delivered to Color Me Read around noon on Thursday. Most of our deliveries came to the bookstore from publishing companies and looked quite ordinary, compared with this box. Our regular delivery guy, Glen, plunked it on the checkout desk and wiped his hands against each other as if they were dirty.

"Glad to be done with this one," he said.

It was a busy morning and we were swamped. I was doing three things at once, and Bob Turpin, a fellow employee, was waiting behind me to ring up a sale. I didn't want to be rude to anyone. I hunched my shoulder up to hold the phone between my shoulder and my ear, thereby freeing up a hand. I counted out change for Coralue Throckmorton, who had bought a dozen of the Halloween coloring books I had drawn, and I was nodding to a woman who was asking if we carried birthday cards and wrapping paper.

Suddenly a scream screeched through the phone. It was so loud that everyone looked at me in shock. The line went dead.

"My word!" exclaimed Coralue. "Who were you talking to?"

"A salesperson. I hope she's okay." I thanked Coralue for her purchases. As she exited the store, I directed the other lady to the stationery display all the way down the hall near the back.

Then I called the salesperson who had been checking on an order we placed. A recording came on, telling me the hours of the business and to leave a message. "Hi. This is Florrie Fox at Color Me Read. I was abruptly disconnected after someone screamed. I just want to be sure everything is okay." I hung up.

Bob was examining the box. "This is so cool. It looks like something Indiana Jones would receive."

Frodo, my parents' golden retriever, who was staying with me while they were on a Rhine River cruise, sniffed the box. He growled at it and backed away.

Studying the square box, I realized that it was actually a wooden crate made of rough planks. It was about three feet wide on both sides and just over a foot high. It was addressed to Professor John Maxwell, who had sometimes been called a real-life Indiana Jones. Professor Maxwell owned Color Me Read but was far better known for his daring adventures in search of historical artifacts.

"Must be something exotic!" Bob turned it around, examining it. "But Frodo doesn't like it."

Glen held out an electronic tablet for me to sign. "I'm just glad I'm not hauling that thing around anymore."

I signed for the package. "I don't get it. It's just a box. Is it heavy?"

He looked at me coyly. "I'll check back with you when I bring your next delivery. Then we'll talk." Glen hurried out the door.

"Bwahahaha," sang Bob, holding up his hands and wiggling his fingers. "Everybody is into Halloween. What do you bet he's saying that to everyone to freak them out?"

"Probably. I'll take it up to the professor if you'll check on the lady looking for wrapping paper."

"Deal."

The phone rang. It was the salesperson to whom I'd been speaking on the phone when she screamed. "Florrie! Is everything all right there? That shriek was the most horrible thing I've ever heard. I was afraid someone was attacking you."

I laughed. "There must have been some kind of glitch on the line. I was afraid something terrible had happened to *you*!"

"That's too funny. I'm glad you're okay. Anyway, I tracked down your order and we're going to expedite it. Sorry about the delay."

I thanked her and hung up. What a crazy day.

I lifted the crate. Although it was made of wood, the package wasn't very heavy.

My sister, Veronica, had found removable vinyl stickers at a local store called Curiosities that we had applied to the stair risers. From the checkout area and the front door, it looked as if you were going to walk into another dimension. Bare limbs hung at the top of a bluish-green mist and odd glowing eyes made us feel they were watching us. Veronica and I had always loved Halloween, and the store showed it. We had placed pumpkins, lanterns, and faux candles among the books throughout the store. The candles and lanterns operated on batteries for safety but the wicks flickered and looked remarkably real.

Frodo followed me as I walked up to the third floor of the bookstore, where the professor kept an office. It was decorated with artifacts he had brought back from his many travels. Cyril Oldfield was seated comfortably across from Professor Maxwell.

"I hope I'm not interrupting," I said as I marched into the office carrying the crate.

The professor was a distinguished man with a well-trimmed

graying beard. As an artist, I was fascinated by the shades of his beard. It was snow white along his sideburns and at the bottom of his chin, but his hair changed to black pepper on top of his head and along his jawline.

Heir to the Maxwell fortune, the professor was a member of one of the oldest families in Washington, DC. His roots ran deep in the community.

Cyril Oldfield had been one of the professor's students, and they remained good friends. Unlike the professor, Cyril was balding. A ring of fluffy white hair circled the back of his head. He wore a gray circle beard that was little more than a mustache and a chin patch. A loyal customer of Color Me Read, he visited the store quite often. He had been widowed for many years but had never remarried, which surprised me because he was quite charming. I put him close to fifty. He adjusted his wire-rimmed glasses and smiled at me. "Hi, Florrie."

"Good morning." I handed the box to the professor, who tilted his head. "What have we here? I wasn't expecting anything." He studied the exterior labels. "Most intriguing."

Cyril leaned forward for a better look. "Unexpected packages are always the most interesting."

The professor pulled out an ornate knife, which had surely come from one of his adventures, and used it to turn the screws that held the wood together. When he lifted the lid, I saw nothing but shredded newspaper. Someone had made certain the contents wouldn't shift or break in transit. The professor lifted the mass out of the box and gently separated the shreds to reveal a skull.